Temptress in Disguise

Rogues of Fortune's Den
Book 2

ADELE CLEE

Temptress in Disguise
Copyright © 2023 Adele Clee
All rights reserved.
ISBN-13: 978-1-915354-33-4

Cover by Dar Albert at Wicked Smart Designs

'Be thou the rainbow in the storms of life. The evening beam that smiles the clouds away, and tints tomorrow with prophetic ray.'

— Lord Byron

Chapter One

The Belldrake was a lesser-known playhouse tucked down a quiet lane in Covent Garden. The home of serious thespians. Actors who spent years perfecting their craft, not a hive for an amateur actress out to attract a wealthy paramour.

It begged the question: how did a woman like Lydia Fontaine secure the role of Hero in Shakespeare's play? More importantly, Aramis Chance wondered why the hell she had summoned *him* to the theatre. It was said she kept a string of lovers, men who danced like marionettes whenever she called. Weak men with generous souls, not a dangerous bastard with a stone-cold heart.

Amid the dark confines of his carriage, Aramis held Miss Fontaine's note to the window and studied the bold script beneath the lamplight.

Join me for supper at the Belldrake tonight.
I shall make it worth your while.

It was the third such note he had received today. The paper stank of cheap perfume. The words carried an illicit promise. If he so desired, he could be buried inside Miss Fontaine before the peal of St Mary's bells.

But something was amiss.

Did the coquette think he was in the market for a mistress?

Worse still, was she in the market for a husband?

As a sworn bachelor, Aramis would rather sever a main vein than shackle himself with a wife. Ever since his brother Christian had married, desperate females were crawling out of the woodwork, keen to be the devil's bride.

Aramis screwed the paper in his hand and sat back in the seat. He'd not come to the theatre to hear the lady's proposition. Only men desperate for cunny could be dazzled into submission. No. Having once suffered at the hands of a Jezebel—and with an ugly scar on his left arm as proof—he wished to ensure Miss Fontaine knew he despised conniving women.

And so, he waited for the patrons to disperse before climbing down from the carriage and striding to the side entrance. Fist clenched, he banged on the paint-chipped door, hoping his annoyance was evident.

A tubby fellow with a bald pate answered. Through suspicious eyes, he scanned Aramis' broad shoulders. "What can I do for you, gov'nor?"

Aramis grabbed the man's meaty paw and thrust the crumpled note into his palm. "I'm here to see Miss Fontaine. That's what I think of the invitation."

The man didn't smooth the paper and read the note.

His face twisted into a perfect picture of unease. "She ain't able to take visitors at present."

Aramis firmed his jaw. "Fetch her. Or I'll find her myself."

"I—I can't. She left with a gent ten minutes ago."

Anger gathered like a tempest in Aramis' chest. No one liked being played for a fool, least of all him. If the woman thought jealousy was a tool to catch a suitor, she was sorely mistaken.

He did not waste time asking for an explanation. "Tell Miss Fontaine I dislike childish games. Tell her, if she means to rile Lucifer she should expect to get burned. Tell her never to contact me again."

He left the lackey quaking in his boots and returned to his carriage.

Godby glanced down from atop his box. "Home, Mr Chance?"

Where else would he go at this late hour?

As part owner of Fortune's Den—the best gaming hell in town—there was always a scandal to keep him entertained. His brother Aaron owned a fine wine cellar. And having once been betrayed so cruelly, Aramis preferred the company of trusted kin to deceitful shrews.

Thank God his brothers knew nothing about his escapade to the Belldrake. They'd taunt him about it for weeks.

"Take me back to the Den. I'll spend the night with a bottle of my brother's best claret." He would take his frustration out on the dissolute lords of the *ton*. Wrestle with a few warring punters.

Aramis climbed into the carriage. He was about to

close the door when a woman darted like a sprite from the shadows. In the blink of an eye, she was inside the vehicle and sitting on his leather seat.

"Mr Chance?" she panted. "Mr Aramis Chance?"

Saints and sinners!

Not another desperate waif seeking a husband?

Judging by her trembling lips and the way she clutched her carpet bag, she was a runaway, out to trap some poor bugger into marriage.

He was ready to curse her to Hades, to tell her in no uncertain terms to get out of his *bloody* vehicle. But he didn't believe in fate or coincidences, and something about her delicate features made him falter. Perhaps his brothers knew he'd come to the Belldrake and had staged a prank.

Devious devils!

Had they hired a buxom wench with sultry eyes and a teasing grin he would have deposited her on the pavement. But this woman was small, graceful and downright terrified. Doubtless a disguise to allay his suspicions.

Keen to test her mettle, and to see if his brothers had wasted their hard-earned coin, he leaned forward and slammed the door shut.

Let's see how she fared as his prisoner.

"I'm Aramis Chance. As you've invaded my vehicle, I demand to know your name, madam." Like the lady herself, he guessed it would be something delicate and unassuming.

Relief flashed in eyes that were a deep ocean blue in the darkness. "Thank heavens you came. I shall explain all once we're on the road. Tell your coachman to drive to the Copper Crown north of Highgate."

The Copper Crown?

What the blazes?

The inn was a den for cutthroats and thieves. No respectable woman in her right mind would enter the yard, let alone grace the establishment.

Aramis smiled to himself. Perhaps this wasn't a prank, and his brothers had arranged a night of debauchery followed by a fistfight at the Crown. There would be a scuffle. A chance to test his pugilistic skills. An opportunity to lift his sullen mood.

Still, he would play the disgruntled brute a little longer.

"This isn't a damn hackney cab." And he was by no means a gentleman. The sooner she realised that, the better. If this woman wanted to dance in hell's flames, she needed to know the devil stoked the fire. "And I'm no spinster's flunkey."

She raised her chin. "I'm not a spinster. I'm three and twenty."

The faint simmer of anger in her tone sparked his interest. He wished she would lower the hood of her cloak so he could study her hair. He imagined it was dull brown and tied in a knot as severe as her expression.

"And a virgin maiden," he stated. Or a damn actress and one of his brothers wrote the notes summoning him to the Belldrake. As always, he would have the last laugh.

"For an intelligent man, you're quick to make flippant assumptions."

Aramis leaned forward and rested his arm on his knee. "Don't disappoint me now. A shrewd woman would know it's a test. A means for me to study your reactions and assess your character."

She gulped. "And what did you deduce?"

"That you're afraid of me." As most people were.

She did not refute the claim. "You're a dangerous man from a dangerous family. You have friends in high places and know the best enquiry agents in town. I risk your wrath and even gaol by taking command of your conveyance."

Taking command of his conveyance?

This lady had courage abound.

Aramis laughed and made a mental note to thank his kin. The minx proved highly entertaining. "Madam, you barely have command of your emotions. You're half my size and lack brute strength. What makes you think I'll drive you to the Copper Crown?"

"If you're so skilled at analysing a woman's character, surely you can work that out for yourself, sir."

A fire burned beneath her demure countenance. It was more glowing embers than rampant flames, but it warmed his blood all the same.

"Perhaps you intend to offer yourself as the reward." He'd have scanned her body were she not shrouded in the drab wool cloak. At a guess, she had a narrow waist and small breasts that might bounce nicely in his palms. "You'll need more than fluttering lashes and a coy smile to lure me into bed."

It was her turn to offer an amused snort. "Don't disappoint *me*, Mr Chance. I'm inclined to think your deductive skills are decidedly poor. I would never trade my body for a ride across town."

"More's the pity," he said, confident he could have her in bed before the first stroke of midnight. "It would have

6

been a ride to remember."

The lady's confidence faltered. She touched the backs of her fingers to her cheek. "It's your brains and brawn I need, not your body. Well, hopefully not your body, though I shall only permit you to bed me as a last resort."

Curiosity warred with anger.

The latter won.

"I'm no one's last resort." Indeed, her comment roused more than his ire. It reminded him of how naive he'd been in his youth. How one could be blind-sided by false words and a pretty smile. How easily one might be used as a pawn in a strumpet's game. "State your name and your business, or get out. I'll not ask you again."

The lady gripped her tatty bag as if she carried the crown jewels. "It's Miss Fontaine, and—"

"Fontaine!" he blurted, the taste in his mouth turning bitter. This was the siren who held half the men in London by the ballocks? This … this diminutive, dare he say fascinating, elfin-faced creature was Lydia Fontaine? "You're the actress who took Lord Bedlow as her lover? You're the famed coquette?"

He would wager every penny this woman had never been kissed, let alone indulged in an illicit affair.

"Why do you sound so surprised?" The lady fought to hold his gaze, though she looked more than uncomfortable with his current line of questioning. "First impressions can be deceptive. I was told to expect a beast, yet you're merely a handsome man with a temper."

A chuckle burst from his lips. "I was told Miss Fontaine had large breasts and was half a foot taller."

A blush flooded her cheeks. "A decent corset can

enhance a lady's assets. And I often prefer a pretty heeled shoe to these practical boots."

To prove she did indeed wear boots as tatty as her bag, she raised her hem a fraction. The ugly footwear did not detract from the delicate turn of her ankle. The combination proved intriguing and annoying in equal measure.

"Then tell me what Bedlow liked to do in bed."

"I beg your pardon?" She swallowed hard. The fear in her eyes overshadowed her attempt to appear offended. "A lady would never discuss intimacies with a stranger. What happens in one's bedchamber is a personal matter. Suffice to say, his lordship had no complaint."

Liar!

The word danced on his tongue, but he enjoyed watching her squirm. "If I'm to take you to the Copper Crown, I must be assured of your identity. As I said, this isn't a hackney, and you're not paying me in kind."

She was undeterred in her efforts to prove she was the haughty actress. "I can recite every one of Hero's lines in the play. Will that suffice?"

"If I'm to go out of my way, I'll need a damn sight more than that. An intellectual could easily quote Shakespeare, and you're definitely more the timid bluestocking than the wicked coquette."

"I shall take that as a compliment."

"Please do. There's no chance in hell I would ferry Miss Fontaine across town. I despise conceited women."

The lady was quick to challenge him. "Yet it took nothing more than a simple invitation to have you scampering to the Belldrake tonight."

He fought to curb his indignation. "I came to tell Miss

Fontaine to stop sending notes. Trust me. I'm not the sort of man who pines or scampers. As my sister-in-law recently pointed out, I don't have a passionate bone in my body."

Through narrowed eyes, she assessed his physique. He waited for her soft sigh or the tantalising stroke of her tongue over her bottom lip. The lady merely looked at him as one would fish at Billingsgate Market.

"Yet you were willing to accept payment in kind, sir."

"Because you've piqued my interest. If you want to climax in a carriage, then come and sit astride me. Don't expect reams of pretty prose and gestures of undying love."

She fell silent.

But it wasn't shock marring her delicate features.

A heavy cloud of sadness swamped the space between them. He wished she would berate him. Call him cruel names. Harsh words slipped off him like rain on a windowpane. But this … this sudden air of melancholy awakened memories he would sooner forget.

"I'm not sure what sort of women you've entertained in the past, Mr Chance, but I'd rather spend a lifetime in silence than listen to an insincere man recite poetry." Her little snort carried a thread of contempt. "As a rose needs sunshine to bloom, love needs trust. Trust is a fool's game, is it not?"

Her words sucked the oxygen out of the air.

His throat closed against painful memories of betrayal. A stepmother and her lackeys dragging four frightened boys from their beds and dumping them in an alley in the rookeries. They'd fought hard to survive, none more so than his older brother Aaron.

Other harrowing memories scrambled for prominence.

I thought I was in love once, he imagined himself saying as an image of Melissa burst into his mind. But love was the devil's own deception. A cruel means to strip a man of hope and bring him crashing to his knees. He bore the scar as a permanent reminder not to be so damn foolish again.

Needing to calm the inner chaos, Aramis leaned forward and opened the carriage door. "You're right. When it comes to women, love and trust are foreign to my vocabulary. That's how I know you're a liar. Miss Fontaine beds men for fame and fortune. She manipulates her lovers and picks her victims wisely. Which is why she did not write the note summoning me to the Belldrake."

Everyone in town knew of his reputation.

No one—and he meant no one—would dare risk his wrath.

He had more than enough money to attract the likes of Miss Fontaine. But he'd donate everything to the homeless refuge before giving the conniving actress a penny.

And so, a few questions remained. Had this woman duped him? If so, for what purpose? Or had his brothers played the prank of the century, and a night of pleasure awaited him at the Copper Crown?

It was time to find out.

"Good night, madam." He gestured to the pavement.

The lady sat rigid in the seat. "Have you ever been so desperate for help you'd do anything to end the nightmare?"

Merciful Lord!

Was she determined to rake up his past?

He doubted she'd ever experienced real horrors.

"Many times. The night my father dragged me out of bed when I was twelve years old. He needed a child to fight in the pit to pay his debt. The opponent was a beast of a man aged thirty-five." Despite nursing bruised ribs and a blackened eye, Aaron had offered himself up as the victim. Hence his brother would always be his hero.

Water glistened in her eyes, though she found no words to console him.

How could she?

"I can give you an example more terrifying than dreadful." Aramis tugged his coat sleeve an inch above his wrist, baring his marred skin. "How about the night someone held my arm over a lit brazier and laughed as I screamed?" He still woke in a sweat, the smell of burning flesh assaulting his nostrils.

She covered her mouth with her hand as she gazed at his ugly scars. It took her a moment to gather herself before saying, "It takes a strong man to endure such hardships."

"Strong? I'm made of bloody steel."

"I'm well aware of your attributes, Mr Chance." Her gaze dipped to examine his muscular thighs like one might assess a stallion at Tattersalls. "It's why I'm forced to take command of you and your fine equipage."

Fine equipage?

It was an odd turn of phrase for a woman. Indeed, her reply convinced him his brothers were behind this sham of a kidnapping. Why else would she use a suggestive innuendo? And she wasn't the least bit fazed by his foul language.

"It seems you have courage abound, madam. Why wait until we reach the Copper Crown to indulge our whims?" Having her might ease the tension and his damnable curiosity. "Put down that ugly bag and let me show you what I can do with my equipage. I assure you, you shall have no complaint."

She didn't berate him or attempt to make a hasty escape. She didn't throw her bag to the floor, hike up her skirts and flash her pretty stockings.

"You mistake my meaning, sir. This is a matter of business, not pleasure. If we're to spend time together, you must learn to curb your tongue and your appetite."

Business? The lady was deluded.

He dealt with lying devils daily.

Why would he add another to the growing list?

"On the contrary. Our acquaintance is about to come to an abrupt end. Good night, madam. You can show yourself out."

When she reached into her bag, he expected her to whip out a bible and flick to a parable about lust and sinners. To lecture him about the dangers of libidinous behaviour. Worse still, he feared she might recite a passage about the benefits of sharing one's burdens.

But no!

The lady pulled a pistol from her drab bag, cocked the hammer and said quite sternly, "If you want to live to see dawn, Mr Chance, you will take me to the Copper Crown."

Chapter Two

Naomi's hand shook as she kept the pistol trained on the enigmatic Mr Chance. The man was a cold-hearted devil who could slay his enemies with scathing words and a Medusa-like glare. Yet his sad stories and scarred arm told a different tale.

Like most people, Mr Chance had locked his trauma in an iron-clad chest. Little wonder he lost his temper when someone rattled the chains. He was rude and disagreeable. But his face glowed when he said something amusing, and his eyes sparkled like stars in the heavens.

Perhaps humour was the key to securing his help.

"I hoped it wouldn't come to this." She had given him fair warning. Desperate people did desperate things, though shooting Aramis Chance would only hinder her cause. "I hoped you would be more agreeable. It's not often a man is kidnapped by a woman half his size. Is it not a tale to tell one's grandchildren?"

Mr Chance arched a dark, sardonic brow. "If one discounts my older brother, I'm the most disagreeable man in London. This is not a kidnapping. I could disarm you in a matter of seconds."

She stemmed her nerves. "Why haven't you?"

"Because to say I'm intrigued is an understatement. Few men dare to look me in the eye. You, madam, seem to think you can ride roughshod over me, and I demand to know why."

"Tell Godby to head to Highgate, and I shall explain all." Now she had to strive to keep him amused and intrigued. But not in the way Lydia would, with coy glances and flirtatious banter. Heavens, one wrong word and he'd throw her out at the first turnpike.

"How do you know my coachman's name?"

"I heard you tell him you wished to go home."

The air of sadness in his voice had tugged at her heart-strings. Guilt surfaced. Perhaps she should have chosen someone else to play her champion. Someone less … less handsome and domineering.

"It seems there's no chance of that."

She failed to suppress her surprise. "Does that mean you'll let me take command of you and your vehicle? If it soothes your pride, I have come equipped with restraints."

"Restraints?"

"Yes, I'm shocked you didn't hear the leg irons clattering in my carpet bag. You'll be glad to know I kept the pistol in an oak case. Heaven forbid I should accidentally trip the hammer. I might have blown a hole in your toe."

The corners of his mouth twitched. "Am I supposed to thank you for your foresight? Should I be grateful I'm not a cripple?"

"No, but as you're skilled at dissecting a lady's character, surely you can deduce something from my need to keep you safe."

Despite relaxing against the squab, he remained a formidable presence. "When it comes to kidnapping, you're supposed to leave the victim quaking in their boots."

"We've already established you could disarm me." Hence the pistol wasn't loaded. She'd not risk getting shot. Though perhaps death would be a blessing in disguise—a quick end to her nightmare. "And I need you alive if I'm to make use of your brains and brawn."

"But not my body." He smoothed his large hands over his thick thighs. "You mean to bed me only as a last resort."

Naomi let her gaze venture over his muscular physique. Aramis Chance could have any woman of his choosing. Having seen him once, Lydia had been desperate to have him as her lover.

One cannot seduce the devil.

It's an impossible feat. Even for someone with my skill.

Lydia had looked at Naomi, her eyes brimming with pity.

He'd eat you alive, my darling.

Use you most dreadfully.

Poor thing, you know nothing about men and their desires.

Naomi had observed how Lydia treated her admirers. Such devious tactics would not work with Mr Chance. Honesty would ensure she prevailed.

"You may excel in the bedchamber, Mr Chance, but such attributes do not fascinate me."

His arrogant snort said he was keen to prove her wrong. "How would a virgin know?"

"One does not need to down ten vials of laudanum to know it's addictive. Lust is a drug like any other."

"You could say that about most things. Happiness is a drug. People are forever chasing that elusive thing that makes them feel whole."

"Happiness is a state of mind. People should look no further than their own thoughts." She removed the handcuffs from her bag and threw them onto the seat beside him. "You can fight and argue and be disgruntled or sit calmly with your wrists in shackles."

He pinned her to the seat with his stony gaze. "I'll not sit here trussed up like a plucked pheasant. And I'll not take you to the Copper Crown until you return the pistol to the box and tell me your name. Be warned. My patience is hanging by a thread."

Naomi's pulse raced.

She would be a fool to trust him. Equally, only a fool would think the threat of violence might sway his decision. Aramis Chance could fight Lucifer's army and return unscathed. He knew she had no intention of pulling the trigger, and though they'd reached a stalemate, she had no option but to surrender.

"Then, I concede." Her heart urged her to have faith. She held her breath while releasing the hammer. Under the power of his penetrating gaze, she returned the pistol to the box. "Let us begin again." She offered her gloved hand. "Miss Grant. Miss Naomi Grant."

Mr Chance stared at her hand. He considered the size and shape as if it were a strange object of art at a museum.

With surprising hesitance, he slid his palm over hers and clasped her hand.

For some strange reason, they both inhaled sharply.

"Well, Miss Grant, you have managed an impossible feat." His warm hand swamped hers as his commanding aura filled the space between them. "You have gained my undivided attention."

She smiled to disguise the internal chaos. "Perhaps this will be amongst your list of most memorable meetings."

"This tops my list of memorable meetings. It's not often one is accosted by a lady bearing shackles." He released his grip on her hand, snatched the locked hand-cuffs and slipped them into his coat pocket. "I trust you have the key."

She nodded. "I didn't plan to keep you a prisoner forever." Once she had what she wanted, she would grant him his freedom.

A sinful smile touched his lips. "No, only until you'd used me for my brains and brawn. Indeed, I should feel quite violated."

"As you have already explained, you've found yourself in worse situations. And you were never in danger of being ravished."

"How disappointing." Even when amused, the man had the presence of a panther—all silky black hair and dark, hypnotic eyes. A striking symbol of power and mastery. "As an actress, I'm sure you could convince me otherwise."

Mr Chance was as quick-witted as he was command-ing. Every sentence was constructed to gain more informa-tion. Though tempted to play along and weave a tale,

Naomi had decided to approach her dilemma with integrity.

"I'm not an actress."

"Then what were you doing at the Belldrake?"

Naomi tapped her finger to her lips before offering him an ultimatum. "I'll say nothing more while we're stationary."

Mr Chance cursed under his breath. He might have protested had fate not handed Naomi a boon. A light tap on the window dragged another profanity from his lips.

"Hell and damnation." He refused to acknowledge the two women peering through the window. "Ignore them, Miss Grant." He thumped the carriage roof with his clenched fist and called for Godby to ferry them to Highgate.

The older woman opened the carriage door before the coachman could whip his reins into action. "Mr Chance. How fortuitous. My brother Henry was due to collect us after the performance but has failed to arrive. And here you are, coming to our aid like a knight of Camelot."

Naomi thought it was a feeble excuse to gain his attention. She would have noticed a woman with a small canary nesting in her hat. And the patrons had left the theatre half an hour ago.

"I am otherwise engaged, Mrs Wendon. Please close the door." The man made no secret of his wish to avoid them.

Mrs Wendon was undeterred. She shoved her daughter into the carriage. "Might we trouble you for a ride to Leicester Square? It's not far and will be no inconvenience. Sit beside Mr Chance, Hester." Amid the rustle of silk, Mrs Wendon climbed in behind her daughter. "She's such an obedient girl, sir."

Poor Hester looked like she'd been picked to be the next Viking sacrifice. Her pale skin turned blotchy, and she couldn't quite catch her breath. She sat so close to the window that the carriage would likely tilt on its axis when they rounded the bend.

Mr Chance gritted his teeth. "We have an appointment across town. Wait outside, and I shall have Godby find you a hackney."

Naomi bit back a chuckle as Mrs Wendon closed the door. "We have time to take a small detour to Leicester Square." She had planned for a delay in case Mr Chance proved difficult. And the Reverend Smollett would be drinking at the Copper Crown until dawn.

Mrs Wendon sat beside Naomi and cast her a sidelong glance. "Hester is acquainted with Mr Chance's sister Delphine. They get along famously. They're practically inseparable."

Hester found her voice. "I've spoken to her twice, Mother."

"Yes, but she gave you excellent fashion advice and recommended her own modiste. Is that not a sign she holds you in high regard?"

"If you're riding with me, I won't mind my manners," Mr Chance warned. "If you wish to save yourself any embarrassment, Mrs Wendon, I suggest you alight."

Hester moved to stand, but her mother hit her with her reticule.

"Sit down. Mr Chance is merely testing your resolve." Mrs Wendon smiled. "We can make allowances, sir. On account it's late and men have the devil in them at night."

Realising it was easier to make the five-minute journey to Leicester Square than to prise Mrs Wendon from the carriage seat, Mr Chance barked instructions at Godby.

The vehicle lurched forward and picked up speed.

"You can say anything to Hester and she'll not take offence. She has the heart of an angel and a backbone of steel."

Hester sat quivering like a perfectly set blancmange.

Mr Chance rose to the challenge and offered a wicked grin. "Mrs Wendon's husband lost his fortune at my gaming hell. Consequently, she means to harass me until I marry her daughter."

"Have you told her that's impossible?" Naomi said.

"At least three times this week."

While Hester avoided touching Mr Chance, Mrs Wendon decided to question the competition. "I suppose you work at the theatre, my dear. Actresses have a tendency to look a little desperate."

"Is that not a sweeping generalisation?"

Mrs Wendon gave Naomi's knee a reassuring pat. "No need to be tetchy. Hester understands a man's needs. She'd not object to a gentleman's pastimes."

"I'm not a gentleman," Mr Chance countered. "And as Miss Wendon looks like she might cry if I untied her bonnet, I won't be bedding her anytime soon."

Hester breathed a relieved sigh.

"Rest assured. She's had instruction in the pleasures of the flesh," Mrs Wendon persisted. "She'll not be shy on her wedding night."

Mr Chance swore. "I'm not marrying Miss Wendon."

"Of course you're not," Naomi said, giving the man a covert wink. "How can you, when you're marrying me? Though, I have had no such instruction on how to please a man and will probably scream like a babe."

While Mr Chance folded his arms across his muscular chest and grinned, Mrs Wendon wheeled out the cannons. "Only a fool would marry a nobody when he can marry the niece of a baron. Actresses are two a penny."

"Only a man in love would marry a nobody rather than the niece of a baron. Is that not so, Mr Chance?"

Naomi imagined Mr Chance would rather sell his soul than admit he loved a woman. For the benefit of Mrs Wendon, he glanced at Naomi and said, "Love should be the only reason a man marries."

"Poppycock," Mrs Wendon countered. "Were that the case, we'd be overrun with bachelors, not rats. No. Love is merely a tool—"

"Enough. I see we've arrived at our destination." Mr Chance sighed with relief when the carriage stopped in Leicester Square.

With skin as thick as an oak trunk, the matron showed great tenacity. "Hester is available to ride out most days. She has lessons from a card sharp on Wednesdays. A lady must be useful to her husband."

Hester cast an apologetic grimace as she alighted.

Before closing the carriage door behind her, Mrs Wendon remembered to say that Hester had attended a bare-knuckle brawl near Camden Town and did not swoon at the sight of blood.

"For the love of God," Mr Chance muttered before

telling Godby to drive to the inn near Highgate. "The only way to silence that woman is to cut out her tongue."

"I doubt that would deter her. I imagine she would stand outside your establishment waving placards." Not that it would do any good. Should everything go to plan, Naomi hoped Mr Chance would agree to marry her once they reached the Copper Crown. "I didn't realise you were in such high demand."

"I'm a man of many talents, Miss Grant. If you'd care to cross the carriage, I shall give you a private demonstration."

"Half an hour ago, you were keen to throw me out." Indeed, she was surprised she'd lasted this long. There was every chance he'd abandon her at the thieves' den once he heard her plan.

"That was before I found you mildly interesting." He raised his hand to silence her. "Don't excite yourself. These rare flickers of emotion soon fade."

Hence she had to do everything in her power to keep him entertained. "Luckily, I'm not looking for a man with a passionate spirit and a penchant for poetry. A cold-hearted blackguard will do."

He laughed, the sound deep and husky. "Tell me. How is such an adventurous and amusing woman still a virgin?" He sounded keen to resolve the issue.

"When a lady finds herself destitute, she must learn to survive or die. I'm like a chameleon and know how to blend into the background."

"I beg to differ. You're the only bright star in the night sky."

The compliment caught her off-guard. She should be

grateful Mr Chance saw her at all, yet doubts surfaced. She needed a scoundrel. A selfish beast. A man with a damaged heart who took pleasure in flexing his fists.

"You don't want to know why I'm destitute?" He might agree to her plan if she could make him see her as an ally, a fellow sufferer of fate's cruel injustice. "I have lost everything because of my stepmother's treachery. Now I must scrape a living with what little talent I possess."

Something she'd said had a marked effect on his countenance.

Suspicion glinted in his hard eyes, and the devil's fury darkened his tone. "I knew my brothers had hired you. Don't think you can play me for a fool, madam. Don't think you can rouse my pity by reminding me of my own tragic past. I feel nothing. I'll always feel nothing."

Naomi steeled herself. Mrs Wendon was right. This man had Lucifer's temper. At any moment, he might stop the carriage and leave her stranded. So why was she not afraid? Perhaps because a lady knew where she stood when a man spoke his mind.

"How much did my brothers pay you?" he snapped, his volatile reaction an indication of how deeply he had once been hurt. "This talent of yours. Does it amount to more than sucking a man's—"

"Mr Chance!" Doubtless he meant to shock her while he gathered his defences. "Speak to me in that despicable tone again and I *will* shoot you in the foot." Naomi glared at him. "Unlike you, I have a talent for prose. Mr Budworth, the theatre manager, paid me to write a short play. It will be performed during Thursday's matinee."

Although, after the incident in his office tonight, he'd probably tossed the script in the grate.

He remained silent.

"Regardless of your opinion, I am a lady of gentle breeding. At least I was until my stepmother stole my inheritance." Determined to prove her point, she tugged down her hood. "I have nothing to hide. And while your brothers' reputations precede them, they did not pay me to… to…" She gestured to the placket of his trousers.

"To what, Miss Grant?" He found her inability to repeat the phrase amusing. "Surely a playwright can express herself eloquently."

"I'm not a playwright but a storyteller of average ability. Mr Budworth pitied me." *Pity* was not the appropriate word. The manager requested private meetings, hoping to sate his lustful cravings. "Hence the play will be performed on the quietest day of the week."

"Still, I should like to hear you stutter over the lewd description. You owe me something for the ride across town."

"I refuse to let you intimidate me." Though her life was a shambles and she needed this man, she would not stoop to his level.

"I intimidate everyone. I'm known by the moniker the King of Spades. What is a spade if not an inverted black heart?"

"You make hostility sound like a medal one should wear with pride. Compassion is a far more attractive trait in a man." She thumped the carriage roof and cried, "Stop the vehicle, Godby."

"What the blazes?" Mr Chance jerked at the sudden

change of plan. He glanced out into the darkness at the scattering of houses nestled amid an expanse of fields. "We must be three miles from the Copper Crown."

"I'm not sure you're equipped to deal with the problems that lie ahead. I shall find another mode of transport. You may return to your gaming hell and enjoy that bottle of claret."

Mr Chance frowned. He was used to getting his own way and evidently disliked the lack of control. "Godby won't stop unless I issue the command."

Naomi smiled. "Then you have a choice, sir. Be warned. This is a game of deception and murder." If that didn't appeal to his thirst for intrigue, nothing would.

"Murder?" he scoffed. "Whose murder?"

Naomi ignored the knots twisting in her stomach.

It was now or never.

"Lydia Fontaine is my sister."

"Your sister! What the devil. You mean half-sister, surely?"

"No. Lydia insists on using an alias. She has been missing for three days, missing presumed dead." In truth, Lydia had probably eloped with a degenerate, but the story helped Naomi's cause. "She retired to her dressing room in the interval and hasn't been seen since. Because we're so alike, Mr Budworth had me play the role of Hero. Her disappearance remains a guarded secret, but I'm convinced my stepmother and uncle are involved."

Naomi had taken a risk remaining at the theatre and their apartment and needed to find somewhere safe to hide. Where better than a thieves' den? Though if she hoped to survive, she needed the protection of a man as powerful as Aramis Chance.

The man in question sat forward, bracing his large hands on the black leather seat. "Why involve me? I've never met your stepmother or your sister. Does your uncle gamble at the club?"

The enquiry agent who told her to seek this man's help said explaining the connection would be the hard part— along with getting him to the altar. Hopefully, a desire for retribution would be enough of an incentive.

Naomi inhaled a calming breath. "I have it on good authority that you know my stepmother. Though I believe you've not seen her for ten years. I'm assured we both have a reason to seek vengeance."

Like the shadows in hell's corridors, a darkness swamped his features. He firmed his jaw, though hesitated before asking the damning question. "What is her name?"

Naomi's pulse galloped. "Melissa Grant. Though you might know her as Melissa Adams. She is currently my uncle's mistress. Together, they conspired to remove me from the house."

In truth, she'd had no choice but to flee but knew the scene would strike a chord with him. As children, the Chance brothers had been dragged from their home and dumped in the rookeries. With their parents dead and their inheritance stolen, they'd fought to survive. Like the myth- ical phoenix, they had risen from the ashes and were born again.

He sat statue-still in the seat, an ominous air swirling between them. "So, you know what that woman did to me? Did she tell you, or did you hear it from the gossips?"

Neither. She'd discovered the truth from another source.

She swallowed hard. "I'll not lie to you. I heard you were in love with her when you were barely nineteen."

"Correction. I thought I was in love with her."

Naomi nodded. How anyone could love such a vindictive woman was beyond her. But he had been young and naive, and now he was simply angry. "Despite being ten years your senior, you didn't know she was married. Her husband held your arm over a lit brazier. Punishment for the insult."

Like Lucifer commanding his minions, he cried, "Enough!"

The battle to contain his emotions marred his flawless features. Regardless of his surly manner, her heart wept for him. She wanted to invent a story, tell him Melissa Adams had cared. That she hadn't used him in the hope he would kill her husband. That he was worthy of love. But he would see through the lies, and the war would be lost before it had begun.

"Sometimes bad things happen so better things can follow."

She believed that. She had to believe that.

His snort rang with contempt. "As you rightly said, love cannot blossom without trust. I'll never trust a woman again."

"I suppose it's a case of one rotten apple spoiling the cart, though I suspect the person you trust least is yourself." When his frown deepened, she said, "You fear your judgement is flawed. When lying awake in the darkness, you torture yourself. How could you have missed the signs? How could you have been so gullible?" It's why the world got to see the dangerous man made of steel, not the vulnerable youth who'd been so easily led.

He averted his gaze to prevent her from seeing the truth in his eyes. "It would seem my first assessment of you was correct."

"How so?"

"You mean to strip me bare, just not in the way I hoped."

"Anger never fades. It festers. Removing any emotional attachment to the memory is the only way to rid yourself of a painful past."

It was easier said than done when one was a victim.

Preachers rarely followed their own advice.

His deep sigh carried the echoes of surrender. "And how do you mean to exact your revenge? I assume you have a plan."

"I prefer to call it justice as opposed to revenge. It sounds morally correct, does it not?"

"Let me rephrase. How do you mean to gain justice?"

Naomi braced herself. She wished she had bound him in shackles, though leg irons wouldn't prevent the beast from howling his objection. "I shall begin by marrying you, sir."

Chapter Three

Aramis needed air.

He needed a stiff brandy and a hard punch to the gut. Something to bring calm to the chaos. Something to banish the surge of painful memories.

Miss Grant was a devious imp out to tear his ordered world in two. A siren disguised as a prim bluestocking. A woman with a clever mouth and magical hands. Why else would he feel a profound spark of attraction from a simple touch?

"Marry me? Have you taken leave of your senses?"

The woman intrigued him. The urge to bed her had left him nursing a throbbing cockstand the entire journey. He'd hire a room and pleasure her until dawn, by which time lust's flames would be nought but dying embers.

But marriage?

Shackled for life?

"Think of it this way," she said, as if his dilemma amounted to nothing more than choosing a dessert at dinner. "It would stop Mrs Wendon harassing you. I believe she's one of many desperate females out to snag a handsome husband for her daughter."

"I could have the face of a gargoyle, and Mrs Wendon would still hound me to the ends of the earth. The desperate females you mention want one thing only —money."

Miss Grant's tempting mouth curled into a smile. "Perhaps they find your kind heart and compassionate nature attractive."

The minx's sarcasm knew no bounds. "Taunt me at your peril."

"I'm not afraid of you, sir."

"Liar."

She raised her dainty chin. "I'm afraid you won't agree to my plan, but I don't believe you would hurt me. I find your blunt manner and honest expressions quite refreshing."

The mention of the *plan* left a bitter taste in his mouth. "What makes you so different from Melissa?" Uttering that name had shame clawing in his veins. Humiliation was a sickness that worsened with time. "You mean to use me for your own gain."

"On the contrary, we can be useful to each other. I will bring my devious uncle to justice, and you will punish the woman you despise. I want nothing from the marriage. Though to show my gratitude, I will give you a share of my inheritance when we part ways."

Aramis scoffed. "I don't want or need your money."

"Then name your price."

He fell silent, contemplating what it would take to sign away his freedom. On reflection, Miss Grant's idea had some merit. A married man could go about his business in peace. And it would be amusing to watch his brother Theo become Mrs Wendon's whipping boy.

"You would never agree to my price." He had an unreasonable list of demands which he would want in writing, preferably in blood.

"Allow me to decide what's acceptable, sir."

He observed her proud demeanour and the wide mouth that held him entranced. It was unusual for such a slight creature to be so courageous. He had been wrong about her hair. It was so fair it might be made of fairy dust. It was pinned loosely. One slight tug and it would tumble down around her shoulders.

It wouldn't take much to unleash her untamed passion.

It wouldn't take much to make her a slave to his will.

"I'll insist you tell everyone it's a love match." He'd not have the lofty lords think him foolish. "You'll make no claim on my assets. I'll provide for you only until we've dealt with your uncle."

"And found my sister," she added.

He had no desire to come to Miss Fontaine's aid but nodded. "If, at any point, you reveal the truth about our bargain, I shall prosecute you. I'll need that in writing. When the time comes to part, I will decide the narrative we use to explain our estrangement."

She laughed. "Anything else?"

"We will live separately, though as your husband, I reserve the right to bed you at my convenience." While the need to have her drummed in his blood, it would likely be twice before he found it tiresome.

The lady's delectable mouth fell open. "If you bed me,

we cannot have the marriage annulled. What if you wish to marry at a later date?"

"I won't." He could not envisage ever marrying. He'd not raise a child in a world he considered cruel and corrupt. So why be lumbered with a burden? "Nor will I allow you to make a spectacle of me in court by suggesting the marriage is a sham. If we marry, it's for life. Those are my terms."

Miss Grant sagged back in the seat. "Well, I have a lot to consider. Indeed, you make marriage sound daunting."

Marriage to him would be challenging at best.

"Count your blessings. Had any other woman suggested an alliance, she would have felt the sharp lash of my tongue." Miss Grant would feel the soft stroke of his tongue in every intimate place. "While you decide, let me offer a word of caution. I'll be dominant in bed. I expect you to accommodate me. To pleasure me at will. That's the price you must pay for vengeance, Miss Grant."

The lady paled.

Rightfully so. He would ruin her for other men.

Seconds passed before she spoke. "If I agree to your price, may I ask for one thing in return? I, too, will want it in writing."

"I'll not give you a child. Don't think you can persuade me otherwise. It's not open to negotiation."

She smiled. A smile so warm and sweet it was in danger of stealing past his defences. "No matter what happens, I ask that you're always honest with me. I shall afford you the same courtesy."

Stunned by her proposal, Aramis dragged a breath into his lungs. She could have asked for a diamond bracelet or a pledge he'd not bed another woman until they parted. She could have asked him to be gentler in bed, and he might have conceded.

"Agreed." He felt like he'd won a coveted prize at auction. "I shall make no allowances for my blunt manner." When a man had been tricked into believing a lie, he made sure everyone understood his meaning.

Her eyes brightened. "It's nice to know we can agree on something. It bodes well for the future."

He might have told her he lived for today, but the carriage rumbled into the yard of the Copper Crown, and he turned his attention to the group of men shouting near the stables.

Two thugs stood, fists raised, engaged in a bare-knuckle brawl. Amongst the rowdy rabble surrounding them, three men held lit lanterns aloft. Another battled to stop his savage dog from joining the fray. A fellow stood on a wooden crate, scribbling in a notebook with a stubby pencil, the bets coming as fast as the punches.

The second Aramis stepped down from the carriage, he could almost taste the tangy essence of blood. "Wait here, Miss Grant."

Excitement thrummed in his veins, coupled with the familiar tinge of fear. Old memories surfaced. Accompanying Aaron to the fighting pits always filled him with dread. His brother fought to put food on the table and clothes on their backs. A win brought a rush of elation. Not because the money helped to fill their bellies but because Aaron hadn't died.

Aramis pushed through the throng of unruly men. The expert cut of his coat marked him as fodder for the felons.

Their greedy gazes found him in the gloom. In their minds, they were already appraising his gold pocket watch, eyeing the large onyx in his sovereign ring.

Woe betide the first man who touched him.

But it wasn't a man who dared to tap him on the back.

"Mr Chance, it's not safe to linger out here. We must go inside at once, or we'll encounter more trouble than we bargained for."

He turned to see the petite Miss Grant standing amongst a crowd of cutthroats. "I told you to remain in the carriage. Do not disobey me, madam." Else they would both be found dead in a ditch come the morning.

"You're not my husband yet," she whispered for his ears only before parting her cloak and revealing the pistol hidden inside a deep pocket. "I have adequate protection."

For the love of God!

This woman would be the death of him.

These villains didn't need to raise a finger.

"Happen you should listen to the lady." A toothless blackguard staggered out from the shadows. "Seems she has the measure of the situation."

"Aye, I'll have that fancy ring off yer finger as soon as blink," came the threat from another quarter.

Aramis smiled to himself. The night was turning into one of the finest he'd had in years. What better way to pass a few hours than to fight drunken imbeciles and bed the delectable Miss Grant?

"I was told there's honour amongst thieves." Aramis hardened his tone. "I'll fight anyone here for a place amongst your ranks. If I win, you'll allow us to come and go as we please."

"You'll need someone to vouch for you," said the scrawny fellow, swigging liquor from a dirty bottle. "Someone to find a worthy opponent."

"You'll do. Make the arrangements. You can have a tenth of the winnings."

Mocking chuckles echoed in the cool night air.

Aramis had gained the horde's attention.

"A tenth?" he cackled. "I'll want half. That's my price."

"You can have it all in exchange for safe passage."

The atmosphere sparked with excitement. The toothless brute almost fell over his own feet in shock. Suddenly, Aramis found himself under the man's supervision and swamped by rogues keen to assess his physique.

"Where's my wife?" Aramis snapped, searching the crowd. He'd not let these brutes think Miss Grant lacked protection. "I want her in my sights at all times, or I'll not give you a damn penny."

The fellow, who explained his name was Duckett because he'd lost his teeth due to poor timing, ushered Miss Grant forward.

"She has a loaded pistol," Aramis said, dismissing the pang of pride in his chest. "But lay a hand on her, and I'll gut you like a fish."

"If you survive," one brute sneered.

Aramis grinned. "You can't kill the devil."

While Duckett scuttled away to find an opponent and rouse the bystanders into a betting frenzy, Aramis shrugged out of his coat and handed it to Miss Grant.

"Sir, I must advise you to reconsider." She ground her

teeth together in agitation. "There are no Queensbury rules here."

Her naiveté might have touched him, were his heart not encased in steel. "I've fought in dungeons and rat-infested cellars." Aaron had ensured his brothers were skilled in the art of pugilism. "Fortune's Den has its own fighting pit in the basement. We host a monthly event. The bouts are often brutal."

The mention of the gaming hell he owned with his brothers had her nibbling her bottom lip. "You live there, I'm told."

"I own numerous properties in town but prefer to live with my kin." Before they exchanged vows, she needed to know he had no intention of leaving Fortune's Den. "Regardless of our arrangement, I shall continue to do so. And my brother Aaron would never permit a woman to live above the gaming hell."

"You have a sister living at home."

"Delphine is the exception."

They were too scared to let their sister out of their sight. Men neck-deep in debt were desperate enough to snatch Delphine and hold her for ransom. And then there was the secret no one spoke about, but that was another matter.

Beneath the soft shimmer of moonlight, Miss Grant watched him unbutton his waistcoat. He'd never had cause to seduce a woman. He'd never cared if a woman admired his physique. Yet he felt a deep ripple of desire when her gaze slid slowly over his muscular shoulders.

"Have you ever seen a man without his shirt?"

"Once." She took receipt of his waistcoat and clutched

his garments to her chest. "Though it is not a memory I care to revisit."

"Turn away if you're embarrassed." He kept an indifferent tone though his blood boiled. Some wicked devil had hurt her. He'd learn his name and visit him in the dead of night. "If we're to marry, you should become accustomed to the sight."

She pursed her lips and nodded.

The glimmer of innocence coupled with her fierce spirit did odd things to his insides. He blamed it on the fact he'd never met a woman as fascinating as Miss Grant. That, and the primal urge to mate was compelling.

He fixed his eyes on hers as he untied his cravat and dragged his shirt over his head. What would she think of his hideous scar?

Miss Grant studied every toned muscle. Her gaze softened as it moved to the disfigured skin covering his left forearm like a tatty leather vambrace. Her lips parted as she followed the trail of dark hair from his navel to the waistband of his trousers.

"You put the marble statues of gods to shame." She made no mention of his scar. "I'm tempted to touch you to see if you are made of steel."

A memory invaded his mind.

The words of a disgruntled husband he'd known nothing about.

The fire's hot, eh?

You'll suffer a second for every time she touched you.

Based on her confession, it's more than ten.

"You'll have to take me at my word," he said, anger

ripping through him like the flames had ripped through his skin. "No one touches me, madam."

The lady jerked her head and looked confused. "Not even your soon-to-be bride? Not the women you bed?"

"No one."

Her brow furrowed as she tried to make sense of his statement.

"Perhaps you wish you'd chosen my younger brother to be your saviour. Theo is known by the moniker the King of Hearts. Women adore him."

Like a lone soldier facing a battalion, she stiffened her spine. "It's of no consequence. Our time together will be brief, though one should never dismiss the power of a genuine caress."

He couldn't help but glance at her delicate hands. For the first time in ten years, he experienced a flicker of regret.

What the hell had this woman done to him?

He'd be damned if he knew.

He didn't have time to contemplate the matter. Duckett came hurrying over, grinning like he'd found King Midas' treasure. "Woods will fight you, though his fists are like *bleeding* mallets." He pointed to the towering brute with mangled ears. "I've bet ten shillings he'll take you in the second round. Take a hit if you're still standing, but don't rouse suspicion."

Aramis grabbed Duckett by his stained neckcloth. "You've mistaken me for a coward. I suggest you change your bet. I'll floor the giant in the first round." He would have Woods on his arse in ten seconds.

"But Woods never—"

"If I'm wrong, I'll reimburse you."

Duckett stumbled away when Aramis released him.

While awaiting the lout's return, he turned to Miss Grant. "If I die, take my sovereign ring to my brother Aaron. Tell him a spade trumps a club. Tell him I've beaten him to the grave. Tell him my dying wish is that he helps you in my stead."

"That's not how this night will end." Miss Grant hugged his clothes to her chest as if he were inside them. "I have every faith you'll live."

He had every faith, too. Still, he looked at her mouth, keen to drink from her sensual lips lest he perish. Ordinarily, he would grip her hair, tilt her head and feed like a beast in need of blood.

Yet he faltered.

This woman had a hidden power.

What if one kiss drew the strength from his bones?

Thankfully, there was no time to consider the point.

The shouts and jeers grew louder. The crowd parted to create an avenue to the makeshift ring. Woods took centre stage, growling and flexing his muscles to incite the mob.

Aramis cupped Miss Grant's upper arm. "If I go down, you're to run. Don't look back. Do you hear me? Godby will see you safely to Fortune's Den."

For the first time since she'd kidnapped him at gunpoint, panic flashed in her eyes. "Don't say that. You're sure to succeed. I've never met a man more courageous."

So, she was a virgin.

Only an innocent presumed it took courage to hit a man.

Aside from the competitive aspects, men fought out of fear.

"Rest assured. It will be over quickly." He put all thoughts of Miss Grant behind him as he followed Duckett through the crowd. Woods snarled and made vile threats. None of it penetrated Aramis' armour.

While he stretched his muscles and flexed his fists, he let the painful images surface. A man fought better when he had a cause. His wasn't vengeance for the scar on his arm. His anger didn't stem from being tricked out of his own inheritance. Whenever he recalled how Aaron had suffered to protect his kin, hell's fury fired through his veins.

"Let the nabob have it, Woods," someone yelled.

"There ain't no place here for *bleeding* dandies," said another.

"Happen his wife might need a shoulder to cry on."

Damnation!

The last comment hit a nerve.

"Any man who touches her will lose his fingers." He goaded Woods and beckoned the giant forward. The sooner he knocked the fellow out, the better.

The crowd continued hurling threats and insults, but Aramis calmed his mind. The key was to strike quickly and to stun one's opponent. Most men aimed for the face first. Indeed, Woods kept his fists high as he barrelled forward, anticipating an obvious attack.

Don't underestimate the element of surprise.

Aramis bounced lightly on his feet, his movements fluid, though he let Woods think he was preparing to deliver an uppercut to the jaw. The halfwit lunged first, throwing all his weight behind a punch capable of knocking a man to the ground.

Aramis ducked and delivered a hard jab to the weak spot between Woods' ribs and upper abdomen. The blow knocked the air out of the brute's lungs. Arms flailing, he fought for breath as the second punch caught him under the chin. Woods hit the ground with a thud. Despite his supporters racing into the ring to rouse him with a few sharp slaps, Woods struggled to stand.

Aramis smiled to himself.

Aaron would be proud.

Amid the stunned silence, Duckett charged into the fray and raised Aramis' hand, quickly declaring him the victor.

"I'll fetch you a drink and find another opponent," Duckett said, chuckling at his good fortune. "Though the odds won't be as good next time, I should still earn a tidy bunce."

"Not tonight." Aramis glanced at Miss Grant. The lady smiled as she held his gaze. Why he felt compelled to join her was anyone's guess. "My wife would never forgive me, and I have business in the inn."

The nature of that business was yet to be determined.

Indeed, he would have to call in a debt to secure a special licence unless the plan meant having the banns read.

Intrigued to know why she'd dragged him to the Copper Crown, he slapped Duckett on the shoulder and made to depart. "Enjoy your winnings. I expect to come and go without incident. Cross me at your peril. I have three brothers equally skilled in pugilism."

He joined Miss Grant, cupped her elbow and directed her to a nearby well. Touching her proved a novelty. Like he'd known her a lifetime, not mere hours.

She watched him raise the bucket and splash water over his face and chest. "I thought there was a no-touching rule. You've touched me twice since we arrived."

He reached for his shirt. "I can touch *you*."

"Because you function best when in control?"

"Because this was the penalty for allowing a woman to touch me." He gestured to the arm she surely found abhorrent. No further explanation was needed.

"What if I accidentally touch you when we consummate our union? Will you bind my wrists or place me in shackles?"

He found himself smiling again. He would pin her hands above her head and ride her hard. "I shall merely bend you over the desk so there need be no mistakes."

Innocent eyes peered up at him, eyes like sparkling blue pools in the height of summer. "From what I've seen, lovemaking is a vigorous activity. Surely you'll make allowances for my inexperience."

He'd not given the matter much thought.

In his mind's eye, he saw himself pounding fast enough to drive her out from under his skin.

"Let's consider the matter once we're wed." There was little point discussing something that might never come to pass. "You've still not explained why marriage is necessary or why we're visiting this iniquitous den."

He set about tying his cravat, but she insisted on coming to his aid. She folded and knotted the silk with ease, a hairsbreadth between her dainty fingers and his jaw —the closest he would ever come to a caress.

"I helped the actors at the Belldrake with their costumes." She spoke as if needing to justify her skill at dressing a man. "As my husband, everything I own becomes yours. I need you to fight for my share of Hartford Hall. One look at you, and my uncle will be shaking in his boots."

Battles were not always that simple.

"But you said you trust no one. Why trust me? I could prosecute your uncle and keep every penny."

She glanced at his cravat and gave a nod of approval. "That's a question I've asked myself many times. What if you betray me and side with Melissa?"

Aramis growled at the suggestion. "I'd rather burn in hell. I'm relying on you to ensure I don't bury her in a shallow grave. I speak figuratively, of course."

"Of course." Like an obedient wife, she handed him his waistcoat. Though a wise man would do well to remember she carried a loaded pistol in the deep pocket of her travelling cloak. "I may be timid when it comes to lovemaking, but I intend to fight for what's mine. I have no choice but to trust you. I have no choice but to leave London. Failure is not an option."

As he had no intention of leaving town, this marriage of convenience would work perfectly. "You must return to the Belldrake while we continue our enquiries and the banns are read."

The lady paled. "That's impossible and quite unnecessary." She scanned the yard before making a confession. "I

43

hit Mr Budworth with a stool when he tried to lock me in his office."

Aramis inwardly cursed. Doubtless Budworth admired more than Miss Grant's acting abilities. "Did he throw you out?"

She worried her bottom lip. "No, I left him groaning on the floor. I locked the door and threw the key into the orchestra pit."

An unfamiliar swell of admiration formed in his chest. "That explains your need to take me hostage." However, if anyone asked, he would say he was a willing participant.

"Once we're married, Mr Budworth will think twice before exacting revenge. I don't know what I'd have done had you not come to the Belldrake tonight."

Being a logical man, he dismissed the idea that their meeting was anything more than bad timing on his part. That said, the lady had offered the perfect solution for getting rid of Mrs Wendon.

A sudden cacophony of cries and jeers erupted as two more men stripped off their shirts, ready to do battle.

"We should head inside." Aramis shrugged into his coat. "I understand your need to marry, but perhaps you might explain what's so important about visiting the Copper Crown?"

"St Augustine's is a quaint church with a unique congregation." She pointed to the sprawling field behind the inn. "The Reverend Smollett drinks in the Copper Crown. For a fee, he will marry us in church. He will provide a Certificate of Banns, listing me as living in the parish. I told him St Mary's is your parish church."

"A godly man with a blackguard's heart. How original." The reverend wouldn't be the first clergyman to bend the law. When Aramis returned to town, he would make enquires into Smollett's background, be assured of his credentials. "Has he given you a date for our nuptials? We'll need a solicitor to draw up the legal documents pertaining to our agreement."

He wondered if Miss Grant had thought the matter through. Indeed, his need to punish Melissa had made him a tad hasty. There was no proof this woman spoke the truth.

Miss Grant looked at him like he'd sprouted horns. "Forgive me. I thought you understood. The Reverend Smollett is to marry us tonight."

Chapter Four

"The reverend cannot marry us tonight," Mr Chance argued as they strode towards the carriage. "The law is clear on the matter. What next? I suppose you'll tell me it's a handfasting ceremony."

"The parish records will say the wedding took place at eight o'clock tomorrow morning." Naomi bit her bottom lip. It was perhaps one lie too many for Mr Chance, but the enquiry agent she'd hired to find Lydia assured her the plan would work.

"Your head is so full with thoughts of vengeance, you're not thinking clearly. This whole thing is absurd."

"If you've had second thoughts, please say so now." Naomi dragged her carpet bag out of the carriage and quickly returned the pistol to the box. In truth, she had her own doubts about the match.

She had not expected Mr Chance to have a list of demands as long as Hadrian's Wall. Nor had she antici-pated the rush of excitement when gazing upon his broad chest. Seeing his dreadful scar had hurt her heart. Amid the maelstrom of emotions, the need to soothe his woes had taken precedence.

You're more fortunate than most, she imagined telling him. *Take heart. People love you. Your brothers would die for you.*

Most shocking of all was why he affected her so profoundly. The smell of his clothes proved irresistible. Perhaps his valet had added laudanum to his cologne. Inhaling the musky scent had quickly developed into an addiction.

"I've not had second thoughts." He spoke in the commanding voice she found comforting. "Though I will need certain assurances before we proceed."

Anticipating the request, she urged him to follow her into the shabby inn. "After the night's events, I'm sure you need a drink, and the Reverend Smollett is awaiting our arrival. I have a few items in my bag that should prove my claim." Her enquiry agent would convince him she spoke the truth.

He marched beside her, a giant against her slight frame.

No one in the yard dared look in their direction.

The moment they entered the dim taproom, all conversation died. Word of Mr Chance's formidable strength had men shifting sideways and stumbling over their feet. Some eyed him as one would a dangerous panther. Others arrogantly assessed the size of his arms, gauging if they had the skill to beat him.

The air reeked of stale smoke and unwashed clothes. Dogs lounged beside the huge stone hearth while their masters' mouths were glued to their tankards.

Dressed in black, the Reverend Smollett sat in a shadowy corner of the taproom, sucking on chicken bones and guzzling ale. Beside him, Mr Sloane—the agent who'd suggested Mr Chance's desire for retribution would make him a valuable ally—sat flipping a coin between his fingers.

Naomi motioned to the men. "Let me introduce you to the reverend and the agent I hired to find Lydia. You can hear what they have to say before making a decision."

Mr Chance gritted his teeth as he eyed the enquiry agent. "I knew it. I knew Daventry was involved." He referred to the master sleuth who owned the enquiry agency.

"Yes. It was Mr Daventry who explained our common interest." Until then, she had not known how Mr Chance had come by the dreadful scar. "And Mr Sloane said he worked with you recently on a case involving your brother and Egyptian artefacts."

"Did Sloane encourage you to kidnap me at gunpoint? Or was it his matchmaking employer who first mentioned marriage?"

She came to an abrupt halt, forcing him to face her. She stared into eyes that were depthless obsidian pools. "Mr Sloane suggested I give you an opportunity to seek retribution for the injustice served. *I* decided to bring a pistol and shackles, and so raided the theatre's prop basket."

He raised a brow. "Prop basket? The pistol wasn't loaded?"

"Of course not. I'm a novice when it comes to abduction. If I'd shot you, I'd never have forgiven myself."

She expected the ground to tremble as his temper rose from its underground lair, but he threw back his head and laughed. "Miss Grant, this business is so farcical I'm inclined to think I'm dreaming."

"Sir, I would pinch you were it not for the no-touching rule." Guilt tugged at her conscience. She didn't want him to think she was as cunning as her stepmother. "The pistol seemed like the best way to gain your assistance. You're free to leave with my humble apology. I shall deal with Melissa myself." She offered him a sincere smile. "On the bright side, has it not been an interesting evening?"

"*Interesting* is one word I'd use to describe tonight's events."

Feminine pride soared in her chest. Few could claim to capture the notice of such a formidable fellow. Lydia would be furious. "*Surprising* might be another. My sister was adamant I lacked the skill needed to gain a gentleman's attention."

His eyes brightened as he studied her face. "I'm not a gentleman. And you had my undivided attention before you drew the pistol."

She held his gaze. Something passed between them. Something warm and congenial, which was odd when one considered his dangerous reputation. "Will you join me in a discussion with the reverend and Mr Sloane? Or shall we part ways here?"

Her pulse raced as she awaited his answer.

In his presence, she did not feel so dreadfully alone.

"Since you risked gaol to get me to the Copper Crown, it would be rude not to stay." His hand came to rest on the small of her back, a gesture for her to lead the way. He didn't remove it until they reached the table.

"Ah, Miss Grant. I wasn't sure you'd return." The reverend barely took his eyes off his dinner. Grease coated his bristled chin. Wine stained his white Geneva bands. "I see you brought the groom."

"Potential groom," she said. "Mr Chance needs more information before he will relinquish his bachelorhood."

Mr Chance glowered at Mr Sloane. "I want a private word with you once we've concluded our business. You might have visited me at Fortune's Den instead of forcing the lady to take matters into her own hands."

Mr Sloane leaned back in the chair and grinned. With his long hair, he had the look of a swashbuckling pirate. "Miss Grant should be commended. I bet ten pounds she'd crumble at the first hurdle." He glanced at her, unrepentant. "No offence, madam. Who knew you could accomplish such an impossible feat?"

"Mr Chance is a logical man," she said, keen to defuse the thrum of hostility. "He saw the sense in my plan. A plan that is to our mutual benefit."

The agent narrowed his gaze. He motioned to the empty wooden chairs around the table and urged them to sit. "You know this would be a marriage in name only, Miss Grant. Only a naive woman would hope to tame the hard-hearted."

Mr Sloane was beginning to sound as cold as Lydia.

You're so gullible, my darling. Like a delicate flower, it wouldn't take much for you to lose your bloom.

"You speak in error, sir. Mr Chance is hard-headed, not hard-hearted." Else he would have disarmed her and thrown her out at the Belldrake. "Hence we're both aware of our obligations."

The reverend stopped slathering over his chicken bones. "Trust in the Lord. He is our refuge and strength." He turned to Mr Sloane. "Might I have another mug of ale?"

Mr Sloane beckoned a serving wench, slipped her a sovereign and ordered refreshment. Mr Chance asked for brandy. Needing a potent drink to calm her nerves, Naomi had the same.

She reached into her bag, found the documents buried beneath the leg irons and handed the file to Mr Chance. "This is a copy of my father's will, given to me secretly a week before he died. As Hartford Hall is unentailed, he wanted his daughters to inherit the house. He left Melissa a cottage on the estate and a small stipend."

Mr Chance scanned the documents. "A cottage?"

"To quote my father's dying words, 'That conniving witch likes to sow oats, let her live in the gardener's cottage'."

A muscle in Mr Chance's cheek twitched. He hardened his gaze. "I assume she was entertaining your uncle while married to your father."

"Presumably so. My uncle Jeremiah Grant moved into the house the day after the funeral. Imagine our shock when the solicitor read the will and Melissa and my uncle had inherited everything."

Naomi had produced the original document, whereby the solicitor explained she was in receipt of an old copy. That the most recent was proved at Doctors' Commons. "I believe they conspired to kill my father, though how does one prove such a thing?"

Mr Chance's snort rang with contempt. "It's quite simple. We attack from the flank. We force them to reveal their secrets. We scare them until they make a mistake."

He sounded so confident in his ability to get the job done it brought strength to her tired limbs. "You will need to school me in the art of warfare."

He leaned closer, his breath hot against her ear as he whispered, "A husband may school his wife in many things. I suspect you'll be a competent student, Miss Grant."

Heat crept up her neck and warmed her cheeks. She suspected he would insist on tutoring her daily. "You might learn a thing or two from me, sir."

"What could you possibly teach someone so seasoned?"

"The element of surprise."

A smile tugged at his lips. He pinned her to the chair with his penetrating gaze. "Oh, you're a master at catching a man unawares."

The serving wench returned with their drinks.

Naomi reached for the small pewter mug and took a large sip to calm her nerves. Liquid fire scorched her throat. "Good Lord." She coughed and hissed to cool the burn.

Mr Chance patted her gently on the back.

"Be careful, sir. Someone might mistake you for a gentleman."

"Or a scoundrel out to get you drunk."

Mr Sloane coughed, too, though it was merely to gain

their attention. "Should you need assistance proving fraud, visit our Hart Street office." He retrieved a black notebook and pencil from his coat pocket and flicked to the relevant page. "I've had no luck locating your sister. Lord Bedlow hasn't seen her for a week. Not since they argued about Mr Chivers' frequent visits to the theatre. Can you think of anyone with a gripe against her?"

Naomi scoured her mind. Everyone loved Lydia, or at least they professed to. "I heard her arguing with the theatre manager. It may have been about money. The manager threatened to throw her out."

Mr Sloane scribbled in his notebook. "And she didn't complain about unwanted attention? She didn't tell you she feared for her life or that she'd made plans to leave London?"

"No. Do you have an older sibling, Mr Sloane?"

"I'm an only child, Miss Grant."

Naomi thought how best to word her grievance without sounding feeble. "Lydia always knows best. My thoughts and feelings count for very little." Lydia believed her experience with men made her superior. "She tells me nothing about her business."

"You're not close," Mr Chance stated.

"No. Unlike your kin, Lydia would not risk her life to save me." The selfish mare was likely promenading along Brighton pier with a lover, keen to teach the theatre manager a lesson. Naomi had grown tired of Lydia's lies and excuses and had hired Mr Sloane to uncover the truth. "Oh, I did find Mr Kendrick searching her room. The actor said she had borrowed his copy of the script and flounced out in a dreadful huff."

Mr Sloane gave a curious hum. "I've spoken to Kendrick but will press him for a detailed statement." He took a swig of ale from his tankard. "I suppose we should return to the matter of marriage. You know the law. It's a simple case of coverture. As your husband, Mr Chance might appeal to have the will overturned. You'll need proof of fraud and a decent barrister. Daventry can help with that."

Naomi cast Mr Chance a sideways glance. It was impossible to distinguish anything from his unreadable expression, but he seemed annoyed whenever someone mentioned Mr Daventry's name.

The reverend dragged himself from his meal and joined the conversation. "I can marry you tonight in St Augustine's."

"You'd be breaking the law," came Mr Chance's angry whisper.

"On the contrary, Mr Sloane's employer obtained a special licence."

"A special licence?" Mr Chance frowned. "Is it forged? I doubt the Archbishop would grant me such a privilege."

Mr Sloane was quick to settle any concerns. "Despite your father's banishment, your uncle is the current Earl of Berridge. Daventry persuaded the Home Secretary to intervene. Solving a serious case of fraud is important to the Crown."

"What made Daventry so certain I'd agree?"

Mr Sloane shrugged. "He understands how the past can haunt a man and believes vengeance is the only cure. I will act as a witness to the proceedings. Your coachman will serve as the second. Did you bring a ring?"

Mr Chance snorted. "I didn't have time to procure one."

With a confident grin, Mr Sloane removed three velvet boxes from his satchel and placed them on the table. He opened them to reveal the gold rings inside—a tiny opal set amongst a cluster of black sapphires, a diamond and pearl cluster, and a ruby solitaire. "They're on loan from Woodcroft Jewellers on Bond Street. Do you wish to purchase one?"

Mr Chance didn't give them a second glance. "Pick one, Miss Grant. I shall settle with Woodcroft's on my return to town."

She faced him, her stomach churning. "You wish to proceed with the plan? I doubt there's a solicitor on hand to record your demands."

He shrugged. "We'll document them ourselves. Sloane and the reverend will witness our signatures."

She scanned the rings that surely cost a king's ransom. "Do you have something simple? A cheap gold band? I do not wish to put Mr Chance to any unnecessary expense."

Mr Chance sat forward. "Money is no object. If it's to remain on your finger, I would rather you choose something pleasing."

Mr Sloane chuckled. "Take advantage of his generosity, Miss Grant. It's not often Aramis Chance considers a woman's needs."

Not wanting to offend him by suggesting she settle the bill when she received her inheritance, she studied the rings on the table.

Being tenderhearted, she opted for the obvious choice. "If it fits, I should like the sapphire and opal cluster."

The white stone was a symbol of hope and purity. Like Mr Chance's dominant aura, the black sapphires represented power and protection. The contrast was striking. Beautiful.

She tried it for size. Much like her betrothed, it was a fraction too big. "Once on, I doubt it will slip past my knuckle. I can have it altered in town."

Being suddenly impatient, the reverend suggested they remove to the church so he might conduct the proceedings. "I have a sermon on gluttony to write, though it will be wasted on this rabble."

Mr Sloane fetched paper and ink and laughed when he heard Mr Chance's list of demands. Still, both witnesses signed the document, which Mr Chance folded and slipped into his coat pocket.

The sombre stone church of St Augustine's stood nestled in shadow between a copse and desolate fields. A lonely place that did nothing to settle her nerves. Amid the stillness of the night, the air was cool, the moon serene, yet every step along the narrow path took immense effort.

Would she come to regret her decision?

In attempting to solve one problem, would she encounter another?

Mr Chance's deep sigh spoke of grave reservations. He trudged beside her like a man in mourning.

"Think of this as a mere business transaction," she said as they passed through the vestibule. "With or without my inheritance, I'm quite capable of making my own way in the world." Still, she owed it to her father to see justice served. "I shall be no trouble. You'll barely know I exist."

"Only a fool would fail to notice you." He cast her a

sidelong glance. "I was anticipating my elder brother's reaction when he discovers I'm married. Be thankful it's one fight you won't have to witness."

She sensed his inner torment. In the absence of parents, one could not help but feel compelled to please an older sibling. "I'm sure he will understand your reasons. If not, ask him to spend five minutes in a carriage with Mrs Wendon. That should warm him to your cause."

Mr Chance's dark eyes glowed with amusement. "You have a talent few women possess, Miss Grant. You can lift a man's sullen mood with a few choice words."

"I merely allude to the truth, sir."

He looked at her like she had sprouted fairy wings and arrived from an otherworldly plain. "Once we're wed, you will call me Aramis. Regardless of the vows we make here, I shall forever be your protector."

The promise tugged at her heart. When a woman found herself alone, it was good to have someone she could depend upon. "As my husband, you may call me Naomi. Regardless of the vows we make here, I shall forever be a shoulder of support."

Who knew what would happen once they'd brought the villains to justice? Perhaps they might become friends, picnic in the park and dine together on Sundays. Hopefully, they would not despise one another as her father had Melissa.

The Reverend Smollett beckoned them past the rows of deserted pews. "Let us waste no more time."

Though the chill of trepidation rippled over Naomi's shoulders, she navigated the aisle, clutching her tatty bag, not a pretty posy. She stopped before the altar and faced the enigmatic Mr Chance. "It's not too late to run," she teased.

He gave a look of stoic resignation. "I believe I'll stay."

"May I have your donation?" The reverend offered his open bible.

"Yes. Just a moment. I shall find the thirty pounds."

She crouched and rummaged in her carpet bag, but Mr Chance cupped her elbow and drew her slowly to her feet. "Allow me to settle the bill."

He bombarded the reverend with questions and demanded to see the licence. "Should anyone have cause to doubt this marriage, I shall hold you both accountable."

Mr Sloane offered every reassurance. "Upon repeating the vows, you will be legally wed. You have my word."

Mr Chance produced the banknotes, which he agreed to sign along with the register. "I'll bring the devil's wrath down on both of you if you're wrong."

The reverend shrugged into his white surplice and slid the notes into the pages of his bible. "Let us begin." He spoke in the lofty voice one would use to address a packed congregation.

Naomi glanced at the empty pews, the echo of loneliness like tight fingers gripping her throat. This wasn't how she'd pictured her wedding day. There were no beaming faces, no people who cared.

"Will your family be annoyed they missed your wedding?"

Mr Chance sighed. "Under normal circumstances, yes."

"But not when you're marrying the woman who

kidnapped you?"

"No. The news will be as welcome as a storm of fire and brimstone."

"I'd rather suffer a storm than deathly silence." She struggled to keep the sadness from her voice. "Though, I'd like to think my mother is watching from heaven, wishing me well."

He swallowed hard. "Perhaps my mother is watching, too."

Desperate to begin, the reverend said, "Dearly beloved—"

"Wait!" Mr Chance drew the proceedings to an abrupt halt. "I need a few minutes." He touched her upper arm lightly. "Remain here, Miss Grant. I shall return shortly."

He marched along the aisle, the clip of his shoes like the drum of a death knell. Was London his destination? Had talk of fire and brimstone made him fear lying before God? Had he suddenly realised the value of bachelorhood?

He wouldn't get far without his coachman, and Godby sat in the pew like a stuffed bear, not the least perturbed.

They waited in silence.

Minutes passed.

Reverend Smollett squirrelled the banknotes into his pocket.

Mr Sloane withdrew his gold watch and checked the time. "At this rate, I'll not arrive home until dawn. Daventry will want a report—"

The sound of discordant song filtered into the church. Men and women piled into the old building and began filling the pews. Though they were all invariably drunk, they sang and smiled and were keen to make merry.

Mr Chance reappeared, herding them like sheep. Soon, they were all seated and staring at the altar. After a quick appraisal, he came to stand before her.

"I know they're not family," he said, straightening his coat, "but I'm sure they'll make for a lively congregation. I sensed you found the emptiness disturbing."

She stared at him, wanting to clasp his hand and press a kiss of thanks to his knuckles. "It's silly, especially in light of why we're marrying, but the atmosphere was so bleak."

He glanced at the grinning rogues. "Be prepared for them to heckle. I imagine a few crude words will pass from their lips."

"Dearly beloved," Reverend Smollett began, evidently tired of the delays. "We are gathered here tonight to celebrate …"

And so it went on—a sermon extolling the importance of love and commitment—words that should have given them every reason to flee.

Despite the crowd's jeers, Mr Chance kept an impassive expression when promising to cherish her always. Then it was Naomi's turn to pledge her troth, to swear before God to love and obey this dangerous man she hardly knew. It was like asking her to ride an untamed stallion, not knowing if she'd feel the rush of exhilaration or the pain of rejection.

"I will," she said beneath the power of Mr Chance's compelling stare.

"Who giveth this woman to be married to this man?"

In the absence of family, the reverend called on Mr Sloane. The agent captured Naomi's cold hand and placed it gently on Mr Chance's broad palm. "I trust you will take care of her."

"I always protect what's mine."

The possessiveness in his tone proved oddly comforting. The mere touch of his skin played havoc with her insides. When he wrapped his firm fingers around hers, she could not recall ever feeling so safe.

"With my body I thee worship." His tone turned husky as he repeated the vow and slipped the ring on her finger. He would insist on touching her intimately, those powerful hands holding her enthralled while she could do nothing but clutch the bedsheets.

But it was too late for regrets.

A mere minute passed before the reverend declared them man and wife. The throng stamped loudly, cheered and gave a rapturous applause.

"Kiss her!" someone shouted.

"Lock yer lips!"

"We should do as they ask," he said while she was trying to come to terms with the weight of the burden on her finger. "Every lady deserves to be kissed on her wedding day."

She could barely breathe. "Not before an audience."

"I'll make it brief." A wicked smile tugged at his lips. "Though you may demand a thorough ravishment at a later date."

"I lack Miss Wendon's knowledge for pleasing men."

"I'm not like other men. Miss Wendon doesn't have the first idea how to please me. You, on the other hand, have an innocence I find bewitching." He captured her chin and drew her closer. "Relax. Let me taste you."

She closed her eyes, felt his breath caress her lips before their mouths met. As expected, he tasted warm like fine wine, rich and instantly intoxicating. While she kept her hands balled at her sides, he drew her into a dance, the melding of their mouths like a slow, sensual waltz. Heat flared deep in her core. Her head whirled. Her pulse raced.

She was out of her depth.

If a mere kiss could drug her senses, what would happen when he wanted more? And there was so much more to come. She could sense him fighting against his restraints.

As if he couldn't help himself, he slid his tongue gently over the seam of her lips before abruptly pulling away.

A slow smile formed as he dragged his thumb over his bottom lip. "Be thankful we have an audience."

The audience were on their feet, clapping and calling for them to continue the celebrations at the inn. Before Naomi could gather her wits, she was jostled out of the church and into the Copper Crown, a cup of strong wine thrust into her hand.

Thieves and cutthroats danced as much as they drank. One man played a fiddle while the landlord made space for others to engage in a jig. Mr Duckett wouldn't take no for an answer and swung her around and around until she was laughing so hard her abdomen hurt.

Her attention strayed to the far corner of the taproom, where her husband sat at a table with Mr Sloane. The agent talked while Mr Chance remained silent, his formidable gaze fixed on no one but her.

Chapter Five

It was past dawn when Aramis helped his wife into Sloane's carriage and closed the door. He disliked the plan. He disliked the plan as much as he disliked the strange emotions filling his chest. When exchanging vows, he'd expected to feel some sense of responsibility for the woman who'd kidnapped him at gunpoint, but the need to possess her left him questioning his sanity.

Naomi tugged down the window and looked at him through sad, nymph-like eyes. "Are you sure you're happy with the plan? I don't have to stay in the Sloanes' cottage. I can make other arrangements."

He'd promised not to lie but wouldn't tell her he was pining like a puppy. It would pass. Doubtless the hours spent watching her make merry was the cause. Her laugh had the power to hold a man spellbound. Her sweet smile could stun a man into submission. Everything about her was so honest and genuine.

But he'd been fooled once before.

He'd not be fooled again.

"You'll be safe in Little Chelsea." Evan Sloane lived in a vast mansion with his wife and infant pirates. "I shall send word once I've made an appointment to see your father's solicitor." On second thoughts, he might break into the office and throttle the truth from the solicitor's lips.

She gripped the top of the window and leaned forward, her delicate face framed like a priceless work of art. "Perhaps you might come for supper tomorrow evening. Mr Sloane may have news of Lydia. And we can discuss what we'll say to the solicitor."

He wanted to accept the invitation.

Say yes to a quiet dinner.

Yes, to a few hours spent together in bed.

But he needed to keep her at arm's length. Needed to reinforce the point this was nothing but a marriage of convenience.

"Threats and intimidation will work well enough." He was confident he could wring a confession from the solicitor in seconds. "I shall see you in a few days. Should you need anything, send word to Fortune's Den in Aldgate Street."

Naomi's weak smile hammered at the steel encasing his heart. "Thank you, Mr Chance. I know marriage is to our mutual benefit, but I appreciate you coming to my aid."

Hellfire!

How was she able to slip past his defences? Why did he imagine holding her, telling her she never need worry again? For ten long years, no one had come close to rocking his foundations.

"We will speak again soon." He gripped the window,

his little finger grazing her thumb. "It's been a memorable evening." One he would never forget.

A strange intimacy flowed between them. At present, it was a trickling brook, but he'd need to strengthen the dam before it became a raging torrent.

Stepping back from the vehicle, he stood alone in the yard of the Copper Crown and watched the carriage trundle away. Knots formed in his stomach when the lady pressed her palm to the window and held his gaze.

In the cold light of day, it was time to acknowledge what he'd done. He'd married a stranger. Aaron would tear him to pieces, try to force him to have the marriage annulled. Fighting a horde of cutthroats was easier than facing his elder brother. The brother he respected and admired.

Exhaling a heavy sigh, he examined his pocket watch.

He would wait at the Copper Crown and arrive in London in time to visit his brother Christian. They could ride to Fortune's Den together. Having recently married, Christian would not be so quick to judge.

He arrived in Ludgate Hill two hours later.

"I'm here to see my brother." Aramis barged past Christian's new butler—Higgins, Buggins or something similar. "I'll have time for coffee before I leave. Make sure it's piping hot."

The ageing servant paled—doubtless a reaction to Aramis' blunt manner. "I—I'm afraid he is indisposed, sir."

"Indisposed?" Perhaps Christian was tending to his morning ablutions. Ordinarily, it wouldn't stop Aramis charging upstairs and lounging on the bed while his brother shaved. But one did not invade a married man's chamber. "Then I shall wait for him in his study. Have Mrs Chance join me for coffee."

The mention of Mrs Chance roused an image of Naomi. The wife relegated to the wilds of Little Chelsea. The beguiling woman who'd charged through his barricade and made camp in his mind.

Aramis took two steps towards the study, but the butler darted forward to block the door. "I'm afraid you can't go in there, sir."

"Step aside, Higgins." He wasn't about to rifle through the drawers and steal important papers. "My brother keeps no secrets from me."

"It's Huggins, sir. But I must inform you the room is currently occupied." The man's eye twitched, and he lowered his voice. "Occupied on a most delicate matter. No one must enter, or the master will drag me by the scruff of my coat and deposit me on the pavement."

A faint banging echoed in the room beyond.

Aramis heard his brother growl, "Love, you know how to drive your husband wild. Must you work today?"

"Mr Purton is expecting me at the museum," Isabella panted.

A feminine moan of pleasure reached Aramis' ears, along with Isabella's plea that Christian complete the task with some expediency.

Suppressing a grin and an unwelcome pang of jealousy, Aramis informed the red-faced Huggins he would wait for his brother in the carriage. "If you must endure this at breakfast, I would insist on extra pay."

Ten minutes passed—minutes spent trying not to think

of all the erotic ways he might make Naomi Chance his wife.

Christian appeared, grinning like the cat who'd found the cream. He climbed into the carriage, dropped into the seat and gave a satisfied sigh.

"You look exhausted, and it's not even ten." And happy, Aramis noted, his brother looked too damn happy. What man wouldn't when he'd made love to his wife on his desk before breakfast?

"Yet I feel oddly refreshed." Christian brushed a lock of golden hair from his brow. He scanned Aramis' creased clothes and frowned. "You look like you've been wrestling with the devil." His eyes widened in recognition. "Tell me you weren't with Lydia Fontaine at the Copper Crown."

What the blazes?

Aramis straightened. "Who the hell told you that?" He'd lay odds it was Lucius Daventry. "I was at the Copper Crown." Exchanging vows and watching his enchanting wife dance with cutthroats and thieves. "But not with Lydia Fontaine."

Christian gave a confident grin. "Daventry seemed convinced you were with the famed actress. I assured him you would never entertain a woman so shallow."

"That man has no business meddling in my affairs."

"He brought Isabella a gift to congratulate her on her new position at the museum. After informing me of your late-night antics, he asked if I'd heard from you this morning."

Aramis' blood boiled. "Doubtless he was keen to hear if his plan had come to fruition. That scoundrel is out to see every man wed." Had Aramis married anyone but

Naomi Grant, he might feel burning resentment. He might feel cheated had his wife not been honest about her motives.

Christian laughed. "Even an agent with Daventry's skill couldn't persuade you to marry, and certainly not a coquette like Lydia Fontaine. You know there's a wager at White's on the likelihood you'll take a bride. One fool has bid against you. I'm inclined to bet an entire year's income you'll be a bachelor until your dying day."

"I suggest you refrain from making the bet." Aramis scrubbed his face with his hand. Not being one to mince words, he came straight to the point. "I am married. I married Naomi Grant at St Augustine's church last night."

I kissed her innocent lips.

I watched her laugh and make merry.

Spent hours wishing I were a different man.

Stunned silence filled the confined space.

Christian stared at him like he had two heads. "Is this a joke?"

"Would I joke about marriage? It's a business arrangement. I shall explain all once we reach Fortune's Den." He'd not tell the same story twice. Still, he prepared himself for a barrage of questions.

"Have you lost your mind?" Christian could barely sit still. "Who is she? Where did you meet her? Why the hell didn't you say something before? Why in God's name weren't we there?"

He thought of Naomi threatening him with a pistol and laughed. "Not all are as fortunate as you. People marry for reasons other than love. Miss Grant offered an incentive. I found I could not refuse."

Christian's frown deepened. "Does it have anything to do with Mrs Wendon snapping at your heels? I hear they'll lose the house if the daughter doesn't marry well."

"Mrs Wendon will have to settle her ambitions elsewhere. But that's not the only reason I married Miss Grant."

Her story had struck a chord with him. Upon their father's death, Aramis and his brothers lost everything to their scheming stepmother. Despite being the grandsons of an earl, they were left to live like vagrants in the rookeries. Perhaps that's why he felt a kinship with the woman he'd married. And then there was Melissa and a dream of vengeance.

Before Christian could question him further, they arrived at Fortune's Den. The family ate breakfast together every morning at ten and discussed the previous night's scandals. Who had lost their fortune at the tables and thrown themselves off Blackfriars Bridge? Who had issued an invitation to a dawn appointment having been accused of cheating?

Today, Aramis' marriage would dominate the conversation.

Sigmund, their man-of-all-work and a terrifying figure in his own right, answered the door and welcomed them inside. His gaze lingered on Aramis. "Aaron knows you weren't at home last night."

Some would think it odd that a man of twenty-nine should report to his elder brother, but they had many enemies amongst the *ton*. Their uncle—the current Earl of Berridge—would love nothing more than to see their lifeless bodies dangling from the scaffold. And they'd made a pact as frightened children. A sacred rule none of them dared break.

You'll tell me where you are at all times.

There must be no secrets between us, no lies.

Aramis patted Sigmund on the shoulder. "Then I shall join my brother in the dining room and put him out of his misery."

Christian chuckled. "And I'll have a front-row seat."

As always, he found Aaron at the head of the table, his mood as dark as his ebony locks. With a gaze that could freeze the fiery bowels of hell, he stared at Aramis. "How good of you to grace us with your presence. It seems Christian's departure from the fold has had an adverse effect on your memory."

Christian raised his hands in mock surrender. "Don't shoot a man for falling in love. Save your strength for our brother's shocking confession. You may want a stiff brandy to hand." He winked at Delphine, who sat eagerly watching the exchange. "It might be wise to move the knives."

Aaron scowled at him. "Aramis? What the hell have you done?"

Aramis sat in the empty chair beside Theo and snatched a piece of toast from the rack. "I married Miss Naomi Grant in St Augustine's last night. It's a marriage in name only. A means for us both to seek retribution for crimes committed against us."

"And to stop Mrs Wendon hounding him," Christian added, dropping into the seat next to Delphine. "Theo, be on your guard. You'll be the matron's next target."

Amid the undercurrent of tension, no one laughed.

Not while Aaron looked ready to bring the heavens crashing to earth. "You mean to tell me a woman we know nothing about bears your name?" There was a deadly edge to his calm tone. "A woman who likely invented a story to trick you into marriage?"

Aramis sat forward, fury twisting inside him. "Don't speak to me like I'm an imbecile. The lady offered terms. We made a written agreement which protects my name and my assets. She offered me a portion of her inheritance, which I declined."

Aaron's glare would make Satan shriek. "You've been planning this for weeks and said nothing? What about your vow to this family? No lies. No secrets. It's the law we live by."

"I met Miss Grant last night and married her two hours later."

Aaron flinched. "You said you married in church. You either had the banns read or applied for a licence."

He explained all that had occurred, except for the part when the lady held him hostage with a fake pistol. "I'll not let Melissa ruin an innocent woman's life. And being married affords me freedom from Mrs Wendon's machinations."

A curse slipped from Aaron's lips. "I should have known Daventry was involved. What is it with the man's need to see every bachelor leg-shackled?"

Though Aramis found Daventry's interference equally annoying, he could not argue with the agent's logic. "Daventry believes every victim needs justice." Not that Aramis would ever openly admit to being a victim. "His motives are honourable, even if his tactics suggest otherwise."

A pained silence invaded the space.

Justice was a word rarely mentioned in front of Delphine. They feared the notion might give their *adopted* sister a reason to search for her *real* family. But who would leave a young girl on the streets with nothing but the clothes on her back? Who had discarded her so easily? Had Aaron not taken her under his wing, heaven knows where she would be now.

A keen seeker of the truth, Delphine broached the subject everyone avoided. "You never told us what happened after Mr Adams burnt your arm. On your insistence, Aaron agreed not to punish the man, but did you ever seek revenge?"

Theo inhaled sharply. "Pay her no mind. Sometimes curiosity gets the better of her," he said in their sister's defence. "Delphine merely asks the question pertinent in all our minds."

A day ago, he would have told Delphine to mind her damn business and stormed from the room. He never discussed the subject that brought him great shame. He'd rather eat rancid food and sleep in piss-soaked doorways than relive the humiliation he'd suffered at Melissa's hands.

Yet, if he was to help Naomi regain her inheritance, he had to be honest about his dealings with Melissa. And his need to prove he was not a gullible milksop led him to make an embarrassing confession.

"I did nothing." The truth of those words tightened his throat. "I let Jacob and Melissa Adams walk free." To do something meant admitting he'd been naive. "I buried them in an imaginary graveyard. Had no plans for an exhumation until Miss Grant insisted on reminding me of my past."

Aaron's hard eyes softened. He knew. He made it his business to know everything, but he had never made Aramis feel like a fool. "I suspect Daventry means to dig up every skeleton. One might ask themselves why, but as you said, he strives to make the world a better place. He prides himself on encouraging people to deal with their nightmares."

Theo sighed. "I wish you'd felt able to talk to us sooner."

"Why seek vengeance now?" Aaron asked.

Aramis glanced at Christian. His brother had changed. He still studied his Egyptian books, kept the gaming hell's accounts and threatened men who refused to settle their debts. But the darkness had lifted. He walked with a spring in his step. Never stopped smiling.

Because I want what he has.

Not love—that was too much to ask—but freedom. Freedom from the chains that kept him shackled to the past. Freedom from the anger that haunted him like Jacob Adams' ghost.

"Because Miss Grant opened my eyes to the depth of Melissa's duplicity." Learning that Melissa's deception was not an isolated incident had caused a sudden shift inside him. "It made me realise I have no reason to bear the guilt."

"You mean Mrs Chance," Delphine said with a playful grin. "She's part of our family now. When might we meet her?"

"Did you not hear what Aramis said?" Aaron interjected coldly. "She will continue to live in Little Chelsea. Theirs is a marriage in name only. We won't be inviting her to dine at our table."

It was true. So why did he have an overwhelming desire to see his wife sitting beside him? Why couldn't he shake the feeling she belonged at Fortune's Den?

"Perhaps she may become a dear friend," Delphine countered.

"You would like her," Aramis found himself saying. "She is interesting company and quite amusing."

"What does she look like?" Delphine chuckled to herself. "Is she dark-haired like me? Is she tall or petite? She must have a backbone of steel. Forgive the endless questions. I never expected you to marry. The shock has left me giddy."

"It's left us all somewhat dazed," Aaron countered.

Aramis poured coffee into his cup. "Imagine walking deep into the forest and stumbling upon the fae," he said, feeding Delphine's excitement. "She is fair, petite and so delicate one might believe she's otherworldly. But then she opens her cloak in a yard full of cutthroats, shows you a pistol and assures you she's not afraid."

"She sounds like Miss Scrumptious." Delphine glanced at Aaron, aware he despised the moniker they used for the lady who owned the gaming establishment across the street. "Aaron spent an hour staring at The Burnished Jade this morning."

A growl of annoyance rumbled in Aaron's throat. "My interest amounts to nothing more than assessing the competition. I noticed Miss Lovelace ordered new furniture. I find it odd her father would venture abroad and leave a woman in charge of a failing gaming hell."

Aramis smiled to himself. He was grateful for the diversion, and it wasn't the first time they had caught Aaron spying on the lady who lived across the street. "Why don't you ask her why he left?"

Theo laughed. "Because Miss Scrumptious is the only person who doesn't cower when Aaron barks. His inability to frighten her rouses his ire."

Aaron tossed back the contents of his coffee cup. "This isn't about me. Let's return to the more pressing topic of Aramis' marriage."

Aramis braced himself. He was not afraid of his brother, but one did not wish to disappoint one's hero. "There's nothing more to say. I will visit the solicitor in Northwood tomorrow and demand answers."

Aaron surprised him by offering advice, not criticism. "Don't mention your connection to Miss Grant until you're seated in his office and he has no means of escape."

"Mrs Chance," Delphine corrected. "Mrs Naomi Chance. It has such a charming ring, don't you think?"

Tired of listening to their sister's teasing, Aaron threw his napkin on the table and pushed out of the chair. "Aramis, I seek a private word."

They retired to Aaron's office.

As soon as Aaron closed the door, his mood changed. "What the hell were you thinking? If you wanted retribution, there are damn sight easier ways than marrying a stranger. You know nothing about this woman."

He knew she had gumption. Knew she'd not lied about

being innocent. Tasting her had been like drinking a healing elixir, something sweet to counteract his bitterness.

"I've proven I'm an excellent judge of character," he countered. "Or do you mean to judge me for the mistake I made ten years ago?"

Aaron released a long sigh. "I don't blame you for what happened with Melissa Adams. You were young and desperate for the love denied you as a child. I was too busy building our empire and keeping the wolves from our door to notice the devil used many disguises."

"It wasn't your fault."

"I bear the guilt all the same."

Failing his family was Aaron's biggest fear. His temper, strict rules and blunt manner stemmed from love and deep-rooted anxiety. Aaron had spent so long caring for his kin he didn't know how to care for himself.

Aramis gripped his brother's shoulder, a gesture of abiding affection. "Things are different since Christian married. Change is on the horizon. Our ship sails a new course. En route, we're being urged to exorcise our demons."

Aaron frowned. He would rather sever his tongue than engage in philosophical babble. "You married for vengeance. How is that progress?"

Yesterday, he might have agreed.

Yesterday, he hadn't been bewitched by the fae.

"Because in punishing Melissa, I might find the part of me I left in that stinking alley. My skin may have healed, but my heart never recovered."

Aaron swallowed hard, the pain of the past etched on

his face. "Were it not for my promise to you, I would have killed them both."

"You'd risked too much for us already. I didn't want you risking your neck. Trust me. With my wife's help, Melissa will get her comeuppance." It was a shame Jacob Adams was fodder for the worms. Hopefully, Lucifer had given him a taste of his own medicine.

With his countenance much calmer, Aaron perched on the edge of his desk. "And is this wife of yours biddable? Will she be a constant thorn in your side or a balm to soothe the wounds?"

Aramis found himself lost for words. How did he describe the woman who'd slipped under his skin? A passionless man should deny these odd flutters of intrigue. But what if the lady was right? What if he was hard-headed, not hard-hearted? What if he was too practical, too wilful to accept he was anything but cold?

"Time will tell." The opportunity to tease Aaron was too tempting to resist. "She's as formidable as Miss Scrumptious and just as captivating. A man might spend sleepless nights thinking of all the ways he wants her."

Aaron glanced out of the window at The Burnished Jade. "The devil sent that woman to torment me."

"Perhaps you should draw the curtains. What the eye doesn't see, the heart doesn't grieve over."

"I hide from no one," Aaron said with steely defiance. "Least of all, a woman with lofty ideas and no care for her own welfare. Though I can see how the proverb suits your unfortunate circumstance. Where better to place a wife you don't want than amid the sprawling fields of Little Chelsea?"

He didn't tell Aaron he hadn't stopped thinking about his wife since they'd parted hours earlier. He was still thinking about her while watching men lose at the card table later that night. He thought about her when he helped usher the last gamblers out and retired to the drawing room to enjoy a glass of Aaron's best claret.

If thoughts had the power to alter one's fate, he was to blame for Daventry's late-night visit. The agent had not come to offer his felicitations or to gloat that he'd snared another bachelor in his matchmaking trap.

Aramis considered Daventry's grave expression. "What is it?" His thoughts ran amok. A vision of Naomi's lifeless body burst into his mind, the image stark and vivid. "What the hell are you doing here?"

"I need you to come to Bow Street."

"Bow Street?" Aramis' blood ran cold. "What the devil for?"

Daventry brushed a hand through his damp black hair. "I need you to give a statement explaining your whereabouts last night."

Aaron came striding into the hall. "What is this about?"

Daventry sighed—Daventry never sighed. He was always calm under pressure. "They found the manager of the Belldrake murdered last night, bludgeoned with a heavy object. I had no choice but to deliver her to the police office."

"Who?" Aaron said.

"My wife." A shiver ran down Aramis' spine.

Daventry nodded. "Mrs Chance is the prime suspect."

Chapter Six

Naomi sat in Sergeant Maitland's cluttered office, her hands clasped tightly in her lap, her mind awash with confusion. She had grabbed the stool and hit Mr Budworth across the arm and back, not the head. The man had fallen to the floor in shock more than in pain. When she left, he was whining like wind through a keyhole.

"By all accounts, you were the last to see Mr Budworth alive." The grey-haired sergeant sat back in the seat, his chubby hands splayed across his paunch. "Miss Matilda Gray said she heard you arguing with the manager. Said you locked him in his office and threw away the key. What do you have to say about that, Miss Grant?"

She might say Matilda was a scheming shrew.

"It's Mrs Chance," she corrected, hoping her husband would be her alibi. "I was married by special licence last night in St Augustine's near Highgate." She gestured to the agent seated on the wooden chair beside her. "Mr Sloane bore witness and can attest to the fact."

Mr Sloane sat forward. "As Daventry explained, Mrs

Chance is far too slight to lift a marble bust of Julius Caesar and hit Budworth on the head. Her clothes would have been splattered with blood."

"She might have changed before leaving the theatre."

"Have you found evidence to support your claim?"

The sergeant drummed his fingers on his bloated belly. "No."

Naomi fought to keep the tears at bay. With her sister missing and her stepmother's treachery, she had enough to fear without the threat of the noose. "Have you questioned the person who supposedly found the key to the office and opened the door? Do they have an alibi?"

The sergeant narrowed his beady blue eyes. "You must admit, it looks mighty suspicious. Your sister vanishes, and you're promoted from scullery maid to the leading role. An hour before you marry, your lover is found dead in a pool of blood."

"Mr Budworth was not my lover!" She would rather die than have that letch put his clammy hands on her person. "What leads you to think I'm that sort of woman?"

The sergeant gave no apology for his vulgar assumptions. "Miss Fontaine has had more lovers than lines. In my experience, younger siblings tend to follow in their elders' footsteps."

"What poppycock," she said, finding her temper. "My husband is the only man I have ever entertained, as I'm sure he will be pleased to confirm. Perhaps your time would be better spent examining the crime scene. I'm sure Mr Budworth had many enemies. I am not one of them."

The incompetent fool rocked in his chair. "You say you

married Mr Chance last night. Explain why you're living alone in a cottage on Mr Sloane's—"

The door burst open, and Aramis stormed into the room, looking dangerously handsome amid the glow of candlelight. "Don't say another word, my love." Like Lucifer rising from the bowels of hell, he glared at the sergeant. "I'm taking my wife home. It's not a request."

A wave of relief swept through her as Aramis captured her hand and urged her to stand. This show of solidarity was surely why he did not relinquish his firm grip.

Sergeant Maitland hauled himself out of the chair. "But she's a suspect in a murder investigation."

"No, she's not. I met her at the Belldrake last night. Speak to Mrs Wendon. She lives in Leicester Square and rode with us from the theatre. Daventry said the manager was hit so hard he died instantly. Does my wife look like she could inflict such horrific injuries? There wasn't a speck of blood on her face or clothes."

Naomi glanced at her husband's arresting physique. In or out of the ring, he was a force to be reckoned with. Only a fool would challenge him. Mr Sloane was right. With Aramis Chance leading the army, one was sure to win the war.

Beneath the weight of Aramis' stare, Sergeant Maitland stuttered, "If you were m-married last night, why was she hiding in a cottage in Little Chelsea? You must admit it's rather odd, sir."

A delightful shiver rippled through her when Aramis slid his arm around her waist. "Did you expect me to take my bride to a gaming hell? I thought renting a cottage would afford us some privacy. I was leaving Fortune's Den to join her there when Daventry informed me she was at Bow Street. I ask you, do I look like a man who would leave his wife unsatisfied?"

Heat rose to her cheeks. If she'd learnt one thing about her husband during their brief acquaintance, he was thorough.

"Half the peers in London owe me money," he growled. "Save yourself the embarrassment. Don't make me call in a debt."

Mr Daventry stepped into the room, as did another man who looked remarkably like Aramis but a little more menacing. He glanced at her, his gaze cold and darkly assessing.

"I've been granted the authority to investigate Budworth's murder." Mr Daventry stepped forward and handed the sergeant a letter. He gave the man time to read it before adding, "Due to my agents' success at solving crimes, the Home Secretary welcomes my assistance. One of my agents will report to Bow Street daily to update you on our progress."

Sergeant Maitland gave a frustrated sigh. He shoved the letter in his desk drawer before speaking in a more congenial tone. "I suppose you'll want access to the theatre. Mr Kendrick is overseeing things there. It seems murder brings in the crowds. They mean to open as usual tomorrow night."

"Do you know who owns the theatre?" Mr Daventry asked.

The sergeant began flipping through his notes.

"Mr George Budworth and his brother Edwin," Naomi informed him. The men argued constantly, often over

Edwin's insistence Lydia get the starring role. Lydia knew how to use her womanly charm to get what she wanted. "They were partners in the venture. Some say they inherited the money to buy the theatre. Some say they were swimming in debt. I'm afraid the details are a little vague."

Aramis snorted. "Is that not a motive for murder?"

A little red-faced, the sergeant averted his gaze. "I'm paid to follow every line of enquiry, sir."

Mr Daventry insisted they wait outside while he conversed with the sergeant.

Mr Sloane led them to the communal office. They stood amongst an eclectic mix of people—drunkards, ladies of the night, a man with a bloody nose, a distraught woman clutching a torn reticule.

Aramis gestured to the imposing gentleman, who was undoubtedly his kin. "Allow me to introduce my brother Aaron." He turned to the stone-faced fellow and said with a hint of humour, "My wife, Mrs Naomi Chance."

She did not curtsey.

Aaron did not bow.

"Doubtless you're worried how this inconvenient marriage will affect your family," she said, believing a man with Aaron Chance's reputation would prefer she be direct.

Aaron raised a sardonic brow. "Worrying is a woman's game, madam. Concern is a less emotive word which carries the desire to find a solution to a pressing problem."

The fact he saw her as a problem came as no surprise.

You're the problem, Naomi. You have the appeal of a dormouse. Who on earth would want to marry you? I suppose I'll have to feed you until I'm in my dotage.

Her stepmother's words slipped into her mind. But the cruel jibes were not the reason Lydia had shoved clothes into a valise and insisted they flee Hartford Hall in the dead of night. It was the only selfless thing her sister had ever done.

"There is no pressing problem," Aramis said in her defence. "None that should concern you. We're married. The focus should be on proving fraud and finding the beast who murdered the theatre manager."

Mr Sloane was quick to offer his services. "I am at your disposal, Mrs Chance. I have another case, but I'm sure Daventry will demand I spare the time."

Aramis was quick to refuse the offer. "We don't need an enquiry agent. I'm more than capable of catching a scoundrel. I'll not have it said I failed in my duty to protect my wife."

"A duty you were reluctant to accept," Mr Sloane countered.

"Did I seem at all hesitant when reciting my vows?"

Keen to defuse any animosity and prove she was in command of her own destiny, Naomi offered her opinion. "My husband is right, Mr Sloane. He is determined, skilled in combat and willing to take risks. Our fates were aligned the moment my father married Melissa Adams. We shall, of course, call at the Hart Street office should we require your assistance."

Mr Daventry appeared, surprising them all by presuming Aramis and his brothers would be tackling the case. "Together, you should be able to catch the villain. Send Theodore to Northwood to investigate the solicitor who forged Mr Grant's will while you question those who work at the theatre."

Aaron Chance muttered a curse. "We'll not be herded like sheep."

"It's merely a logical suggestion. Sloane will attempt to locate Miss Fontaine. I've a man watching your apartment, Mrs Chance." He reached into his brown leather portfolio and handed Aramis a note. "The Home Secretary gives you permission to oversee the case. Suspects will be required to answer your questions or face arrest."

While her husband read the note, her brother-in-law's black eyes clouded with suspicion. "I can't help but think you're scheming behind the scenes. What if Aramis had refused to marry Miss Grant? What would you have done then?"

Unperturbed, Mr Daventry shrugged. "Sloane would have dealt with Budworth's murder and the case of fraud. Aramis may have lived to regret never bringing his persecutors to justice." He glanced at Naomi and smiled. "Instead of raking up the past, consider what happens to Mrs Chance. She needs a safe place to reside. With her sister missing and the manager dead, she may be the villain's next target."

Naomi's heart lurched. "Can I not return to the cottage in Little Chelsea?" It was quiet and quaint. The gardens were vast, filled with trimmed topiary and extravagant mermaid fountains. The views of the countryside reminded her of happy times at home. But the estate was ten miles from Fortune's Den, and the distance would be a problem when the murder suspects lived in town.

Mr Daventry glanced over his shoulder before

lowering his voice. "Though Peel sought to eradicate corruption amongst his police force, many here would take a bribe. Whoever killed the manager may target you, madam. For your own safety, you must remain with your husband."

"I'm sure that's unnecessary," she said, slightly panicked. Heat coiled in her stomach whenever she thought about spending time alone with Aramis. The mischievous glint in his eyes had the power to bring a helpless female to her knees.

"Extremely unnecessary," Aaron Chance added.

Aramis disagreed. "Daventry is right. In getting rid of Naomi, the villain can frame her for murder without fear of rebuttal. But it's too late to find suitable accommodation." His gaze dipped to her lips. "We'll stay with Mrs Maloney tonight. As she's the closest thing I have to a mother, it's only right she should meet my wife."

"It's too late to wake Mrs Maloney," Aaron snapped.

Aramis slapped his brother playfully on the back. "Mrs Maloney will curse me to Hades if I wait until tomorrow. Besides, it's reside at the bookshop or Fortune's Den."

Aaron looked like he'd rather deliver milk on a yoke than permit her to cross his threshold. "There's always Mivart's hotel."

"My coachman Gibbs will assist you." Mr Daventry motioned to the window and the burly man seated atop a black coach. "He and the vehicle are at your disposal. As you're aware, he's a valuable asset in battle."

No one raised an objection.

Indeed, both Chance brothers seemed pleased.

They parted ways with the agents, agreeing to keep

each other informed of their progress. Once outside, Aaron drew Aramis aside and spoke in a hushed but irate voice.

Naomi took the opportunity to speak to the stern fellow in the oversized greatcoat, their driver for the next few days. "Good evening, Mr Gibbs." She introduced herself and mentioned the unusually wet weather.

"If we're to work together, Mrs Chance, know I'm not one for small talk. Odds are you'll find me rude and my manners coarse. But I get the job done."

"Then let us agree to be frank."

"Suits me fine, ma'am." The man shuffled in his seat.

"Don't get down, I can climb in unaided."

"If you can't use the handle, you've no hope of solving the case. I'm paid to keep you safe, not open doors and carry pretty hat boxes."

She bit back a grin. "That's good to know. I may be small, but I'm stronger than I look. I give my opinion freely and won't hold a grudge."

The man doffed his hat. "Happen we'll get along nicely."

"I'm sure we will." Naomi opened the door and climbed into the conveyance. She relaxed against the cold black leather.

Aramis joined her a minute later. The vehicle rocked on its axis as he dropped into the opposite seat and shut the door. "I told Gibbs to head for Mrs Maloney's bookshop in Lime Street. Say now if you have another suggestion."

What options were there for a woman of no fixed abode?

"I'm not sure who Mrs Maloney is, but if she's impor-tant to you, it's only right I meet her." If the lady was the closest thing he had to a mother, would she be disappointed he'd not married for love?

The carriage lurched forward and picked up speed.

Although hardly any time had passed since she'd persuaded Aramis to take her to Highgate, it felt like a lifetime. Conversation flowed easily between them. She felt safe in his company. Though he was known for being cold and heartless, the air was alive with other sensations. Excitement. Intrigue. Dare she say desire?

When she asked how he met Mrs Maloney, he stared at the passing buildings, a little lost in his own thoughts. "Despite Aaron's best effort to take care of us, we would have died on the streets had Mrs Maloney not given us a place to stay." He sighed deeply. "I'll never forget how good it was to sleep without the fear of being robbed."

Lydia's comments entered her mind as she listened to his impassioned tale. *There's no substance to him. The man fights and fornicates. Though they say he's a master at both skills.*

While the latter was undoubtedly true, Aramis Chance was far more complex than one might imagine. An enigma one felt compelled to examine. Was it foolish to think something magical lay beneath his dangerous personae? He oozed a potent masculinity, but there was a softer side she'd been privileged to glimpse.

"It must have been difficult to adjust after living in Mayfair. Mr Daventry told me your father's family disowned him and paid him to change his name."

"My father was born without a conscience. He lived without a conscience and died without a thought for anyone but himself."

"And yet his sons are loyal, honest men."

He studied her intently, his dark eyes like the depths of a forbidden forest. "We strive to be everything he was not."

"Yet people say you're cold." She'd thought twice before speaking her mind, but she would rather offend him than lie. "You feel nothing. You said so yourself."

He inclined his head. "Then forgive me for not explaining myself properly to a stranger. Sentiment makes a man weak. I avoid lowering my guard with everyone other than the people I trust."

Then you must trust me, she thought.

Why else would he offer an explanation?

She held his gaze. "Are we strangers?"

"Not anymore."

Something in his velvet-edged voice made her heart flutter. She didn't know how to define their relationship. They'd not known each other long enough to be friends. They were not lovers. Yet she felt connected to him in ways she could not explain.

"You kept your vow tonight." She referred to the oaths they made before reaching the altar. "When I needed you most, you were there."

"I promised to protect you."

"And I said I would be no trouble."

His gaze turned hot, his grin sinful. "I knew you were trouble the moment I laid eyes on you. You're my kind of trouble. Trouble I'm well-equipped to handle."

The air grew so tense it was electrifying.

She glanced at his strong hands. He would want to touch her soon. He would want to consummate their union.

Nerves had her asking the obvious question. "Have you considered the sleeping arrangements for tonight? We are married. I can't help but wonder what you have planned."

"Rest assured. I'd never bed a woman who doesn't want me."

She should have breathed a sigh of relief. One chaste kiss had left her giddy. And yet she'd spent all day imagining more.

"You're a handsome man, but the intimacy lovers share would only serve as a distraction." It was foolish, but she'd always hoped to give herself to a man she loved. And every moment should be spent dealing with the monumental tasks ahead.

"Sex can be gratifying without being intimate."

She bit her lip. "I wouldn't know."

"Perhaps you'll allow me to show you."

"Perhaps."

He must have sensed her embarrassment, and so changed the subject. "Aaron said to bid you good night."

She arched a brow. "We agreed not to lie."

He smiled. "He says I shouldn't trust you. He doesn't want you at Fortune's Den and doesn't want you upsetting Mrs Maloney. She has a kind heart and a tendency to become too excited."

That explained the cross words shared outside the police office. "Trust must be earned. Your brother will come to learn I am not the enemy."

His expression turned quizzical. "When attacked, most people deliver a punch intending to maim. You take time to assess the situation, to play peacekeeper."

"Not always. You forget I hit Mr Budworth with a

stool." And she had fought for her life the night the devil stole into her chamber and pinned her to the bed. "But your brother is right to be cautious."

"Life has taught him to expect the worst."

They fell silent as she contemplated the harrowing series of events that had led them both to this point. Perhaps bad things happened to force a person onto a different path. A better path. A route that had already been plotted and mapped for the greater good.

The carriage turned into a narrow lane and rattled to a stop outside a quaint bookshop. The hour was late, past midnight, though the comforting glow of candlelight glistened from within.

Aramis sat forward. "Wait for me here. I would rather explain the circumstances of our marriage to Mrs Maloney before she meets you. In my absence, Gibbs will be your protector."

She nodded. Why would she object? The gesture meant he cared about the lady's feelings. It proved Aramis Chance wasn't the savage beast Lydia had described.

Minutes passed before he returned. The boyish grin on his face said Mrs Maloney had given her blessing, given him something he probably didn't know he needed— acceptance and love.

"Mrs Maloney is keen to meet you." Aramis offered his hand.

A knot of nerves twisted in her stomach as she anticipated touching him. He kept his gaze locked with hers as he held her hand and assisted her from the carriage. The promise of something wicked flashed in his eyes. Something that stole her breath.

The musty shop smelled of dust, old leather and a hint of stewed apples. An elderly woman stood ready to greet her with a warm smile.

Mrs Maloney stepped forward, her wrinkled hands outstretched. "In all my blessed days, I never expected my boy Aramis to marry." She gripped Naomi's hands and searched her face. "But I can see why he was enchanted."

Unsure what Aramis had told the woman, she said, "Perhaps he's never met anyone who shared his ambitions." The ambition to see Melissa Grant transported for fraud.

"'Tis a miracle for sure." Mrs Maloney's tired eyes shone like stars in the heavens. "You'll be good for him. You'll be just what he needs."

"Ours is a marriage of convenience," Aramis said with a hint of frustration, though he looked at the lady as if she were the only angel on earth. "I warned you not to invent your own narrative."

Mrs Maloney gave a knowing grin. "And flowers grow in the most unlikely places." She released Naomi and clapped her hands together in glee. "You can have the room upstairs. It's sparse but clean. The bed's small for a man of Aramis' size, but it won't be a problem for newlyweds."

The image of her squashed next to a naked Aramis Chance left Naomi trembling to the tips of her toes.

Aramis sighed. "As I've already explained, I shall sleep in the attic or sitting room tonight. Naomi may have the bed."

"But you didn't sleep at all last night," Naomi said, suffering a pang of guilt. They had a momentous task ahead of them tomorrow and needed a full grasp of their faculties. "Please have the bed. A chair will be more than adequate for someone of my size."

"I'll not have my wife sleeping in a chair," Aramis snapped.

Mrs Maloney tutted. "You're not children. A married couple can surely sleep in the same bed. Besides, it's bitterly cold down here, and I'm convinced I saw a rat last night. You'll not want it nibbling your toes. You might catch the plague."

Aramis raised both brows. "You're a terrible liar."

"And you're a practical man." Mrs Maloney failed to stifle a yawn. "Come now. It's late. Get yourselves off to bed. If you decide to stay tomorrow, I'll prepare the attic room." She lifted her chin defiantly. "If you want to stay here, those are my terms."

"You're a hard taskmaster, but I must defer to my wife in this matter. The decision is hers."

Naomi looked at the man whose presence was all-consuming. She wasn't afraid to be alone with him. She was afraid of how he made her feel. Safe. Desirable. Afraid of how her traitorous body longed for his touch. Afraid she would come to care for him, that he lacked the ability to care for her, too.

Chapter Seven

Beneath the armour he wore with pride, Aramis' heart skipped a beat. The pain of past memories was the probable cause. The small bedchamber above the bookshop had been his refuge, a haven from the violence he'd encountered on the streets. And the place where Mrs Maloney had stitched Aaron's wound while Aramis fought back tears, fearing his brother might die.

His gaze moved to Naomi, standing at the washbowl, wiping her hands and face with a linen square. The muscles in his abdomen tightened, hardening as he watched her unpin her hair and brush the silky golden locks.

Cursed saints!

He wanted her.

He wanted her more than he'd ever wanted a woman. Hunger writhed in his veins. A lust so potent he could barely stand still. Since the reverend had declared them husband and wife, he'd battled the need to own her. Own her in every damn way he could imagine. And by God, there were many.

"Do you want me to sleep in my clothes?" he said, hoping conversation would banish his craving. "I can always make a bed on the floor." Wherever he laid his head, he'd not sleep a damn wink.

She turned to him, her hair framing her face like a golden halo. "Mrs Maloney is right. We're married. We're sensible adults who are about to become embroiled in a dangerous affair. I think we can—"

"Dangerous? I may be savage out of bed, not so when I'm chasing pleasure." That said, his blood pumped fast at the thought of pressing his mouth to her satin skin.

"I was referring to the case of murder and fraud."

He laughed. "We'll worry about the investigation tomorrow. We need rest. And we need to banish this air of awkwardness if we're to allay the sergeant's suspicions." He slipped out of his coat and draped it over the chair. "I shall undress and climb into bed. Avert your gaze, if you must."

This whole situation was a novelty.

And yet there was honesty in her unease.

"I shall sleep in my shift tonight." She hugged herself, though he suspected it was to ease her nerves, not to chase away the cold.

"Do what pleases you."

She moved into the shadows to remove her stockings and boots. While he stripped off his shirt, he watched her stretch to tackle the concealed hooks and eyes on the back of her unflattering blue dress.

"Let me help you." It would distract him from the

memories of being in this room, memories that haunted him like wraiths in the darkness. He came to stand behind her, smiled when he brushed her hair over her shoulder and heard the hitch in her breath.

So much for keeping her at arm's length.

So much for curbing his desire.

"There's no need. I've become quite skilled at undressing without a maid." Despite the tremble in her voice, she allowed him to free the hooks.

The first glimpse of her bare skin hardened his cock.

He breathed her in, the smell of jasmine assaulting his senses.

Mother Mary!

He'd not had this reaction to a woman since he was twelve and spied the footman undressing the maid. Perhaps it was the lure of the forbidden. Perhaps once he buried himself inside her, these strange stirrings would fade. Sadly, it wouldn't be tonight.

With her dress gaping, he said, "Shall I continue?" He imagined slipping the garment off her shoulders, sliding it past her hips, his mouth following the glide of his fingers.

"Continue what, Aramis? Inhaling the scent of my hair? Brushing your fingers across my nape? Doing things to make me pant and shiver?"

His smile broadened. "I make you pant and shiver?" He liked this game. Who knew honesty could be so arousing?

"Don't be coy. You know the effect you have on women."

He brushed his mouth against her ear. "I only care about the effect I have on you."

She swung around to face him, her gaze dipping to his bare chest, the heat of desire warming her intelligent blue eyes. "Why do you care?"

The question caught him off guard. "You're my wife."

"In name only."

He glanced at her plump lips, lips he was desperate to devour. "We both know it's more complex than that. We're destined to be lovers, and not because you'll let me bed you as a last resort."

She blinked quickly while trying to accept what was obvious to him. Then her baffled frown eased into a look of resignation. "I should chastise you for your arrogance, though I cannot deny the power of this unexpected attraction. In which case, a few questions remain."

"Which are?"

"How and where do we start? How will it work when I lack experience and you insist on being dominant? What happens to us when we tire of each other? When lust's thrill loses its lustre?"

They were valid concerns.

As Mrs Maloney had attested, he was a practical man with a logical mind. On occasion, a stray emotion caught him unawares. Much like the ache in his chest when he barged into Bow Street and noted his wife's teary gaze.

By God, he'd wanted to tear the place asunder.

"We'll begin slowly," he said, confident there was nothing complicated about seeking pleasure. "We'll be honest. I'll be mindful." Ease into her gently until she became accustomed to his strength and size. "We'll agree to be lovers only until we've solved the case. I doubt either of us will tire of the situation before then."

Pensive lines appeared on her brow. "When this is over, we will go our separate ways. Return to our old lives. Look for love elsewhere."

Every muscle in his body tensed. While he could not argue with her sensible statements, something foreign slithered through his veins. Something capable of threatening his robust reserve.

"Let's not race ahead of ourselves." The desire to brand her, to ruin her for any other man, had him plotting her seduction. He'd make sure she never forgot coming around his cock. "We'll take one day at a time."

Naomi nodded nervously before her mouth curled into a smile. "I'm still not sure how we'll begin, but I shall follow your lead."

He glanced at the bed and shocked himself by suggesting sleep should be their priority tonight. "It's late, and we have much to do tomorrow." Having her was not an option. Once he'd tasted the forbidden fruit, he might gorge until dawn. "We must examine the crime scene, interview the witnesses and make a list of suspects."

"If you think that's best." She averted her gaze and stepped back, keen to widen the distance between them now he had no plans to strip her naked. Like water being poured on glowing embers, the crackle of attraction died.

Navigating a woman's virginity proved problematic. If he suggested beginning immediately, she might call him a libertine. In being mindful of her inexperience, he was guilty of an unnamed offence.

They finished undressing in silence.

He spoke first merely to issue a warning.

"When I'm tired, my dreams are vivid." He didn't meet

her gaze but pulled back the sheets and climbed into the cold bed. "I may say things you'll find disturbing."

With hesitant steps, she came closer, her pert nipples visible through the thin shift. "Should I attempt to wake you?"

"I don't know." He wasn't sure how he would react when pulled from a dream in the dead of night. Might he mistake her for the villain who'd dragged a crying boy from his bed? Might he think her a thug out to rob a sleeping child's pockets?

She scanned his bare shoulders. "What do women usually do?"

"I've never spent the night with anyone other than my kin."

"Oh." Her voice broke on that one word. There was no sign of the smile that usually disarmed him. "I think I have the measure of the situation. You feel drawn to me because you see me as a sister."

What! How the devil had she drawn that conclusion?

"A sister? Why would you think that?"

"The women you're used to must be extremely alluring. And it would explain your desire to protect me. Explain why you're not as domineering in my company. I cannot help but sense your reluctance to—" In the absence of words, she waved her hand back and forth between them.

"To what?"

"To kiss me." She blushed and gave a half-shrug. "You wanted to sleep downstairs. And there a noticeable hesitance in your touch. Your words and actions are misaligned. You speak of being lovers yet refuse to look in my direction." She paused only for breath. "I understand. I forced you into this unfortunate arrangement. You had no choice but to rescue me from Bow Street. But if we hope to be friends, Aramis, the time for honesty is nigh."

Fortunately, he had a sister and knew these garbled statements amounted to nerves and a lack of faith in her ability to please. Someone had fed her insecurities. Someone had made her feel less than whole. He'd wager his share of Fortune's Den that Melissa Adams or Lydia Fontaine were to blame.

"Then permit me to correct any misconceptions." Without a thought for his nakedness, he climbed out of bed and strode towards her.

Her wide gaze dipped to his broad thighs and flaccid manhood. "W-what do you mean to do?"

"Leave you in no doubt of my intentions." He captured her hands, pinning them to her sides. "Let you glimpse the fire I'm having a hard time keeping at bay."

He set his mouth to her soft, pillowy lips and moved in slow, hypnotic strokes to drug her senses. With honed skill, he lured her closer to the flames—warming her at his will, waiting to unleash an inferno.

But she was no ordinary woman.

This was no ordinary kiss.

She parted her innocent lips, coaxing him to enter her mouth. The first touch of tongues dragged a growl from deep in his throat. That's when he lost all grasp of reality, and his lust blazed out of control.

He couldn't catch his breath. He couldn't kiss her deeply enough to satisfy his craving. No matter how hard he feasted, he was ravenous.

He gripped her wrists and pulled her closer, trying his damnedest to ignore his throbbing erection every time it grazed her cotton-covered belly.

Confusion reigned. He'd learnt to master his emotions. Desire never ran this deep. Sweet Mother Mary! The need to part her thighs and drive home drummed a constant beat in his blood.

He dragged his mouth from hers and tried to regain his sanity. "It would seem we're compatible in every regard. I trust you're left in no doubt of my intentions." He sounded calm, in complete control, though a wildfire rampaged through his body.

Naomi stared at him, her tongue sliding over the seam of her lips as if she'd found the experience thrilling. "I must confess, I didn't expect to enjoy kissing quite so much. I cannot recall ever feeling so hot and dizzy."

Her candid assessment stoked passion's flames. He wanted to kiss her again, make her his wife in more than name, but strange words entered his head like the whispers of the dearly departed. The echoes of a heart he thought had died.

Hold me.

Touch me.

I suspect you're the only one who knows how.

Keen to banish his inner voice, he glanced down at his erection and grinned. "A man cannot hide how he feels about a woman." Who knew kissing an innocent could have such a marked effect? "The same cannot be said for you, hence I appreciate your honest appraisal."

Her smile warmed the room. "Be in no doubt. I should

very much like to kiss you again, but for now we should do as you suggested and sleep."

He released her hands, found himself brushing the backs of his fingers across her porcelain cheek, unable to step away and break this indomitable bond.

What had this woman done to him?

How did she manage to hold him entranced?

Life was precarious. One's fate could change in a heartbeat. He should be used to navigating uncertain ground, but even as they said good night and he lay still in the darkness, one thought plagued him.

Against the odds, he liked having Naomi as his wife.

Aramis woke to find himself alone in bed, the sheets girding his hips and covering his morning erection. The chamber door was ajar. The smell of coffee and toasted bread wafted upstairs to tease his nostrils. But his wife's lingering scent caused him to inhale deeply and give a broad smile.

She'd wanted him last night.

Her passionate reaction proved promising.

Had she woken him before dressing, a kiss may have led to her straddling his hips and easing the throbbing tension. A wise man knew to keep his wits. Thrusting his tongue into her mouth had been a unique experience. What if he lost himself in her delectable body and accidentally sired a child? An innocent his enemies could use to defeat him. A helpless being treated like a pawn in a wicked game.

The thought was enough to make him throw back the sheets and suffer the cold. He washed and dressed quickly, set his mind to solving a murder, not the outlandish notion of making love to his wife. A man of his ilk did not indulge in sentimental nonsense.

"Good morning." He strode into the sitting room, his armour in place, though as soon as he sat beside his wife at the table, stirrings of contentment threatened his steely resolve. "You should have woken me."

"You were sleeping soundly and needed the rest."

"Did I mutter strange things last night?" If he had, he was blissfully unaware, though her tired eyes said she had suffered disturbed sleep, too.

"You did, though the words were mostly incoherent." She stared into her cup like a crone reading tea leaves, avoiding further discussion.

Mrs Maloney didn't need an excuse to tell tales of her *boys*. "He used to keep them all awake," she said, handing Aramis a plate of kippers slathered in herb butter. "You'd think he was fighting a heathen army, though he lay there, as unmovable as a stone effigy. I tried all sorts of remedies. None worked."

Aramis patted the old woman's hand, not as an apology for the trouble he'd caused in his youth but because she had prepared his favourite breakfast. "Christian said it's worse since Jacob Adams held my arm over the brazier."

"I curse that man to the devil." Mrs Maloney made the sign of the cross. "I hope he's rotting in hell."

Naomi struggled to look at him and continued

103

buttering her toast. "The latent mind is powerful. Perhaps once you've wrought vengeance on those who've hurt you, the nightmares may cease."

Her odd reaction told him all he needed to know. She must have heard every word he'd uttered. Had she lain in the darkness, too scared to touch him, not knowing what to do?

Guilt weighed heavily in his chest. "It doesn't happen every night," he assured her. In a week or two, it wouldn't matter. He'd be sleeping alone, with no thoughts of his estranged wife. "Tiredness is often the cause. I'm sorry if I kept you awake."

Her faint smile failed to reach her eyes. "You didn't. Since fleeing Hartford Hall, I've found it increasingly difficult to sleep. And it's hard to relax when in a strange bed."

Her choice of words raised his hackles and a host of important questions. Had she left Hartford Hall because her life was in danger? Did it have any bearing on her sister's disappearance or why Lydia used the name Fontaine? Instinct said Naomi had a secret, a secret she'd failed to reveal when convincing him to marry her.

It was not a conversation to have in front of Mrs Maloney. Indeed, the lady watched them with marked interest and hadn't stopped grinning since welcoming them into the bookshop last night.

"It won't get any easier." Mrs Maloney dropped a lump of sugar into her tea and stirred it slowly. "If I know Aaron, he'll be pacing the halls like a god of war. He'll not like the lack of control and will insist you reside at Fortune's Den. At least while the murderer is at large."

Mrs Maloney certainly had the measure of the man who'd almost bled to death on her bedchamber floor. Though when it came to family, Aaron's bark was worse than his bite.

"Aaron prefers to reach his own conclusions." No one told Aaron what to do. "Mrs Maloney is right. Be prepared to sleep above a gaming hell tonight."

"You won't hear any complaints from me." The lady reached for another slice of toast to feed her healthy appetite. "Had you not agreed to marry me, I'd have nowhere safe to rest my head."

Though they went on to discuss the plans for the day, her comment plagued his thoughts as he finished his breakfast.

His wife had heard him battling his demons as he slept, waging a war he never won. But what of her nightmares? They amounted to more than being defrauded out of her inheritance. What villainy disturbed her repose?

He was determined to find out.

Chapter Eight

The Belldrake Theatre
Bedford Street, Covent Garden

Aramis stood watching her, studying her intently as they waited in the dank alley at the Belldrake's rear entrance. Ever since she'd mentioned fleeing Hartford Hall, his eyes had burned with curiosity. It was only a matter of time before he asked the question Naomi dreaded. Before he wanted to know why she woke upon hearing the faint creak of the boards, why she lay awake in the darkness, her terrified gaze scanning the shadows.

He hammered the stage door with his fist for the third time in as many minutes. "You're sure someone will be here at this hour?"

"Yes. If they plan to stage the play tonight, there's much to do." She stood on tiptoes, wiped dust from the small viewing window and peered through the pane. The dim corridor was deserted. "We should try the front door, though I doubt anyone will hear us from the auditorium."

"As patience isn't amongst my many virtues," he began with some amusement, "I've a mind to kick down the door."

She looked at the formidable man she'd married, who only last night proved he could be surprisingly gentle. "That's why we make such an excellent team. There's an easier way to enter the premises. One that affords the element of surprise."

He grinned. "You certainly know how to surprise a man. Who knew you could leave a rogue breathless after one kiss?"

Her heart fluttered at the memory of their passionate clinch above the bookshop. Kissing amounted to nothing more than the touching of lips. Yet when Aramis claimed her mouth, every cell in her body sprang to life.

"You're not a rogue. You're honest and have principles. You just scare everyone with your short temper."

"Everyone except you."

Why was that? Mr Ingram had left her shaking like shutters in a storm. "I've always been an oddity." Lydia had said so many times.

"You're not an oddity. You're unique."

Her breath caught in her throat. She met his gaze, unsure if he was teasing her or being sincere. "In a good way?"

His tongue grazed his bottom lip. "In an extremely good way."

"Have a care. Kind men are rarely considered dangerous."

He clasped his hand to his heart. "I trust you won't tell anyone."

"A wife must be loyal to her husband."

She would rather spend the day exchanging compliments than questioning Mr Kendrick. But the fear of being framed for murder had kept her awake most of the night. And so, she led Aramis to the Belldrake's modest entrance and beckoned Mr Gibbs to join them. The coachman hauled his heavy frame down from the black unmarked carriage and crossed the street.

"I believe you're skilled at unlocking doors, Mr Gibbs."

The man studied the lock. "I presume you've tried knocking."

"Indeed. Mr Chance is keen to rip it off its hinges, but I'd rather not attract undue attention."

Mr Gibbs reached into his greatcoat and removed a ring of strange metal objects. "If anyone asks, it was open."

They sheltered him while he crouched beside the lock, springing the mechanism in seconds. He didn't wait to open the theatre door for her but trudged across the street back to the carriage.

Upon entering the building, they paused in the small foyer. Three staircases led in different directions: one to the circle, another to the stalls, and one to the refreshment room where lords often surrounded Lydia after the performance and showered her with compliments and champagne.

The muffled sound of conversation reached Naomi's ears, along with the thud of something heavy hitting the boards. Mr Kendrick's frustrated cry followed, as did a command for Matilda to recite the line again.

Naomi led her husband along the red-carpeted corridor and through a set of double doors into the auditorium. Mr Kendrick stood on a box in the orchestra pit, his purple banyan billowing as he jabbed a silver-topped walking cane at a snivelling Matilda, standing alone on the stage.

"A pretty face won't cut the mustard. Acting is about more than batting your lashes and reading the lines." Mr Kendrick's dramatic hand gestures showed his displeasure. "This is a play about deliberate deceptions. The audience must feel the weight of injustice. Hero is supposed to faint when publicly denounced."

Aramis leaned closer, his hot breath tickling her ear as he whispered, "Perhaps I should call you by the moniker Hero. You know as much about deception and injustice as I do."

She turned her head, her mouth a mere inch from his. "I'm a novice when dealing with treachery, whereas you're a master. That's why you'll always be my hero. And the fact you've saved me on two occasions."

He stared at her, his Adam's apple bobbing in his throat. She expected a teasing remark, but he couldn't muster a word.

Matilda sniffed. "When a man accuses a lady of being a *common stale*, she should fight to clear her name, not collapse like a ninny."

Mr Kendrick covered his eyes with his hand and sighed. "My dear, have you not read the play? Have you not grasped the theme?"

"You said I had to read Hero's lines." Matilda's gaze moved past the irate thespian. She pointed at Naomi and cried, "Miss Grant? What are you doing here? You're supposed to be in gaol."

Mr Kendrick swung around and almost toppled off his box. With a dramatic shake of the head, he whipped his wild brown locks off his face. "And here she is, a bright light in the darkness. Our saviour."

"He's not wrong," Aramis uttered. "I said you were the only star in the night sky."

Mr Kendrick jumped off the box like a man of twenty, not a forty-year-old who had dedicated his life to his craft. He beckoned them forward, glancing at Aramis as a starving man would a sumptuous piece of cherry pie. "My dear, I assume they've not charged you with murder. Thank heavens. We were in danger of being pelted with rotten tomatoes tonight. You'll play Hero, of course, and our reputation will be restored."

Matilda stamped her foot on the boards. "You said I could play Hero."

Mr Kendrick gave a nonchalant wave. "I'll find you another role."

Naomi ignored Matilda's bout of hysterics. "I'm sorry to disappoint you, but I'm here with my husband to investigate Mr Budworth's murder." She made the introductions. "He has a letter from the Home Secretary confirming our appointment."

Mr Kendrick read the letter Aramis thrust into his hand, then blinked. "Husband? How is this possible? You work day and night and are always alone. Why are we just hearing about this now?"

Aramis snatched back the letter. "We're private people. I assure you there's no mistake. The lady is my wife."

It took the thespian a moment to catch his breath. Then he gave a beaming smile and cried, "You shall have a seat in the best box tonight. You should see her command the stage. If you weren't in love with her before, wait until you watch her crumble beneath the weight of such treachery. I'd defy any man not to rush to her aid."

In light of his employer's murder, some might question Mr Kendrick's enthusiasm. But nothing mattered more than a perfect performance.

"Be assured, I'm the only man she needs." Aramis slipped the letter into his pocket. "We're here in a professional capacity to inspect the crime scene. No one can leave the premises until we've taken their statement."

Mr Kendrick scampered to find a solution to his pressing problem. "If I tell you everything I know, might Miss Grant play Hero tonight?"

Aramis firmed his jaw, but she spoke before he said something offensive. "Let us deal with the matter of murder first, Mr Kendrick."

Accepting the challenge, the man clapped his hands. "Come with me to Mr Budworth's office. It's been locked since the coroner left, and I'm the only one with a key." He called to a glum Matilda, "Keep practising, my dear."

As they followed Mr Kendrick through the auditorium, Aramis cupped Naomi's elbow to stall her. "You should have put Kendrick out of his misery. I imagine he's a match for Mrs Wendon when it comes to getting what he wants."

She smiled at that. "It might help our case if I do play Hero tonight. Lydia's admirers always attend the performance and don't know she's missing. Besides, what if a member of the cast has a secret and would rather share it backstage?"

"What if the murderer's objective is to silence you?" he countered.

"You'll be here. Your family could offer their assistance." She doubted Aaron would oblige. He preferred to remain at home, guarding the gates of Hades. "From what you've told me about Delphine, she would enjoy a night at the theatre."

"I don't wish to play the dominant patriarch, but I can't protect you here," he said, proving he was not as reckless as Lydia had claimed. "I can't be in the audience and on stage. I'd not forgive myself if something happened to you."

How could one argue with the voice of reason? Aramis Chance was a pillar of strength. A titan amongst men. A word or touch could put her at ease. Should she not try to be strong for him?

"Then I defer to your better judgement. We'll find another way to get the statements we need."

They caught up with Mr Kendrick outside the manager's office. "Brace yourself, my dear," he said, unlocking the door. "It's the scene of a violent struggle. The killer was like a bull on the rampage, destroying everything in his path."

From his impassive expression, Aramis had looked upon such carnage before. But one scan of the room had horrid images flashing into Naomi's mind. There was blood. Too much blood. Blood smeared over the walls and on every surface. The once-white bust of Julius Caesar lay on the floor, the sculpted hair a deep shade of crimson. The villain had emptied every cupboard and tossed the contents on the floor.

"Good lord! Why would anyone think I was capable of this?" She moved into the room. The lingering stench of bodily fluids almost made her retch. "Mr Budworth had his faults but did not deserve to suffer such a horrific death."

"Would you like me to deal with matters here?" Aramis' hand settled on her back, moving in soothing strokes. "You could begin by interviewing Miss Gray."

She resisted the urge to wrap her arms around his waist and sag against his hard chest. "No. I shall need a witness when taking Matilda's statement." The shrew would throw a tantrum and seek to avert suspicion to those threatening her advancement up the ranks. "And I must steel myself against such horrors if I'm to deal with Melissa and my uncle."

Mr Kendrick retrieved a few papers from the floor. His gaze narrowed as he handed her the blood-spattered pages. "They're part of the script for the short play you wrote. It appears Mr Budworth had decided against staging it during Thursday's matinee."

She understood the veiled implication. As plain as day, someone had scribbled cancelled across the opening scene. "I did not kill Mr Budworth because he decided not to stage my play. Doubtless that was the price for spurning his advances." But who would trust her word?

"What's the play about?" Aramis asked while rifling through the desk drawers. Nothing in his tone suggested he shared Mr Kendrick's suspicions.

"Betrayal." She paused, unsure what he would make of the plot. "It explores an important question: why people fear footpads and scoundrels when the villains are often closer to home."

Aramis glanced at her. "I can relate to that."

"Most people can."

"I'd be interested to hear more." He knew she'd drawn on personal experience and wanted names and precise details.

"It's a story you know."

"I'm not sure it is." His gaze turned pensive as he studied her face. "Permit me to remind you of the clause in our contract. A clause you added. A clause about truths."

I ask that you're always honest with me.

I shall afford you the same courtesy.

"I have no intention of ever breaking my vow. As it has no bearing on the case, we will discuss the matter later." Not wanting to give him a reason to doubt her, she would tell him about Melissa's sordid plot to ruin her.

"Tonight?" he pressed.

"Tonight."

"You can use Miss Fontaine's dressing room after the performance," Mr Kendrick suggested. "I'd advise against leaving the building straight away. Those keen to visit the scene of a gruesome murder will be packed into the stalls as tightly as soldiers in a Trojan horse."

Aramis was quick to address the man's illusions. "Given recent events, I've advised my wife against taking to the stage. I suggest you leave us to conduct our investigation. Use the time to coach Miss Gray. That's an order, Kendrick, not a request."

Aware Aramis could not be intimidated or his opinion easily swayed, Mr Kendrick said he would be in the auditorium if they needed him. "Your heart would swell with pride if you saw her perform."

"Our relationship is based on truths," Aramis barked, "not the ability to put on a show." He rounded the desk, ushered the actor into the corridor and slammed the door. "Now we might examine the scene without interruption."

Naomi's gaze dropped to the papers scattered across the rug. "We have a dilemma. The comment on the script gives me a motive for murder. We have no choice but to mention it to Sergeant Maitland."

Aramis seemed unfazed. "We will gather the papers and take them with us. We'll give Maitland the evidence once we're close to catching the culprit. I'll not give the fool a reason to doubt your innocence."

His desire to protect her confirmed he was a gentleman, not a rogue.

"The blood splatters suggest the pages were thrown to the floor before the murder. The evidence points to an argument about my play."

A shadow of annoyance darkened his features. "Did Budworth mention the play before you hit him with the stool?"

"Of course. He tried to use it to seduce me."

Aramis scanned the floor. "Where is the stool?"

She inspected the room, a little alarmed to find it missing, for it added an element of doubt to her tale. "When I hit him, I threw it on the floor and left. Perhaps the coroner moved it."

Aramis rubbed his temple but said nothing.

Still, she saw a flicker of suspicion in his eyes.

"I didn't do this, Aramis." When a man had been betrayed by someone close, he approached every situation with an air of mistrust. "You have no reason to believe me, but I pray you've learned enough about my character to know I speak the truth."

A tense silence ensued.

"Don't ask me to explain why," he eventually said, "but I believe you. Tonight, when we're alone, you will tell me everything. Everything about your life at Hartford Hall. Everything about your sister and the reason you fled."

Naomi swallowed hard and nodded. She wasn't the only one guarding her emotions. He had secrets. Hidden feelings that would plague him if he did not give them a voice. "And you will tell me why you call for Aaron in your sleep. Why you plead with him and beg his forgiveness."

The man who professed to be made of steel paled and braced his hands on the desk. "You said my words were incoherent."

"I didn't want to discuss it in front of Mrs Maloney." It wasn't just the words that had made her heart weep. The anguish clinging to every syllable had added to the torment.

"And I don't want to discuss it now."

In the name of fairness, most people would demand he concede. But if she was to win his trust, a different approach was needed.

"I vowed to be a shoulder of support. Remember that if

you ever want to talk about your nightmares. Regardless, I shall tell you whatever you want to know about my life."

She watched the tension leave his shoulders, the lines on his brow disappear. He quickly changed the subject. "I see nothing out of the ordinary here. We should question the actors and stagehands. We'll collect the discarded papers before we leave."

"Being a small theatre, most actors play two roles. Still, interviewing everyone will take most of the day."

"Not if you permit me to lead the interrogation." With his demons safely back in their cage, his vigour was restored. "I'll play the devil. You can be the angelic voice of reason. We'll begin with that fop Kendrick."

They found the thespian in the auditorium, attempting to help Matilda act like anything but a shrew. With his frustration evident in every swirl of his silk banyan, Mr Kendrick was glad of the distraction.

"There's no hope for that girl," he said as they moved to the farthest seats in the house. "She sounds more like an irate harpy than a passive maiden. How on earth is she to gain the audience's sympathy?"

Naomi snorted. "The same might be said for my sister, sir."

"Like a chameleon, Miss Fontaine can adapt to any situation."

"I doubt she would appreciate being likened to a lizard."

Mr Kendrick laughed, unaware Aramis was about to hit him with an accusation. "I'd wager you killed Budworth. You had much to gain from his death. Like

Thespis, you longed to step out from the crowd and take centre stage."

Mr Kendrick's eyes widened in shock. "That's where you're mistaken. This theatre is my life. Why would I risk it closing? I've merely accepted the role of manager until our fate can be decided."

"By whom?" Aramis snapped.

"By Mr Budworth's brother Edwin. He cares about one thing—money."

"Where is Edwin? Why is he not here attempting to find his brother's murderer?"

"He rarely v-ventures to town. He has a house in Uxbridge. I assume someone sent for him."

Aramis towered over the actor. "Do you have an alibi?"

"Yes. I was at the Dog and Duck with Miss Gray. With Miss Fontaine missing, she hoped to take a more senior role and desperately needed a tutor."

"I watched them leave," Naomi said in Mr Kendrick's defence.

But Aramis came at the man with another timed swipe. "You have a key to the premises and could have returned."

"No one other than Mr Budworth has a key. He kept the spare set in his apartment above the theatre. I took them when we decided to open tonight."

"Then who found the body?"

The questions came so quickly Mr Kendrick couldn't catch his breath. "Maddock. He helps with props and staging, sorts the costumes for laundry and takes in deliveries. He lives across the road, above Mrs Boyle's Emporium.

He said he saw a figure darting from the alley and found the theatre door open."

Aramis turned to her. "Do you have any questions?"

As always, her husband had been quite thorough. "Who do you think killed Mr Budworth?"

The man averted his gaze. "I—I thought you, Miss Grant. Miss Gray heard you arguing about your play, and I feared there'd been a scuffle. It's common knowledge Mr Budworth uses his position to get close to the leading ladies. No one would blame you for protecting yourself."

A growl rumbled in Aramis' throat. "My wife is innocent."

"Then it might be one of Miss Fontaine's gentleman friends blaming Mr Budworth for her disappearance."

Fear's icy hand wrapped around Naomi's heart. Before Mr Budworth's murder, she'd convinced herself Lydia had escaped to her lover's retreat. Lydia was often dramatic. Liked to do drastic things to keep her admirers keen. But what if something awful had happened?

"That's all for now," she said, keeping her worries at bay. Mr Kendrick looked like he'd been wrung through a mangle. "Inform Miss Gray we would like to ask her a few questions."

Flustered, Mr Kendrick scampered along the aisle and summoned Matilda Gray from the stage.

"We'll swap roles," Aramis said like a Bow Street interrogator. "You attack Miss Gray, and I'll play the dashing hero. Disregard anything I say. I'm merely reciting lines."

She smiled.

"What's so amusing?" he said, smiling too.

"I thought you preferred being the dangerous devil. Perhaps you should ask Mr Kendrick if he has a spare banyan."

"I'd rather walk the streets naked than wear a silk robe. And I am a dangerous devil. I only play the dashing hero when helping you." He glanced at the approaching Miss Gray, who made a point of swinging her hips as she walked. "You can thank me later. I have a feeling this will be painful."

Naomi fought to keep a stone-like expression as she prepared to greet the red-haired beauty. "Miss Gray. Will you sit?"

Matilda came to stand beside Aramis. "No, thank you, Miss Grant. I can only spare a few minutes. As I'm to play Hero tonight, I must perfect my performance."

"You seem more than capable, madam," Aramis said in a voice she didn't recognise.

Matilda melted at the mere hint of flattery. "I'm glad you think so, sir. Mr Kendrick mentioned you work for Bow Street." The lady touched his coat sleeve. "Perhaps you might attend the performance tonight. I can arrange for a private tour backstage."

She meant a tour of her underskirts.

Aramis firmed his jaw and pulled his arm away.

Aware he was struggling to keep his demons caged, Naomi intervened. "Why did you lie to Sergeant Maitland? You know it wasn't an argument. Mr Budworth tried to manipulate me into accepting his lewd proposal."

Matilda shrugged. "I heard raised voices. Be thankful I didn't mention you stole props from the basket."

"Be thankful I didn't tell Sergeant Maitland I saw you leaving Mr Budworth's apartment in a state of dishabille."

The lady did not bow her head in shame. "What do you expect? To get ahead, your sister flaunts herself at every man. I merely took advantage of her absence to secure an important role in the play."

"One must use the talents God gave them," Aramis said.

"Precisely, sir." Matilda batted her lashes. "I knew we were of like minds the moment I laid eyes on you."

"And yet he gave me the role," Naomi countered. To keep the crowds coming, Mr Budworth had begged her to take Lydia's place.

"A temporary solution because you look like your sister. You're paid to clean and assist the actors."

"And in your frustration, you killed Mr Budworth."

Matilda clasped her hand to her heart and staggered back. "Only a fool would kill their employer. Edwin Budworth means to sell the Belldrake to the highest bidder. Now his brother is dead, there's no one to stop him. He's the sole beneficiary."

It was news to Naomi. Had Lydia known? Had she heard the gossip in the interval and left to confront Edwin in Uxbridge? Having built a career from nothing, Lydia would rather be anything but destitute. "When did you last see Edwin?"

"He was in London on business last week. I saw him enter Mrs Boyle's Emporium, though he never came here."

Aramis straightened. "Then we need to speak to Maddock."

"Mr Maddock left to visit his sister in Hounslow and won't be back until tomorrow."

So, Mr Maddock had found the body, and Edwin Budworth visited his lodgings. Though he lacked the heart to commit such a crime, Mr Maddock was as strong as an ox and could easily crush a man's skull with a marble bust.

They spent the next few hours taking other statements. None of the actors knew about Edwin's threat to sell the theatre. Most presumed Naomi had killed the manager while warding off his advances. No one could shed any light on Lydia's disappearance.

"We should check the upstairs apartment." Although Matilda had revealed important facts, Naomi couldn't help but feel deflated. "Hopefully, we will find something to shift suspicion from my door."

She wished she knew what Aramis was thinking.

As time ticked by, he became more subdued.

She could feel his gaze burning her back as he followed her into Mr Budworth's apartment. Was his faith in her waning? Had he been swayed by the actors' damning opinions?

The sitting room looked like an office and library, with books and manuscripts stacked in every available space. The bedchamber was not a tranquil place where one might settle beneath warm wool blankets and read. With clothes strewn across the floor, an empty wine bottle and two dirty glasses on the nightstand, it was more like a den of iniquity.

Aramis picked up a white chemise trimmed with pink lace and held it between two fingers. "It seems Matilda left her undergarments."

Naomi looked at him, fear slicing through her heart like an executioner's blade. Her inner voice urged her to lie. The truth would drive a wedge between them, make him doubt her more than he did already. But she could not break a solemn vow. Fate would guide the way.

"Aramis, that's not Matilda's chemise. If you examine it closely, you will see the monogram bears only one person's initials. Mine."

Chapter Nine

Frozen in disbelief, Aramis stared at the stranger he'd married. She paled. Panic flashed in her eyes while it rioted through every cell in his body. He held the crumpled chemise in a pincer-like grip, his thoughts turning to crippling memories of betrayal.

Your father is dead. But not before he squandered every penny. I promised to care for you, but I've barely money to buy gowns and keep a coach. My friends will take you to join the other guttersnipes. Go quietly. Best not cause trouble.

While Natasha stole everything of value from the house, her thugs dragged four frightened boys from their beds and dumped them in an alley with beggars and thieves. How he wished his stepmother had been thumped with a bust of Caesar and not choked to death on a chicken bone.

"Aramis?" Naomi approached him, visibly shaking. "The chemise is mine, but I swear, someone stole it and planted it here. Someone has been to my apartment with the sole purpose of framing me for murder."

He tried to breathe but couldn't.

In his warped mind, he saw Melissa standing there.

Surely, you're not so naive that you believed everything I said. Lovers often spout flowery words in the heat of the moment. Most people lie to get what they want.

"Aramis? Please talk to me." A lone tear trickled down Naomi's cheek, the sight tearing him in two. "From the moment we met, I've been honest with you. I know this looks like—"

"Like you used me as your alibi?" He swallowed past his gut-wrenching disappointment. "Like you needed a dangerous bastard to play your hero? Like you've manipulated me at every turn?" Like he'd been played for a damn fool.

A sob caught in her throat. "Yes. Like a scene from a play, it's all staged to look a certain way." She slumped to the floor with a cry that had the power to rock his foundations. "I don't know how to ease your fears. I don't know how to prove you can trust me."

He didn't know either.

He was a second away from storming out of the room, from breaking a vow and turning his back on the woman he'd married, from letting humiliation devour what was left of his bleeding heart.

But this was different.

Her desperation was a palpable thing, prodding his conscience.

She wasn't gloating or goading him. She wasn't hurling vile threats. She was a crumpled heap sobbing on the floor, as broken as he was inside. Then she uttered words he never expected to hear from another living soul. Words that affected him in ways he couldn't explain.

"Please don't forsake me. I need you."

She needed him.

Him! Not Aaron.

Not the Chance brothers and all their collective might.

"You need me to do what, Naomi?"

She looked up at him through red-rimmed eyes. "To trust me. To tell me this nightmare will soon end. To be my friend. My confidant. The only person in this entire world who understands me."

"What makes you think I can be anything but a brute?" What could she see that others couldn't? Where was this invisible chink in his armour? He'd be damned if he knew.

"You let me choose the ring I wanted. You filled the pews to please me. When you kissed me at the altar, everything felt right."

Something shifted inside him.

A heaviness he'd not known existed.

Despite a fear of looking foolish, he took a small step forward. A giant leap of faith. "We're leaving." Ignoring a pang of resistance, he scooped Naomi into his arms and held her tightly to his chest. He had never held a woman this close. She was light, as fragile as the fae. "Wrap your arms around my neck."

She sagged against him, gripping the collar of his coat to avoid touching his skin. She didn't speak, only cried. Flood waters finally bursting the bank. A torrent lapped the distant shores of his heart.

Cry for me, too, he uttered silently, stealing himself lest his own defences faltered and unleashed Armageddon.

"Good heavens!" Kendrick called as Aramis stormed through the auditorium. "Is Miss Grant unwell? Will she return to play Hero tonight? We're sure to have a packed house."

"I'm playing Hero," Miss Gray asserted.

Aramis ignored them. He marched through the foyer, kicked the playhouse door open and emerged onto Bedford Street, the daylight almost blinding. With the carriage in his sights, he shouted for Gibbs. "Open the damn door."

The coachman jumped into action. "Shall I fetch a doctor?"

"No. We need privacy, not a physician."

Except Kendrick was determined to scupper the plan. He came darting out of the Belldrake waving a letter. "I forgot to mention the note for Miss Grant. It was in Mr Budworth's office. I took it for safe-keeping."

Aramis released Naomi, supporting her until her feet were planted firmly on the ground. "Kendrick has a letter for you." A letter he had most likely read. A letter he used to delay their departure.

Naomi dashed tears from her cheeks. "A letter?" She took the proffered note, her eyes widening upon reading her name written in elegant script. "When did you find it?"

A blush flooded the man's face. "This morning. Tucked inside Mr Budworth's journal. He kept secret notes about the play, the staging and the actors. He presumed no one knew he'd hidden it under a loose board."

"We need that journal." Aramis prayed it didn't contain damning evidence relating to his wife. Aaron would call him an idiot for believing her. "Show Gibbs to the office. He will gather the evidence we left there." He referred to the blood-stained script, not the creased chemise he'd have Gibbs secretly remove from the bedroom.

"About the play tonight," Kendrick began. "I wonder—"

"No!" Aramis shooed the man away and gave Gibbs a brief list of instructions before assisting Naomi into the conveyance.

"Do you think the letter is from Lydia?" Naomi stared at the folded note in her hand. "It looks like her handwriting."

Aramis closed the door and settled into the seat. "Would you like me to read it for you?" She looked bone-tired, so weary he considered returning to the bookshop, feeding her hot broth and tucking her into bed.

"Perhaps that's best." She handed him the missive, their fingers brushing gently, though the merest contact made her jump. "Forgive me. This is all so confounding."

"Daventry said the key to conducting an investigation is to continue asking questions. The truth always prevails."

"I'm not referring to the case, but the awkwardness that surrounds touching you. It's like tiptoeing through a pit of sleeping vipers. I'm scared of making a wrong move in case you bite."

He expelled a weary sigh. Rules were about control. A way of coping with trauma. A means of preventing pain. But for the first time since he'd set the boundaries, he had to admit the lines were blurred.

"I don't want you to fear me. You're my wife. Forget the rule." He ignored the warning voice in his head. This woman had the power to destroy what was left of his bruised heart. "Be yourself, and we'll muddle through somehow."

His comment drew a smile from her lips, lips made for kissing no one but him. "As God is my witness, you can trust me, Aramis. Fate forced us together for a reason. I truly believe that."

Fate had wrapped them in its tight tendrils and refused to relinquish its grip. For the first time in years, he wasn't hacking at the vines in a bid to escape.

He sat back in the seat. "Before I open this, we should discuss what keeps *you* awake at night." Her tears amounted to more than being framed for a crime she did not commit. Sensing her hesitance, he felt the need to make a small confession. "All my life, Aaron has taken every punch meant for me."

The guilt was immeasurable.

She met his gaze, her eyes holding an empathetic smile. "You don't have to tell me. Not if it's too painful."

His shrug was a means of convincing himself it didn't matter. "The skin on my arm has healed, but the fire rages on in my brother's chest." The sudden break in his voice confirmed it mattered a great deal. "The pain of failing to protect his kin hurts more than any blow he's ever suffered. I could have sought vengeance. I could have helped to heal his heart and conscience, but I thought it better buried."

"And so you ask for forgiveness at night when he cannot hear you?" Tentatively, she reached out and touched his knee. "You say what you cannot bring yourself to say to his face?"

"I don't know what I say at night." But he knew it was an accumulation of his many failings. Pitiful words that should not leave a dangerous bastard's mouth.

"I could tell you."

"I'm not sure I want to know."

Silence descended, though her hand remained on his knee.

Heat warmed his thigh. A feeling that proved arousing and unnerving in equal measure. A new kind of lust. One he was keen to explore.

"Melissa had a plan to get rid of me." She closed her eyes briefly as if reliving the memory, the colour leaching from her face. "She held a party to celebrate the new year. Persuaded one particular guest to enter my chamber. She paid him to ruin me, to kidnap me and keep me a prisoner in his house amid the wilds of Dartmoor."

Anger rumbled inside him as violent as Thor's thunder. He should have dealt with Melissa long ago, before she could ruin other innocent lives. But a lover's deception was not grounds for a stint in Newgate. "I need his name."

She gulped. "Mr Ingram. He's a friend of my uncle's."

The thought of any man touching her hit like a hard punch to the gut. "How did you foil their plan?"

"Lydia suspected something was amiss. She burst into the room and chased him out. She untied me and—"

"Untied you?" Ingram was a dead man walking.

"I was sleeping deeply and didn't hear him enter. It all happened so quickly. It's why I couldn't fight back." Her brows knitted in confusion. "I thought I'd locked the door. But then Gibbs has proven how easy it is to trip the mechanism."

Or Melissa had given Ingram the spare key. "And so you left Hartford Hall." Aramis clasped her hand to reassure her she would never have to deal with the likes of Ingram again.

"We left for London that night. Lydia's modiste made costumes for the Belldrake and introduced her to Mr Budworth. The rest is history."

The dislike he harboured for Miss Fontaine eased a little. "I suppose your sister deserves some credit for assisting you. Doubtless she's done what was necessary to put food on the table."

Naomi's frown deepened. "Lydia spends all her earnings on new clothes and fripperies. I work to pay the rent and buy food and coal. I'll not lie. Lydia can be unpleasant when deprived. But heaven knows where I would be had she not come to my aid."

He did not reply.

He was too busy trying to rein in his errant thoughts, thoughts that had no place in a cold man's mind. The devil rode a beast; he did not sweep in on a white charger and provide for his wife's every comfort.

"While on the subject of your sister, I should read the letter."

She snatched back her hand and closed her eyes briefly. "What if I'm wrong and she's suffering somewhere?"

Instinct said that wasn't the case. He doubted Lydia Fontaine was cowering in a dark corner. But why leave her sister behind?

Aramis peeled back the folds and scanned the missive.

"It's from Lydia, though there's no mention of a forwarding address."

"What does it say?"

He read it twice, the chill of contempt sweeping through him. "She believes she saw your uncle in the crowd during her last performance at the Belldrake. Fearing what he might do, she fled."

While his blood boiled for the way she'd been so cruelly abandoned, Naomi sagged in relief. "At least Lydia is alive."

Her response told him everything he needed to know about her character. She placed the feelings of those she loved above her own.

"She left you to deal with the matter alone." His brothers would never be that selfish.

"Yes, but it would be dangerous to remain together. My uncle cannot afford for us to challenge the will. If he cannot control us, he'll want to get rid of us for good."

Aramis tried to curb his mounting frustration. They should be in Northwood threatening the solicitor, not solving a murder for the fools at Bow Street. Still, proving his wife's innocence took precedence over money or a personal need for vengeance.

"Lydia suggests you use the small amount of money you saved and find other lodgings." He handed Naomi the letter. "She explains she is working to secure an offer of marriage and will contact you again soon."

"She always said we'd need a capable man to help prove fraud. It's why I approached you." Naomi lifted the letter to her nose and inhaled. "How strange. Lydia's perfume is like a calling card. I could map out her day just by following her scent. This smells of nothing."

"You said she left suddenly, without her personal effects."

"Trust me. She would have returned to our apartment to collect perfume and rouge." She read the letter, then snorted. "No wonder Mr Budworth hid it in his journal. She urges me to leave the Belldrake. Explains she will send any future correspondence to Mrs Boyle's Emporium."

Suspicion surfaced. Had Lydia seen her uncle in the audience? Or was it a ploy to abandon her sister and seek fame and fortune elsewhere? Had she been kidnapped and forced to write the note? And did it have anything to do with the murdered manager?

Naomi worried her bottom lip. "If my uncle has found us, why has he made no attempt to contact me? In the days before we married, I kept to my usual routine."

"It's another question to add to the growing list. Before we leave, we should speak to Mrs Boyle." Was it a coincidence that the woman's name had been mentioned three times in the last hour? "It would be helpful to know why Edwin Budworth visited her emporium."

Naomi nodded and summoned a smile. "I'm sorry for earlier. I don't know what came over me. I didn't want you to think I had lied."

"Life has dealt you a poor hand." There was only one difference between them. He had spent years fooling his opponents and perfecting a disguise. "One can only wear a mask for so long."

Her playful chuckle eased his tense muscles. "You must teach me how to be a hard-hearted devil."

"Hard-headed," he corrected. "I wouldn't want to change you. I find there's something endearing about your honest emotions."

Their eyes locked amid a breathy silence.

He didn't need to let his gaze fall to the enticing aspects of her figure. Her hypnotic blue eyes seduced him all on their own.

"That's the nicest thing anyone has ever said to me." She swallowed deeply—an apparent battle with nerves. "As you appreciate the truth, I should tell you that I hope we may do a little more than kiss in bed tonight."

"I'm quite certain we will." The urge to haul her onto his lap and indulge every wicked whim stirred his blood. He might have succumbed to his desires and delved beneath her skirts had Gibbs not knocked on the damn window.

The coachman opened the door and dumped the pile of blood-stained papers on Aramis' lap. "That's everything from the office floor." He placed Naomi's folded chemise beside her on the seat, along with the tatty leather journal. "I spied the fop in the banyan, whispering to a red-haired woman in the corridor. He warned her to keep her pretty mouth shut, or they'd both be dining in Newgate."

Dining, not hanging? It was an odd choice of words. Whatever crime they'd committed, it couldn't amount to murder.

Naomi sat forward. "You're quite certain?"

"People make the mistake of thinking coachmen are

deaf and disloyal. The fool slipped me a shilling when I left and thanked me for tidying the papers."

She faced Aramis. "We should demand an explanation."

"They'll deny it. We must find another way to gain a confession. We'll visit the Dog and Duck. Pray there's a flaw in their alibi."

"It's one more thing to add to the mountain of tasks," she said, somewhat deflated. "I hope Mr Daventry is right and evidence to prove my innocence will soon come to light."

Gibbs cleared his throat. "Daventry asked me to give you a message. He saw me while on his way to the Hart Street office."

The office was a mere stone's throw from the Bell-drake. "I'm surprised he didn't burst into the theatre and take over the investigation." The agent liked to pry into everyone's affairs.

"He has a case in court but said Miss Fontaine's known lovers will be at Lady Stretton's ball in Mount Street tomorrow night. He can get you an invitation. Said it will save you the time and trouble."

Aramis inwardly groaned. The only balls he attended were those hosted by the demi-monde. He had no desire to mingle with men who owed his club money.

Naomi offered her excuse. "It's been years since I danced, and I've never attended a society ball. I've nothing suitable to wear."

Her reluctance should have been a blessing, yet it stirred his temper. He would not have his wife feel she was in any way inadequate. And he would enjoy seeing the *ton* crumble beneath the weight of his stare.

"Let's speak to Mrs Boyle before we decide." He placed Naomi's script on the seat beside him and alighted. "Bring the journal," he said, offering Naomi his hand. "We must keep it safe until we've read Budworth's notes."

They entered Mrs Boyle's emporium—a shop selling everything from walking canes to petticoats and pipes. Upon hearing the tinkle of the overhead bell, a middle-aged woman with a mass of red hair appeared from a door behind the oak counter.

"Can I help ye?" she said in a broad Scottish accent. Her green gaze scanned their clothing, quick to assess if they had money to spend. Then recognition dawned. "Bless the Lord. 'Tis good to see ye, Miss Grant. There's nae need to say any more. I ken why ye've come."

"It's Mrs Chance. I married recently."

Mrs Boyle offered her felicitations and rounded the counter. "Well, isn't that the best news? Have ye had any luck finding yer sister?"

"No, but she sent a letter assuring me all is well."

Being distrustful of most people, Aramis came straight to the point. "You said you knew the reason for my wife's visit."

"Aye. Once she made the discovery, I knew she'd come knocking."

Making a quick assessment of their surroundings, he approached the Scotswoman. "Are you referring to Mr Budworth's sudden demise?"

"Och, I'm nae speaking of murder. The man had

wandering hands. 'Twas only a matter of time before a disgruntled husband sought revenge."

He quickly dismissed the image of a vengeful Jacob Adams. "Is that what Maddock told you? Or did you hear it from Edwin Budworth when he visited your premises secretly last week?"

Mrs Boyle tutted as if he were an errant boy she'd caught scrumping in the orchard. "Yer mind is running away with ye. I'm nae gossip, but I'm sure it's nae secret that Mr Maddock keeps an eye on Edwin Budworth's investment."

Clutching Budworth's journal to her chest, Naomi stepped forward. "You say you knew I'd come. What other reason would I have for calling?"

The lady's bright smile warmed her features. "Because Mr Maddock said yer a kind lass with a generous heart. I knew ye'd find a way to gather the funds. 'Tis why I never sold them."

Naomi cleared her throat. "Sold what?"

"Yer mother's ruby brooch and earrings."

Mrs Boyle's reply had Naomi stumbling back.

Aramis slid his arm around her waist to steady her balance. "Explain yourself, madam. As you can see, my wife is somewhat confused. Why would you have her mother's jewels?"

"I'll explain once I've found ye a chair." Mrs Boyle hurried to the door, turned the key in the lock and pulled down the blind.

"There's no need." Naomi gathered herself. "Forgive my shocked reaction. My mother's jewels went missing the day my father died." She turned to him and whispered,

"Melissa was furious and interrogated me at length, but the last I knew, they were locked inside my father's safe."

"Would you recognise them if you saw them?" he said. The last thing they needed was another mystery to solve.

"Most certainly."

He turned to Mrs Boyle. "May we see the brooch and earrings? Then you might explain how they came to be in your possession." The answer was obvious, though he would wait for Mrs Boyle to break the news to Naomi.

"Aye, of course."

The lady left the room.

Aware his wife was about to feel the stab of betrayal, he drew her around to face him and captured her chin. "Whatever untruths we uncover, it has no bearing on your character. Your heart is open and whole. Don't let someone's selfish actions affect how you behave."

He sounded like the worst hypocrite.

But it was too late for him. The damage was done.

His heart suffered the first blow when his mother was found dead at the bottom of the stairs. The punches kept coming until he grew numb to the pain.

She looked deeply into his eyes. "I don't want to believe what I suspect is true. I don't want to blame my sister for keeping secrets, but lies have a way of poisoning the past."

He bent his head, his mouth an inch from hers. "Life brings its trials and tribulations. Every experience has led you to this moment." He was always cynical, never philosophical. This woman messed with his mind. It was as if their paths were aligned, as if they were each other's guides and teachers. "There's no place I would rather be than here with you." No detour he would have made en route.

Naomi came up on her tiptoes and kissed him. The slow melding of their mouths tightened every muscle. Her lips were soft and sensual, her reaction so natural she had him bewitched.

The patter of footsteps forced them apart. Mrs Boyle appeared, carrying a square of red velvet, which she laid gently on the counter. She peeled back the folds, revealing the red rubies she'd mentioned.

"I dinnae usually buy valuable items without provenance, but yer sister begged and pleaded, said she was desperate for funds."

Naomi ran her finger over the gems and gave a wistful sigh. "My father bought these for my mother during a trip to London." She held an earring up to the light. "They could be made of tin, and she would have loved them just the same." She looked at Mrs Boyle, tears coating her lashes, but she kept them at bay. "That's the mark of true love. How sad that things must change."

"Life is an ever-evolving cycle," the woman said, offering no further wisdom.

Aramis asked the most obvious question. "So your sister never mentioned taking the jewels from Hartford Hall?"

Naomi looked at him, her disappointment evident. "No."

"Yer sister seemed loathe to sell them and asked if I could make sure they went to a good home. Sometimes, tough decisions must be made. Perhaps she feared ye didnae have the heart to part with them."

Naomi returned the earring to the red velvet. "Would it be too much to ask you to keep them for a while longer? I'm due to claim my inheritance and—"

"I shall purchase the jewels for my wife," Aramis said. They were important to her, and it was a small price to pay to lessen the blow of betrayal.

She swung around to face him. "I can't let you do that. It's too much to ask of—"

"What sort of man would I be if I let you leave without them?"

He'd be the man everyone believed him to be.

A devilish rogue with a heart of stone.

A dangerous brute without a conscience.

Titles he feared he could no longer claim.

Chapter Ten

Fortune's Den
Aldgate Street

Having been summoned to Fortune's Den by Aaron Chance, Naomi joined her husband at the candlelit dining table and sat amongst his kin. With all eyes upon her, nerves should have left her shaking in her boots, but Aramis' solid thigh rested against hers beneath the table.

Aaron Chance—whose gaze had the power to freeze one's blood—stared at her over steepled fingers. He listened to Aramis explain what they had learned during their investigation.

"We've examined the journal. It contains nothing but derogatory comments about the actors' performances and personal lives."

Aaron's snort dripped with mockery. "Kendrick sounds like a proud performer. If someone called me a preened peacock, I'd hold them to account. Men often have much to say when trying to hide their guilt."

Naomi found the courage to speak up. "Before we left the emporium, Mrs Boyle said she saw a man lingering in the alley on the night of the murder." She described him as tall with a broad frame but could not see his face. The lady had been reluctant to say any more. "She places him there at midnight, about the same time witnesses can place us at the Copper Crown."

They had visited Bow Street and relayed the information to Sergeant Maitland, who confessed to having no new evidence. They made no mention of the journal or finding her chemise tangled in the bedsheets.

"How convenient." Aaron's tone rang with mistrust.

"By witnesses, you mean the rogues fighting in the yard," Theodore said. His sinful smile could make a nun's heart flutter. "I'd have liked to see the look on their faces when you put the giant on his arse."

Aramis grinned proudly. "When this is over, I say we visit the Copper Crown and ask for a rematch. You can fight the giant this time. That way, the stakes will work in our favour."

Naomi remained silent.

When this was over, where would she be? Living at Hartford Hall with Lydia? Left to fight her own battles, win her own wars? The thought filled her with dread, not hope. Without a husband or children, she shivered against the stark vision of a lonely existence.

Quick to douse his brothers' fiery excitement, Aaron said, "Theo has just returned from the solicitor's office in Northwood. Farquhar retired five months ago. No one has seen or heard from him since. Without an admission of guilt, it will be impossible to prove fraud."

The news came as a dreadful blow. She struggled to catch her breath against the rising panic. Mr Farquhar was in his forties. Where did he get the funds to retire? "Surely his replacement has access to the files. Perhaps the clerk can attest to the solicitor's dishonesty."

Aaron gestured to Theodore, who sighed and said, "There are no files. The office is closed, and the windows are boarded. I spoke to the landlord of the local tavern. Farquhar's clerk moved to London, though no one can recall his name."

Tears gathered behind her eyes. She fought to keep them at bay while thinking of a solution. "For a small fee, we can examine a copy of the will at Doctors' Commons. It will provide us with the names of those who bore witness to fraud."

"Fraud carries the death penalty," Aaron said smugly. "And a proctor at Doctors' Commons must have proved the will in the Prerogative Court. Lawmen at that level won't risk their neck to save their conscience."

Aramis came to her defence. "But a witness might. We gather the names and use one against the other to secure a confession." He made intimidation sound simple.

Aaron reached for his wine. He took a sip, savouring the taste while lost in thought. "Theo will assist you and gain the information from Doctors' Commons. The sooner this matter is dealt with, the better."

He wanted rid of her.

He wanted her gone from the table and their lives.

An awkward silence descended, one broken by the sudden sound of raised voices in the hall. Naomi strained to hear the argument.

Aaron's lethal stare remained fixed on the door.

It swung open, and an attractive woman no older than thirty marched into the room, her golden hair fastened in a simple chignon. With a flash of anger in her eyes, she stormed to the head of the table and threw a handbill in Aaron's lap.

"Forgive me for spoiling your dinner. But as you refuse to see me at a reasonable hour, I had no choice but to force my way in." She gestured to Delphine, who looked more than intrigued. "Miss Chance said I should be persistent."

Aaron glanced at his sister. "Did she?"

Sigmund appeared, offering his own apology. "While I'd happily throw a man to the pavement, I'll not lay my hands on a woman."

"We have a viewing hatch for a reason," Aaron countered.

"Miss Lovelace seemed upset."

"I am upset," she said without compunction.

Aaron snatched the handbill and stood slowly. He perused it for longer than necessary. "You're upset because men wish to fight in my basement? We hold a monthly contest. The prize draws contenders from as far afield as Lancashire."

The lady stared into his obsidian eyes. "I'm upset because that's the night I plan to reopen The Burnished Jade. The Denson Quartet is to perform a recital. Madame de Rosso is to sing. How are ladies meant to relax in tranquil surroundings when men are shouting and brawling in the street?"

Aaron's mouth curled into an arrogant grin. "You

144

should have opened your ladies' club elsewhere. How are men meant to relax when being spied on by spinsters?"

"Spinsters?" Miss Lovelace stepped forward, her face so close to Aaron's their breath surely mingled. "Only you could make freedom sound demeaning."

The close proximity had a marked effect on Aaron Chance. His Adam's apple bobbed in his throat, and he inhaled deeply. He tried to step back, but the chair blocked his retreat.

"I've no intention of altering my plans, madam."

Miss Lovelace raised her chin. "I've no intention of altering mine."

"We will discuss this tomorrow."

"No, we won't. You'll refuse to see me."

"I told you. I'll not make concessions."

Miss Lovelace stared at him. "Very well. As we cannot negotiate peacefully, let us go to war."

Without another word, she stormed from the room, offering Sigmund an apology for his master's lack of faith in him.

Amid the stunned silence, Theo chuckled. "You may want to retire briefly, brother, and adjust your trousers. I might join you. Miss Scrumptious has a way of firing a man's blood."

Naomi turned to Aramis. "Miss Scrumptious?"

He leaned closer, his hand resting on her knee as he whispered, "It's the moniker we use for the only lady who has the power to affect my brother."

The warmth of his hand raised her pulse. "Why does he fight his feelings?"

Aramis' hand slid higher up her thigh. "Like me, he

thought himself immune to a woman's charms. It comes as a shock to find he feels something other than anger. It takes someone special to turn the tides."

Heat coiled in her belly. Aramis looked like he was seconds away from kissing her senseless.

Aaron dropped into the seat and tossed back his wine. "I'll have no more mention of that woman, not tonight, not ever." He turned to Aramis. "Your wife will reside here until the case is solved and Melissa has her comeuppance. I need you in the card room tonight. She will remain upstairs."

"Her name is Naomi," Aramis growled. "And we'll remain here only if she agrees. Being accused of murder is daunting enough. I'll not subject her to your foul moods and short temper."

Keen to bring an element of calm to the situation, she touched her husband's arm. "Your brother has a right to air his concerns. No one here knows me as you do. Trust takes time."

Everyone stared at Aramis as if eyeing a smoking volcano, waiting for it to erupt. When he said nothing, Theodore and Delphine shared bemused glances.

His expression tight with disapproval, Aaron stood and snatched the crystal wine carafe. "Aramis barely knows you. He'd do well to remember that."

Aramis pushed out of the chair. Before he could speak, Aaron was at the door, cradling his claret. "Christian will be here in five minutes. I need you to devise a plan to watch Pelham tonight. I suspect he's counting cards. Delphine will keep your wife company and see to her needs."

Aramis made to protest, but again, Naomi played peacekeeper. "I shall wait up for you, and I'd like to spend some time with Delphine."

"Excellent." Delphine clapped her hands together. "We can take our refreshments upstairs." In the blink of an eye, she was pouring two glasses of sherry at the drinks table. "Perhaps I might help with the case."

As Naomi made to leave, Aramis captured her elbow and drew her so close the contact melted her insides. "I'll try not to be too late. I'll wrestle the lords out if need be. If you're sleeping, I won't wake you."

His thumb moved over her skin in teasing strokes. Since sharing two passionate kisses, she longed to kiss him again. Since he'd insisted on purchasing her mother's jewels from Mrs Boyle, she longed for something far more intimate.

"I'll wait up for you," she said for his ears only. Trying to pretend he didn't arouse a deep desire in her was pointless. Why would she avoid the inevitable? Bedding her was part of their agreement. "If I'm sleeping, I insist you wake me. I'd like to hear about the night's scandals."

He held her gaze. "Then I shall tell Aaron I won't be joining him for our usual drink." His voice was like a panther's purr. "Know I'll need to expend my pent-up energy before I can sleep."

In the dim light, his eyes were like a forest's forbidden realms. Somewhere hidden in their depths was a secret path that led to forever. All a lady need do is learn how to navigate the darkness.

"Perhaps we might partake in a midnight stroll," she

teased. "A walk to the Royal Exchange and back will surely tire you out."

"Why visit the Exchange when there's bartering to be done here?" He pressed his mouth to her ear, his hot breath sending a shiver down her spine. "I intend to trade something more satisfying than stocks."

Had they been alone, she might have touched him, let him know she welcomed his attentions. "I have a pistol and may use it as a bargaining tool."

He looked at her, his lazy grin the most mesmerising thing she had ever seen. "I know it's not loaded. You forget I possess a charming pair of handcuffs."

"For which I have the only key."

"I had Gibbs unlock them. The thought of keeping you imprisoned in my bedchamber will warm my blood for the next five hours."

She glanced at his mouth. "Five hours is a long time to wait."

"I guarantee it will be worth every second."

They parted on that promise.

As Naomi closed the dining room door behind her, she heard Theodore taunting her husband. "Who the hell are you? And what have you done with my brother?"

"The man you know is alive and well. My wife is an angel able to temper hell's flames."

Naomi was still smiling at his reply when she entered Delphine's boudoir on the upper floor. The lady had gowns in every shade of blue and was determined to find something to fit Naomi.

"I'm two inches too short." Naomi held one dress against her and gazed at her reflection in the looking glass.

"It's been a long time since I've worn anything so pretty."
She'd left her clothes at Hartford Hall the night she fled.
It's why she couldn't blame Lydia for squandering money
on new gowns.

"Midnight blue works splendidly with your golden
hair." Delphine found a velvet choker sporting a teardrop
pearl. "Something about the colour reminds me of the sea
on a stormy night."

Naomi hardly recognised herself. "Have you always
loved blue? With your exotic features, you would look
spectacular in red."

Delphine stared absently at the gown. "Blue reminds
me of the sea. On the surface, it looks serene, so easily
discernible. It's nothing but a disguise to hide its
unknowable depths." She glanced at the locked door and
lowered her voice. "What has Aramis told you
about me?"

As Aramis had not sworn her to secrecy, she returned
the dress to the armoire and explained what she knew.
"They found you crying in an alley with no memory of
who you were. They've taken care of you since you were
ten."

Delphine suddenly reached for Naomi's hand and
gripped it tightly. "Might I speak to you in confidence? I
cannot burden Mrs Maloney, but I have a dilemma and
don't dare mention it to my brothers."

"Of course." She knew what it was like to mull over
problems for days. "Let's sit on the bed, and you can tell
me what troubles you."

They sat. It took a moment for Delphine to decide
where to begin. "Have you ever had a recurring dream that

felt so real it's like you were there? A crone at the fair said dreams are a doorway to one's destiny."

Naomi thought to say that crones spouted nonsense, but since meeting Aramis, perhaps one's destiny was written in the stars.

"Not a recurring one, no." She'd had nightmares. The theme was the same—a case of being plagued by an invisible entity—but the setting was always different. "Do you wish to tell me about the dream?"

Delphine worried her bottom lip and shuffled closer. "I'm walking along a riverbank amid beautiful fields. On the other side is an elegant man. I cannot see his face, but every cell in my body urges me to follow him."

It was normal for an unmarried woman to fantasise about men.

"I know he's important to me, but when I call to him, the wind drowns out my words. Out of sheer desperation, I jump into the river, determined to swim to the other side. That's when he disappears, and I realise I'm out of my depth, about to drown."

The dream sounded more like a nightmare, a deep-rooted anxiety. "And it's the same dream every time? The same man?"

"The same dream. The same man. The same location." Delphine pressed her palm to her chest to calm her ragged breathing. "In my heart, I know him. I belong with him. What if it's my father? Worse still, what if I have another brother? A blood brother?"

The lady's fear was as palpable as the violent entity of Naomi's nightmares. "Can you recall anything from your past?"

"No. Aaron said I had a lump on my head when they found me. Delphine was the name sewn into my dress." Tears slipped down her cheeks. "No one came forward to claim me. What if my parents were visiting from abroad? What if they'd spent a lifetime searching for me and died broken-hearted?"

What if she was an orphan left to wander the streets?

A waif no one wanted?

Naomi gathered Delphine close and let the lady cry on her shoulder. "And you've not told your brothers because you fear they'll be hurt?"

"I love them and owe them my life. How can I tell them they're not enough?"

"I'm sure they would understand." Though when a man had lost everything, could he suffer another blow?

Delphine pulled away and dashed tears from her eyes. "I cannot hurt them on a whim."

"It doesn't sound like a whim." She brushed Delphine's hair from her face, her heart aching because she knew how wonderful it was to have a father who'd loved her. "I cannot imagine what it's like not knowing who you are. Perhaps you might hire an investigator to uncover the truth."

"My brothers know all the best enquiry agents in town."

"Which is why I think you should tell them."

Delphine shook her head profusely. "No. I could lose the only people who matter to me." She muttered something to herself as she clutched her abdomen. "Everything is changing. Christian is married and loves Isabella deeply. And Aramis—"

"Married me to seek vengeance on those who hurt him." For her, it was slowly becoming more than a marriage of convenience. She enjoyed his company, liked their honest conversations, heated stares and passionate kisses. If she didn't guard her heart, she might come to care for her husband.

Delphine patted Naomi's hand. "One might be fooled into thinking there's more to your relationship than that. Aaron thinks so, or he wouldn't be so angry." Delphine's lips curled into a half-smile. "Though lately, his temper has much to do with Miss Scrumptious."

The owner of The Burnished Jade seemed like a determined lady.

Doubtless, Aaron was downstairs preparing for war.

"And what about Theodore? Is he the only brother without a wicked temper?" When a man went by the moniker the King of Hearts, surely he was a master of kindness and compassion.

"Those who present themselves as optimistic are often the most damaged. Theo loves everyone, hoping it will make him forget the one woman who spurned him."

A light tap on the door made Delphine jump.

"Delphine, it's me," came a sweet voice.

"Just a moment, Isabella!" In a mild panic, Delphine gripped Naomi's hand. "Please, say nothing to Aramis. Not yet. He's been hurt so terribly. I'll not be the cause of more pain."

"If you decide to hire an investigator, you can find Mr Flynn at the Old Swan in Long Lane. He used to be a runner for Bow Street but now finds missing people." The only reason Naomi hadn't hired him was because Mr

Sloane offered his services for free. "I can make enquiries on your behalf. I can speak to Aramis and explain your longing for the truth." She could not keep secrets from her husband when he'd already suffered a great betrayal.

Delphine moved to answer the door. "Let me think about it for a while. I'm in no rush to decide."

With the arrival of Christian's wife, all conversation turned to Aramis and their shock at discovering he'd married.

"He'd sworn to die a bachelor," Isabella said, her brown eyes warm and friendly. "Though the thought of seeking vengeance on the woman who hurt him surely proved too tempting to resist."

"Mrs Wendon helped my cause. He'd grown tired of her constant harassment." Poor Hester had sat quietly, blushing with humiliation.

"I saw Mrs Wendon lingering outside The Burnished Jade this morning," Delphine said, amused. "She was waiting for Aramis to leave, not knowing he'd spent the night with his wife at Mrs Maloney's bookshop."

Heat crept up her neck to warm her cheeks. She liked being his wife. She liked his fervent kisses. Just thinking of what the night would bring roused excitement and nerves in equal measure.

Noting her reaction, Isabella touched Naomi's knee and offered words of caution. "At all costs, you must protect your heart. While Aramis is a very charismatic man, he lacks depth when it comes to romantic relationships. I told him so only recently."

Delphine grinned. "You may revise your opinion once you've seen them together. She touched his arm tonight, and he didn't flinch. I don't know how to explain it. I just know there's something different about him since he married Naomi."

She wished she could offer a reason for the strange connection they shared. Was it that they felt safe with each other? Was it nothing more than a physical attraction that would soon wane?

"How do ladies usually hold his attention?" The question had nothing to do with being desperate to please him. She could not make false protestations like Lydia or feign feelings for her own gain. It was merely a means of learning more about the man she'd married.

"They don't. I've never known him to give a lady a second glance. That's what makes this so remarkable." Delphine sprang to her feet. "I have an idea." She was rummaging in the armoire before Naomi could catch her breath. "Why don't I curl your hair? I've got a pretty nightdress you can borrow. It's trimmed with gold lace. You can wear my perfume from Paris."

Isabella fed off Delphine's enthusiasm. The ladies began offering suggestions as to how she might seduce her husband.

"When Aramis comes upstairs, he might find you relaxing in the bathtub, one lithe limb dangling over the edge." Isabella chuckled. "The last thing you want to do is sit waiting in bed like a virgin bride."

"You could be in bed, wearing nothing but a velvet choker." Delphine presented said choker and wiggled her brows.

It was apparent that Delphine used clothes and adornments to create a perfect persona. She wanted to show the world a certain version of herself because she didn't know who she was inside.

For Naomi, the opposite was true. She knew herself but didn't care if she projected that image to the wider world. Aramis was one of the few people who truly saw her, which is why she knew there was only one strategy that would excite her husband.

She would be honest.

And she would be herself.

Chapter Eleven

Aramis mounted the stairs slowly, mentally exhausted from the night's events. Having studied Pelham for hours, he'd caught him doing more than counting cards. Through a series of covert facial movements, the blackguard was collaborating with his friend Perks. It took nothing more than a threatening look to drag a confession from the men. Once word spread through the *ton*, no one in London would gamble with the cheating devils again.

Aaron was furious he'd not noticed sooner, blaming his lapse on the stress of Miss Lovelace reopening The Burnished Jade.

Aramis chuckled to himself.

There was a word to describe his brother's mental state —addled.

One question remained.

Did Aaron's concerns relate to business, or was he suffering from the same crazed longing that had plagued Aramis for the last five hours? His blood raced southward whenever he thought about bedding Naomi. As the card room emptied and patrons left to chase pleasure elsewhere, he was busy considering how he might seduce the woman he'd married.

Yet, as he reached his bedchamber door, he paused.

An unexpected feeling flickered in his chest.

One he was forced to acknowledge as fear.

It had nothing to do with his ability to please her. He'd make her come so hard she'd forget her own name. No. When making their bargain, he'd not considered what he might lose once they parted. An intriguing companion. A dear friend. A passionate lover. The only woman who didn't shy away from the truth.

Christian's words filled his head.

You will know when you meet someone special. There's an undeniable connection. You're drawn to her in ways you cannot explain. Physically, it's so intense ...

Naomi was exceptional. He'd known it the minute he laid eyes on her. She deserved someone exceptional, too. A man with a huge heart. A man like Christian. One capable of feeling abiding affection. Not a broken beast. One irreparably damaged.

His throat tightened.

It was not too late to walk away.

They could have the marriage annulled.

She could save herself for someone more deserving.

So why did the thought leave him nauseous?

Lost in a whirl of confusion, he stepped back, but the bedchamber door flew open, and his gaze settled on the vision of his beautiful wife pointing a pistol at his chest.

"Sweet Mary," she whispered, her determined gaze softening as she lowered her weapon. "You've been standing there for so long I feared the murderer had found his way into the club."

All reservations vanished the instant she smiled. Her magnetic pull was a force beyond his comprehension. "We pay Sigmund to ensure no one ventures upstairs."

She beckoned him inside his own bedchamber. "Then what were you doing lingering outside the door? You were there an age."

"Thinking." Wondering what it would take to become a better man.

Upon entering the room, he took a moment to study her. The plain nightgown swamped her and was so long the hem gathered dust from the boards. Her golden tresses were not caressing her shoulders but woven into a simple braid. His wife looked dainty. Demure. Divine.

"Before you say anything, I know the nightgown looks like a shroud, but Delphine insisted I borrow one." She closed the door and turned the key to lock the world out. It was just the two of them alone at last. "It was this or one with ridiculous frills and ghastly ribbons. Tomorrow, I must visit my apartment and fetch more clothes."

The heaviness in his chest eased. "You didn't think your husband would like to see you in something more alluring?" She could wrap herself in a hessian sack, and he would want her with the same fervency.

Her gaze met his and held him riveted. "I knew I wouldn't be wearing it for long and couldn't imagine myself in something frivolous. You accept me as I am. I saw no need to play the coquette."

"So you mean to sleep naked?" he teased.

She arched a brow. "Isn't that what happens when a

couple make love? If you'd prefer, I keep it on until—"

"No." Every muscle hardened at the thought of setting his hands to her soft skin. He'd never made love to a woman. He'd never allowed his emotions to run free. In one respect, they were both virgins. "If I may, I shall remove it myself." After he'd untied her braid and kissed her while fisting his hand in her silky locks.

"Is that before you bind my wrist to the bed with iron shackles?"

He laughed, though quickly dismissed the idea. "I wouldn't dream of doing anything to suppress your passionate nature and feminine instincts." Nothing about this night should be sordid or staged. Regardless of what happened next week or next month, he knew the memory of having her would always remain with him.

She placed the pistol on the chair. "I'm glad you said that, though it poses a small problem."

"Which is?"

"What if I want to touch you?"

Jacob Adams' ugly grin burst into his mind.

For the pleasure of her touch, I'll make you suffer, lad.

Naomi must have noticed him stiffen. "You can trust me. I will abide by any decision you make. But I will be forced to suppress a part of myself if you insist on setting boundaries."

"As I said, we'll muddle through." The thought of having half of her, not every delightful morsel, was enough to make him consider his position. "And because I want you with a desperation that defies logic, I'm willing to make concessions."

Fear raised its head again.

He liked this cosy intimacy. He liked the intense hunger beating wildly in his blood. He liked the unfamiliar glow of happiness warming his chest. What if having her ruined everything? What if he was too damned rough in bed?

But the fae had the power of enchantment. A means of making a man's woes disappear with one sinful suggestion.

"Then you won't mind if I undress you while we talk. I've poured clean water into the washbowl and noticed oil of frankincense next to your shaving soap. It might help to ease the tension in your shoulders."

Her eagerness to please hardened his cock. "The oil softens the tight skin on my forearm, but I'm sure it has other uses, too."

"Then sit while I remove your shoes."

"You don't need to do that," he said, but this woman intrigued him, so he perched on the edge of the bed.

She knelt on the floor and undid the buttons on the blucher boots he favoured. "Appease me. It may sound silly, but if we're to do more than kiss, I need to feel close to you, Aramis."

It didn't sound silly. Whatever happened in this room tonight would amount to more than mere gratification. If anyone was out of their depth, it was him. Since gaining his scar, he'd become immune to seduction. But his wife was a temptress in disguise.

"Relinquishing control must be difficult." She smiled as she tugged off one boot and massaged the ball of his foot with her tiny thumbs. "Don't be nervous."

Nervous? He might have laughed, but there was truth

to her statements, and the neckline of her nightgown gaped, giving him the first glimpse of her soft breasts.

Saints and sinners!

He'd never witnessed a sight so arousing.

"You're one of the few people whose commands I'd follow." In his present state, he'd run naked through the streets of London if she so desired. Indeed, he wondered when she'd notice the hard length throbbing in his trousers.

"You would?" she said proudly. "Because I believe our time would be better spent at the Belldrake than at Lady Stretton's ball. All the suspects, bar Edwin Budworth, will be gathered under one roof."

The suggestion should have doused lust's flames, but she rose between his parted legs like a goddess from the sea and pushed his coat off his shoulders.

He tugged his arms free while watching her unbutton his waistcoat. "We'll discuss our options during breakfast tomorrow," he said, determined nothing would spoil his current mood.

"I've been studying Mr Budworth's journal." Her nimble fingers slipped the last button. She met his gaze, holding him rigid as she tugged his shirt slowly from his trousers. Then the minx slid her dainty hands beneath the garment and touched his bare chest. "May I continue? I understand if it's all too much."

He hissed a breath, the distinction between pleasure and pain blurring. "I'll say if I want you to stop." His heart thumped harder than a blacksmith's hammer. "There's always an alternative. A caress with the mouth isn't touching."

"It's good to know a lady has options." Her fingers moved over his skin, light like the flutter of fairy wings. Her voice was smooth and warm, a balm to soothe his senses. "You're so hot. I'm sure you won't mind if I remove this."

"Not at all. I'm at your command."

She divested him of his waistcoat, her hands following the contour of his biceps. Drugged by desire, her blue eyes glazed as she untied his cravat. Her breathing quickened as she looked at his bare throat. "Is it always like this?"

"Like what?" Like he might come from her fumbling with his neckcloth? Like he couldn't rouse a rational thought and doubted he'd last five minutes, let alone the next hour?

"Is it always so … so intense? So consuming?"

"Never." This was a unique experience. He could see how logical men became enslaved by addiction. "I doubt we'll get as far as using oil. Not tonight, at any rate."

"We don't have to rush." Her velvet voice tugged at the muscles in his abdomen. Despite her claim, she dragged his shirt over his head and tossed the garment to the floor. Her fingertips found a home amid the dusting of dark hair on his chest. "We could talk about Lydia's lovers and why Mr Budworth knew the names of all the gentlemen except one. One he referred to as the man with many faces. It seems my sister kept plenty of secrets from me."

Not wanting to spoil the moment by discussing Lydia Fontaine, he slid his hands over Naomi's hips and gripped her buttocks. They were soft and ripe and his for the taking. "Let's talk about how I'm so hard for you I'm not sure how long I can endure this erotic teasing." The fact he'd not burst his trouser seams was a testament to the expert tailoring.

Her eyelids fluttered as he fondled her. "Show me."

"See for yourself."

A coy grin touched her lips as she settled her hands on his solid thighs. "You have the most powerful legs." Her shaky fingers edged higher and stopped an inch from his rigid cock. "Forgive my hesitance. I've coped with my nerves quite well until now."

"Remarkably well." He took hold of her hand, his breath hissing through his teeth as he moved her palm over his hard shaft. "This is what you do to me, Naomi. I need to be inside you like I need air to breathe."

"I feared you'd find my inexperience tedious."

"Nothing about you gives cause for complaint."

"Good. I'm keen to explore our connection."

"Then trust me and turn around."

With one last stroke of his cock through his trousers, she turned to face the looking glass he'd moved five hours earlier.

He stood, watching her reactions in the glass as he removed his trousers and his erection sprang free.

She gulped. "You will be patient if it hurts?"

Blood filled the empty chambers of a heart he thought had perished. "I promise you, nothing about this will be painful." He'd not hurt her for the world. "While it's evident I want you, we don't have to make love tonight. You don't have to do this just because we're married."

Her heated gaze roamed over every inch of his engorged flesh. "Aramis, I'd want you even if we weren't married. I can't fight this. I'm like a moth drawn to your flame."

"You're a damn sight more beautiful than a moth. But I agree. Something unexplainable exists between us. Something so powerful we're both slaves to its will."

He stepped closer and untied the bow securing her braid. A hint of jasmine teased his nostrils as he combed his fingers through the golden strands.

"Does my scar bother you?" The question had never left his lips before tonight. He'd never cared what women thought of him. Yet she encouraged him to be a better man. "Do you find it abhorrent?"

"Not at all. It adds a certain ruggedness to your character I find appealing. We all have scars and blemishes."

Yet he knew when he studied her naked body, he would find utter perfection. Theo was right. He had changed. He'd morphed into someone he hardly knew, one he might one day come to respect.

He brushed Naomi's hair over her shoulder and kissed her nape. God, she was soft and warm and smelled divine. "Shall I remove your nightdress, or would you rather wait a while?"

She met his gaze in the looking glass. "What would you prefer?"

He wanted her hot and naked and writhing on the bed but was mindful of her inexperience. "I want you to do what pleases you. Don't worry about me. This tops my list of most memorable meetings."

Her lips curled into a blinding smile. "You mean it beats being kidnapped by a woman half your size?"

"That night, you captured my attention." And she had

held him hostage ever since. "Tonight, you hold me enthralled."

Her eyes sparkled in the candlelight—a glow of confidence in her allure. "It's right what they say about you. You're a master of seduction."

"The gossips know nothing. You're the only woman I've ever tried to seduce. And I need to know you're not bedding me as a last resort."

Her gaze caressed him through the glass. "Forgive me. You're no one's last resort. But I didn't know you then." As brazen as the night she'd held him at gunpoint, she drew her nightgown over her head and let it fall to the floor. "I feel differently now."

He stood there, all dry mouth and throbbing cock, staring at the beautiful woman he had married. Everything about her was so damn perfect. Skin pale and smooth as alabaster. Breasts full and ripe, with the prettiest pink nipples. She was small, her hips narrow, and would likely break in two when he pounded her into the mattress.

"Aramis, say something."

You're mine!

Do you hear? Mine!

He was struggling against a primal need to possess her. A strong desire to lock her in his bedchamber and never set her free.

"I've never wanted a woman as badly as I want you." The honest statement left his lips while his thoughts ran amok. He needed to chase his pleasure, not dwell on the host of peculiar feelings. He needed to release the tension. Pray he'd have a grasp of his faculties once sated. "Can I touch you?" His hands were shaking.

Amusement danced in her eyes. "How are we to make love if you don't? You will need to be my guide. You must talk to me. Tell me your darkest desires and deepest secrets."

He laughed. "I could spend days describing all the ways I want you. I've spent the last five hours living every fantasy in my mind."

She turned away from the mirror to look at him directly, removing the barrier he had unconsciously erected. "Show me how to ease the ache. Do it now before nerves get the better of me."

He slid his arm around her waist and drew her close, relishing the heat of her skin. Thrusting into her sumptuous body would be the death of him. "I'll try my damnedest not to rush." His cock was already weeping. "I don't want this night to end." The words came from somewhere other than his rational mind. Hence, he added, "Not until you've experienced every pleasure."

She kissed him unexpectedly, wrapping her arms around his neck as if waiting proved painful. Her body moved in time with her mouth, slow and sensual.

The kiss was unlike anything he had ever encountered.

Simple. Soft. Sweetly hypnotic.

But he tasted more than lust on her lips.

She wanted him. Not his face or physique. Not his fame or fortune. Not his skill between the sheets. But a desire to know him in every intimate way. It was there in the stroke of her fingers on his nape. In the gentle hum in her throat. In the way she moulded herself to his mouth, like nothing could tear them apart.

She was a siren luring him to his doom.

Tempting him with the one thing no woman ever had.
Herself.

If a chaste kiss could hold him prisoner, what would happen when he pushed into her, when she sheathed his cock and urged him to pump harder?

Desperate to regain control, he cupped her buttocks, lifted her off the floor and encouraged her to wrap her thighs around his hips. "I'm taking you to bed."

She pushed his hair from his face, caressed his stubbled jaw, and stared at him through eyes so beautiful they chased away his ghosts. "I wouldn't want to share this moment with anyone but you," she whispered, bewitching him with words now. "Everything about this feels right."

It felt right and so damn perfect he prayed they'd not tire of each other soon. By God, he needed to repeat the experience over and over. Once would not be enough.

He laid her down on the bed, his own personal feast. "You must tell me what you like, what you dislike. Your penchant for honesty applies to lovemaking."

She blinked rapidly. "I'll try, but it's hard when one is a novice."

"Watch me. Tell me where you feel the ache. Don't be shy."

He stood at the edge of the bed and ran his palm over his muscled abdomen before gripping his swollen shaft. A groan left his lips as he stroked himself and imagined her honey-sweet mouth swallowing the crown.

Her eyes burned hot with approval.

She panted, her breasts heaving, but said nothing.

"Tell me where it throbs, love. Show me."

Her smile conveyed intrigue, not innocence. He almost

spurted his seed over the coverlet when her dainty hand grazed her breast.

"Here," she said, her breath quickening as she touched her erect nipple. "And here." Her fingers slipped through the folds of her sex. Not once or twice but three times, every touch a potent aphrodisiac. "It aches so terribly here, Aramis."

"As your husband, I'm duty-bound to soothe all your woes." He climbed over her, his desire to have her so powerful his control hung by a thread. "Forgive me. By the time I've worked my way down, the ache will be unbearable."

He claimed her mouth in fierce possession, his tongue thrusting deep into the wet depths to stoke lust's flames. Needing to taste every inch of her, he moved to the graceful column of her throat.

She shuddered beneath him as he sucked the sensitive spot behind her ear. "Aramis." The pretty hum on her lips was so damnably arousing. "I—I pray I'm enough for you."

The words were a sword to his soul, while the compulsion to mate drummed an incessant beat in his blood. "You're more than enough." He was the one lacking. He was the one floundering in a sea of inadequacy. "You're so desirable. You're a sweet addiction I cannot deny."

She smiled as he kissed her lips. "You're always so kind to me. How could anyone ever think you were heartless?"

He was everything people claimed—ruthless, aggressive, domineering—except when indulging his wife. She spoke to the man he kept hidden … even from himself.

"I'm different when I'm with you." He worshipped her with a trail of kisses down to her breast. "When we're alone, I forget the rest of the world exists." He preferred this world free of falsehoods. With Naomi, he was not chained to bitter memories. He was no longer a prisoner of the past.

The need to claim her rose inside him.

The need to banish the thoughts of her loving another man turned his mind back to seduction. It was up to him to ensure this was the most satisfying experience of her life.

He blew softly over her nipple before taking the bud into his mouth, every swirl of his tongue earning the desired reaction.

But he did not stop there.

He teased her with whisper-like kisses against her thigh. Drugged her senses with a slow exploration to her sex.

As expected, embarrassment had her drawing her knees together. "You can't kiss me there."

"I can. I guarantee you'll love every second. You'll beg me to do it nightly. Close your eyes and relax. Trust me."

She looked doubtful.

"Trust me," he reiterated.

She parted her legs, surrendering herself to him.

The first taste of her musk-scented flesh was his undoing. He fought the urge to bury his face and feast until dawn. He'd been a fool to think he might be her tutor. Every artless jerk of her hips fed his desire. Every sweet moan sent his arousal spiralling.

She came hard.

Convulsing and calling his name.

Unable to wait a second longer, he came up onto the bed, took himself in hand and made sure she wished to continue. "Do you want more, love? Or have you had your fill of pleasure tonight?"

Their eyes met.

The dazed look of satiation was beautiful on her. He couldn't get enough of this woman. Everything about her drove him wild.

"Be gentle," she said, beckoning him closer. "Be patient."

"I'll not hurt you." He'd kill anyone who harmed a hair on her head. "You must say if you want me to stop."

When she nodded, he braced himself and eased into her slowly. She was warm and wet, so snug she sheathed him like a glove. He withdrew, rolled his hips and pushed a little deeper, steeling himself against the urge to pump hard.

Mother of all saints! She felt divine.

He'd never taken a woman like this. He never cared to look at them, always sought to remain detached. But Naomi insisted on tearing down his barriers. She was determined to stare into his soul and remove every barricade.

"Aramis," she panted, clutching the coverlet in her small fists. "I—I need to touch you. If only for a moment."

He gritted his teeth, aware he was about to become a captive of the fae. "Very well. When I've pushed past your maidenhead, I need to thrust hard. Hold on to me. Take all of me, love."

Everything changed when she wrapped her arms and legs around him and held him close. He was twice her size, yet her embrace had the power to knock a man down in the first round.

He had suffered many unwelcome surprises in his life. Who knew a virgin who'd held him hostage at gunpoint would break his spell of bad luck?

He began moving again, driving slowly in and out of her, angling his hips to better the sensations, while his enchantress traced circles on his back. Her touch conjured strange thoughts and impossible dreams. No more night-mares—but glorious days and happy endings.

"Do it now, Aramis." She cupped his cheek, encour-aging him to watch her reaction as he thrust to the hilt.

His throat tightened as he sank deep. He expected to see her wince in pain, for a visible sign she disliked the intrusion. But the light of happiness danced in her eyes.

You belong to me, he wanted to say. "No court in the land would annul our marriage now."

As always, she said something heartfelt, something special. "I'd not want to share this moment with anyone but you."

Their mouths met with carnal urgency. Every deep slide into her proved exquisite. But as lust's coil wound so tight he could barely breathe, and he spurted his seed over her belly, worrying thoughts entered his head.

A man could be a dangerous bastard when he had little to lose.

Now, the stakes were high.

What if the devil had marked him?

What if happiness was meant for other men, never for him?

Chapter Twelve

Tuttle's Silversmith
Villiers Street

When Naomi entered the silversmith's, she found Mr Tuttle sitting behind the counter, polishing the plates he'd removed from the bow window.

The white-haired man looked up from the tedious task, saw her and blinked in shock. "Miss Grant? I thought you were visiting relatives in Northwood. That's what I told the gentleman who called last night. Evidently, I spoke in error."

"What gentleman?" Though her heart galloped, she pasted a smile and avoided drawing attention to the landlord's frequent lapse in memory. "I know few people here in town. Perhaps he meant to ask for my sister."

Or Edwin Budworth heard she was a suspect in his brother's murder and wished to know why she wasn't locked in a dank cell in Newgate. Worse still, was her devious uncle on the prowl?

"He asked for you by name and wished to speak to you urgently. I told him you had joined your sister in Northwood. Forgive me. When you didn't return home, I presumed my memory had failed me."

She was at fault for lying about Lydia's whereabouts.

"Did this gentleman leave a name or calling card?" Aramis moved to stand beside her, his broad frame casting the ageing man in shadow. "I shall need a detailed description."

Mr Tuttle's brows knitted in concentration. "He didn't give a name, but he was tall, forty and of medium build. I'm certain he had brown hair, though he wore his hat pulled so low I could barely see his face."

"Did he say what he wanted with my wife?"

"Your wife?" Mr Tuttle almost slipped off his rickety stool.

"Mr Chance is my husband." She gestured to the intimidating figure of the man she had married. The dangerous man who'd cradled her in his arms last night and stroked her hair. The troubled man who'd woken twice before dawn, begging his father to take him to fight instead of his badly beaten brother. "Ours was a relatively quick engagement."

So quick she was still catching her breath.

Mr Tuttle dabbed his forehead with his handkerchief and offered a beaming smile. "Then I wish you well, my dear. I trust you no longer need the apartment and have come to give notice."

"No. I—"

"Yes," Aramis interjected. "I shall pay you two months' notice, by which time we should know whether

173

my wife's sister wishes to continue renting the rooms or live with us."

Naomi nudged his arm covertly. "Let us not be hasty." What if they failed to prove fraud and secure her inheritance? It was almost impossible to find a decent place to stay in London. "My sister is extremely independent and will want to reside close to the Belldrake."

Mr Tuttle scratched his head. "Forgive me, my dear. It doesn't take much to confuse me these days, but your sister is upstairs packing her things. She said her betrothed wants her to live in a grand house in Mayfair, though she made no mention of your wedding."

"Lydia is here?" Her pulse thumped in her throat.

"Yes. She said it was up to you to give notice." He gestured to the door leading to the upper floors. "I'd go now, as she's in somewhat of a hurry. Then let me know what you want to do about the rent."

Naomi nodded, but the thought of seeing Lydia made her nervous. "What is Lydia doing here?" she whispered to Aramis as they climbed the first flight of stairs. "She is supposed to be hiding from our uncle. Do you think she's really accepted a marriage proposal?"

He shrugged. "We're about to find out."

A sudden thought struck her when they reached the landing. Lydia might not speak openly in front of Aramis and would turn doe-eyed as soon as she glimpsed his handsome countenance. "You should wait in the hall. I shall enter the apartment and attempt to learn what she has planned. She may be too afraid to speak in front of a stranger."

"I'm not leaving you alone with her."

174

Surprised by his volatile reaction, she was quick to ease his fears. "Lydia can be officious and sometimes unkind, but she would never hurt me. I assure you, it will please her to know I'm safe."

Aramis' mouth twisted in unease. Most people would nod, but he insisted on expressing his opinion. "As your husband, I must protect you. I don't trust her. She left you to the wolves. Don't expect me to take tea with her and pass pleasantries."

She brought him to a halt on the landing. "I'm glad she did, or I would never have enlisted your help." She dared to cup his cheek. His dark eyes softened as they had last night when their gazes locked and he buried himself deep inside her. "Aramis, I'd spend ten years in Newgate if it meant sharing one more night with you. But I cannot abandon Lydia."

He drew her hand to his lips and pressed a lingering kiss to her palm. "Your kindness and faith in others are amongst the things that make you beautiful to me. I'm at fault for trying to force you to think otherwise. God knows I've failed my brother many times over the years. I wouldn't want you to live with the same guilt or regret."

It seemed incredible to her that a man who had been hurt so cruelly could continue to punish himself. Self-flagellation didn't solve the problem. It kept the wounds weeping and raw.

"You were a child, then a young man. I'm certain you did the best you could at the time. Talk to Aaron. Tell him how you feel. His reaction may surprise you."

He snorted. "Aaron keeps painful memories locked in

a crypt guarded by hellhounds. Only a fool would venture below ground and goad them to bite."

"Then steal the key and slip past the beasts when they're sleeping." Miss Scrumptious managed to sneak through Aaron's defences. Did that not prove the titan known as the King of Clubs was human?

A loud bang in her apartment brought the conversation to an abrupt end. The sound was akin to the lid of a trunk hitting the boards, not gunfire. Still, it was imperative she spoke to Lydia before she burst out onto the landing and caught her in a clinch with Aramis Chance.

"Wait by the door. I shall leave it ajar so you can listen to our conversation. I'll get Lydia to tell me her plan before I call you inside."

This time, he nodded. As she moved to walk away, he captured her wrist. "Be careful. Call me if you encounter any difficulty."

The tense lines on his brow made her heart skip a beat. She hoped her smile would reassure him. Yet strange thoughts plagued her as she turned the iron doorknob and crossed the threshold.

There was a major flaw in her plan to gain her fortune.

She wasn't supposed to care deeply for her husband.

"For goodness' sake. It must be here somewhere." Lydia's distressed plea came from the bedchamber.

Naomi found her sister sitting on the bed, rummaging through a pink reticule. "Have you lost something? Perhaps you're looking for our mother's ruby ring. I'm told Mrs Boyle pays a handsome price for family heirlooms."

Lydia's head shot up. Her eyes widened as she clasped

her heaving bosom in her usual dramatic fashion. "Merciful Lord! What have I told you about creeping up on people? I might have died of apoplexy."

"I'm hardly to blame for being light-footed."

With a huff of frustration, Lydia stood and threw the reticule on the bed. "How I do despair. I told you not to return to our lodgings. Do you not understand the meaning of unsafe? All you had to do was follow one simple order."

Ordinarily, Naomi would ignore her sister's mindless rant. Yet, since spending time with Aramis, she had developed a spine of steel. "I'm not a child. You left the theatre without saying a word. How—"

"I left a note."

"A note Mr Budworth stole because he wanted me to fill your shoes and play Hero. I've spent sleepless nights worrying about you. Is there to be no apology for the grief you've caused?"

Lydia stared at her like she had two heads. "Have you been drinking? Since when were you prone to sudden outbursts?"

Naomi firmed her jaw. "Since you left me at the Belldrake. I was taken to Bow Street and interrogated about Mr Budworth's murder."

Lydia had the decency to look a little ashamed. She closed the gap between them and drew Naomi into an embrace. "Oh, my poor darling. Who would think you capable of murder? You're like a sweet little butterfly flitting about in the background. One wrong move, and you would snap a delicate wing."

Naomi inwardly groaned. This sort of veiled condescension would not warm Aramis to his sister-in-law. "I've developed the devil's tenacity and temper in your absence. Did you know of Mr Budworth's fate?"

Lydia moved to sit on the bed, the fight leaving her temporarily. "Yes. I read about it in the broadsheets. I presumed one of the cast had plucked up the courage to air their grievance. George was such an odious man. So morally superior when in truth he was a brainless toad."

"Were you lovers?" she dared ask. How else had Lydia secured a position, having never taken to the stage? That said, most men came to the theatre to look at her breasts and ankles. The praise received was not for her heartfelt depiction of a kind and gentle heroine.

"Lovers!" Lydia put her hand to her mouth and retched. "Oh, please. Even desperate women have limits. And before you accuse me of murder, remember why we're here. I could be dining amid the splendour of Hartford Hall, not scrambling about the *ton* looking for a powerful man to marry."

Guilt raised its head. She would always be thankful for Lydia's intervention on the night of Mr Ingram's attack. It's why she tolerated her sister's foul moods.

"Mr Tuttle said you're betrothed. Is it true?" Lord Bedlow coveted power and wealth. He might bed an actress, but he would marry an heiress, a daughter of the *ton*. Was that why Lydia had spent months discussing ways they might reclaim their estate?

"Not quite. Chivers has rented an apartment in Mayfair. A little love nest that will do for the time being. Sadly, he lacks the strength and fortitude required to tackle our uncle."

"Perhaps I can help with that. Finding a capable man, I mean."

Lydia's face softened as pity clouded her blue eyes. "My poor darling, I only wish you could. We've discussed this many times. We need the devil on our side. Someone who can stop a man's heart with a stern look. Any of those wicked Chance brothers would do, but such men wouldn't give a naive country girl a second glance. Not without good cause."

Naomi's throat constricted as tears welled. The gathering of emotions had nothing to do with her plight. It had to do with the way the world saw her husband. Not loyal, honest and considerate, not so beautiful on the inside she could cry, but a scarred beast, a monster.

"I went to Hart Street to visit the enquiry agents whose card I found in your dressing room." Lydia had considered hiring Mr Daventry to prove a case of fraud but couldn't find time to visit the office. "Mr Sloane has been trying to find you but to no avail. Mr Chivers told him he'd not seen you."

It seemed odd that a skilled agent who had solved the most complex cases couldn't find a famed actress in town. Perhaps Aramis was right. Lydia had secrets, like the one mentioned in Mr Budworth's journal—the mysterious man with many faces. That said, Mr Budworth had a vivid imagination.

Lydia stuck her nose in the air. "Dearest, it sounds like you're accusing me of lying. I stayed two nights at The Three Feathers in Kingsbury before moving to The Crown in Cricklewood. Not knowing who to trust, I told Chivers not to reveal my whereabouts to anyone. He's waiting in a carriage outside if you'd care to ask him."

This time, guilt mingled with suspicion. She wanted to trust Lydia, but how could she when her sister had sold their mother's jewels?

"I visited Mrs Boyle and bought Mother's brooch and earrings. I understand why you stole them from Hartford Hall, but nothing would have persuaded me to part with something so precious."

Lydia gave a mocking snort. "Under the circumstances, I'm certain Mother would have approved. Let's not forget why we're suffering in this godforsaken pit." She tutted and shook her head. "I suppose you spent your savings on sentiment. That's why you disobeyed my orders and returned here."

"I came for clean clothes." Sensing Aramis was but a few feet away in the corridor and catching a faint whiff of his cologne, she said, "My husband bought Mother's jewels as my wedding gift."

Aramis had held the rubies against her ear and said the red stones would always remind him of her lips.

"Your husband?" Lydia's eyes widened in horror. "Who in God's name did you marry? Evidently, someone with money. I'd have thought George Budworth were he not dead. He loves controlling the meek."

"I married Aramis Chance by special licence," she said, aware the man who made her heart flutter was about to fill the doorway. "He agreed to help me deal with Uncle and Melissa."

Lydia looked like she might vomit. "Aramis Chance married you?"

Aramis stepped into the room, his impenetrable eyes fixed on Lydia. "I'm curious about something, Miss Fontaine. Did you know of my history with Melissa when you told my wife I'd be the ideal person to help with your plight? Surely you based your assumption on more than a man's reputation."

Beneath the weight of his stare, Lydia stood with regal bearing. She brushed her skirts and patted her hair while her gaze caressed the man she'd confessed to desiring. "Tell me my sister is delirious, sir. Tell me there has been a mistake. It's said you swore an oath never to marry."

"There's no mistake. How could I not be captivated by your sister's innate beauty?" Like a dutiful husband, he stood beside Naomi and slid his arm around her waist. "You didn't answer my question."

Lydia's lips parted as she gawped at Aramis' impressive physique. "I've never believed the adage opposites attract. There must be some commonality for a relationship to work. Oh, but forgive me. Doubtless you married my sister so you could claim her share of the inheritance."

Aramis stiffened. "As you seem to know a lot about me, you know I don't need my wife's money. Now answer the damn question. Did you know of my history with your stepmother?"

Lydia's coy shrug was a silent admission. "Melissa may have mentioned you when she spoke about her first husband. A brute of a man who met his end in a dark alley."

Naomi froze. Time slowed, though her thoughts raced. "Why did you not tell me? You let me believe you'd

181

singled Aramis out because of his courage and formidable strength."

"I'm sure I did tell you," came Lydia's flippant reply.

"Mr Daventry told me. He can attest to my surprise." The last thing she wanted was for Aramis to think she'd lied.

"What did Melissa say?" His tone was as sharp as an Arctic wind.

Naomi held her breath, praying it wasn't something unkind. Other thoughts entered her mind. Why did he care about Melissa's opinion? Had he been lying to himself for ten years, convincing himself he felt nothing? Was this marriage doomed long before they'd exchanged vows?

"Melissa said you were too weak to fight for her. Too weak to defend yourself against her husband. That you were a fool who—"

"Stop!" Naomi cried. She faced Aramis, who stood like a stone monument to hatred. "Do not give that Jezebel's opinion a second thought. You're not the man she describes."

He met her gaze, every tight facial muscle relaxing. "I know. I merely wondered if she'd shown any remorse. I could have killed Jacob Adams. In doing so, I would have become Melissa's puppet. Part of me felt I received the punishment I deserved."

Uninterested in their conversation, Lydia quickly turned to the matter of the forged will. "So, what do you mean to do about her? How can you help us regain what is ours by rights?"

"Do you not think proving your sister is innocent of Budworth's murder should be the priority?" Aramis said.

He was right. Sergeant Maitland was waiting for an excuse to arrest her. One piece of damning evidence would see her confined to a cell in Newgate.

"Of course. No one in their right mind would believe she's guilty." Lydia's voice turned catlike. "I would love to help save my dearest darling, but Mr Chivers wishes to avoid any scandal lest his mother learn of our cosy arrangement."

A sudden emptiness filled Naomi's chest. Had Aramis asked his brothers for assistance, they would have raced to the armoury, ready to stand beside him, pistols and pikes at the ready.

She had no one to depend upon but Aramis.

"Maybe there's something I can do while remaining incognito." Though Lydia tried to sound helpful, her tone lacked conviction.

Instinct said Lydia would cause trouble for her and Aramis. Jealousy was not a coat her sister wore well. Somehow, she would seek to gain the upper hand.

"You can begin by answering a few questions." Naomi forced herself to remember Lydia had once saved her life. Surely that counted for something. "In his journal, Mr Budworth referred to one of your admirers as the man with many faces. Is he referring to one of the actors?" It certainly sounded like a metaphor for a theatrical performer.

Lydia frowned and tapped her finger to her lips. "Are you certain he mentioned me? I know he wrote a lot of old nonsense in his pathetic little book, but you've born witness to all the men who wished to court me."

Courting was not the word Naomi would use to

describe the men's ambitions. "Not always. You refused to let me visit the modiste with you. You've taken many a drive about town without mentioning your companions."

"Had I known I would be under such heavy scrutiny, I would have kept a list."

"Do you recall the name of Mr Farquhar's clerk?" Aramis said.

"Mr Farquhar?"

Naomi groaned. Was Lydia remotely interested in reclaiming their family home? "The solicitor who presented a fake will to Doctors' Commons. The office is closed. Both men have vanished."

"Oh! I recall thinking his name matched his snout of a nose." With a flourish, Lydia recited a few examples. "Hogson. No. Pigford. No. Piggot. Yes, Mr Piggot. He told the maid he used to live with his aunt next door to the Herald's office near St Paul's. Mentioned something about being plagued by pigeons."

Naomi couldn't help but give a relieved sigh. Lydia had been surprisingly helpful. "Might you visit his aunt and see if she knows his whereabouts?"

Lydia screwed up her nose. "I can't be seen where there are crowds. I've no transport, and Chivers is tired of this sorry business. I hope to persuade him to support our cause, but these things take time. Can you not take Mr Chance?"

Aramis cursed beneath his breath. "We're wasting our time here. Your sister cares more about feathering her nest than punishing Melissa for stealing your inheritance."

Lydia harrumphed. "We cannot rush these things. One mistake, and we lose our chance of making an appeal."

"You're missing the point," Aramis yelled. "My wife is the prime suspect in Budworth's murder. By rights, she should be in a cell while the useless oafs at Bow Street scramble to find evidence. I'll not dally while her life hangs in the balance."

He was right. Without Mr Daventry's influence with the Home Secretary, she would not be free to walk the streets.

Equally frustrated, Lydia stamped her foot. "What has Budworth's murder got to do with our inheritance?"

"Nothing. Everything. Until we investigate further, we won't know." Aramis drew a calming breath. "You saved your sister from Ingram's evil clutches. I expect you to help save her now."

Lydia's eyes grew wide. "You told him about Mr Ingram?"

"Of course. I keep no secrets from my husband."

"For pity's sake, he's not your husband in the true sense of the word. He is using you as an excuse to visit Melissa." She glared at Aramis. "How convenient this is for you, sir. Perhaps you hope Melissa harbours secret feelings. Perhaps you mean to frame my uncle for fraud and live with our stepmother."

"Were you anyone but my wife's sister, I would tell you what I thought of your pathetic comments."

Naomi couldn't bring herself to believe Aramis would be disloyal. "My husband is not capable of such a wicked deception."

"I think I know more about men than you do, my darling. Take him to see Melissa and seek the proof for yourself."

Like Lucifer rising from the underworld, Aramis straightened to his full height. His dark eyes hardened as he looked down at Lydia. "Don't presume to know me, madam. To hell with your inheritance. I don't give a damn who owns Hartford Hall. My wife will have whatever her heart desires, while you will always be a vulture picking scraps from a dead man's bones."

Lydia's throat worked tirelessly as she tried to keep her composure. Aramis was unlike the gentlemen her sister courted. He could be rude and blunt and coldly cutting. If he raised his defences, no one could break through the barrier.

"You will send word to my wife at Fortune's Den, informing her of your direction. I'll not have her lying awake at night fretting about you." Aramis turned to face her, the fury in his eyes dimming as he captured her hand. "Gather what you need, love. I shall have a private word with Chivers and wait for you outside."

She nodded and waited for his footsteps to recede before offering Lydia a word of caution. "Mr Chance has been good to me. I wouldn't be standing here were it not for him."

Lydia scowled. "You'd be living amid the wilds of Dartmoor were it not for my foresight and intervention."

Naomi ignored her sister's need to play the martyr. "And I've worked myself to the bone to repay you. But things are different now." Their paths diverged the moment Lydia left the Belldrake without saying a word. "I don't know what the future holds, but I'm not the same woman you abandoned."

She was a stronger version of her old self. She was no

longer Lydia's poor little darling, the one made to feel like a useless burden. In truth, she could not share Hartford Hall with Lydia. If she did find proof of fraud, she would have to place her share of their father's estate in trust.

But who would be her beneficiary?

There was no one.

No one but the man who made her heart sing.

No one but the wonderful man she had married.

Chapter Thirteen

Aramis had a newfound respect for Lucius Daventry. How the man kept abreast of his cases, taught his sons to fence and ride, and kept a permanent smile on his wife's face was anyone's guess.

Having spent hours yesterday trying to locate Lord Bedlow and visiting Mrs Boyle's emporium looking for the missing Maddock, the night ended with trouble in the club.

He had crawled into bed in the early hours and lay on his side in the darkness, staring at the golden-haired angel sleeping soundly on his pillow. Lust's tightening coil urged him to wake her. God, how he longed to indulge in every wicked pleasure. He craved her smile, her touch, the intimacy that flowed between them whenever their eyes met. But the lack of answers to the mounting questions had left her weary. And since confronting her sister, Naomi had been subdued.

It's why, with the optimism of a new day, he suggested they stop delaying the inevitable and visit Hartford Hall.

He didn't want her thinking he held an ounce of affection for the woman who'd used him so cruelly.

"You don't have to prove anything to me," Naomi said from the confines of the carriage as it rattled along Cornhill. "If you had any feelings for Melissa, you would have sought her out before now."

She was right. He had nothing to prove, but he'd be damned if he'd add to his wife's worries. "I assure you. I feel nothing but contempt for the woman who tricked me. Had I known she was married, I would never have entertained her."

"Melissa is a desirable woman."

"She's rotten to the core." He'd heard rumours it was Melissa's insatiable need for attention that had led to the death of Jacob Adams. There was reason to believe she had caused the death of Naomi's father, too, though it would be impossible to prove. "Like your sister, Melissa wears many masks to fool the unsuspecting."

Naomi fell silent. She sat stiff in the seat and hadn't stopped nibbling her bottom lip since they'd left Fortune's Den. Did the thought of seeing her stepmother fill her with dread? Did her anxiety stem from a lack of faith in him?

Not being one who avoided awkward questions, he addressed the issue. "Do you trust me, Naomi?"

The blunt question had her jerking to attention. "I—I recall we both said we'd trust no one again. Trust is a fool's game."

Having faith in a woman had seemed as possible as escaping one's shadow. Yet he knew, beyond any doubt, his life was safe in her hands.

You'll know when you meet someone special.

Christian had failed to say it would hit like a bolt from the heavens. That thoughts of her would consume him and invade every waking hour.

"What we said the night we met and what we feel now are by no means the same." Somehow, amid the chaos of two amateurs trying to solve a case, he had come to care about his wife.

She swallowed hard. "Can I be honest with you?"

A knot of fear tightened in his chest as he anticipated her confession. "I'm your husband. You can tell me anything."

I don't want you.

I've never wanted you.

This is nothing more than a business arrangement.

"I'm afraid, Aramis."

A mocking snort escaped him. "Not of me?"

He was the monster of many a man's nightmares.

Could he ever be the hero of her dreams?

"Of course not. You would never hurt me, not intentionally." A blush touched her porcelain cheeks. "My heart is not as hard as yours. It's like a stranded lamb on a hillside with nothing to shield it from the elements." She waved her hand between them. "What I'm trying to say is, I'm not sure what is happening here."

"I'm not sure either." Strange thoughts and feelings assaulted him like ruthless footpads in the darkness. No matter how hard he tried, he lacked the strength to avert an attack. "But I trust you. I want you in my life, by my side, in my bed. What comes after that, I cannot say."

Her shoulders relaxed. "I feel the same way."

A wave of relief almost knocked him off the seat, as

did the fierce need to kill the devil plotting to send her to the gallows. A burning desire to find the culprit overshadowed any personal need for vengeance.

"Then let us agree to live in the present moment and not worry about tomorrow." It was easier said than done. Someone sought to ruin her life, but who? Melissa? Miss Gray? Lydia Fontaine? Until they discovered her identity, every moment together might be their last. "I think we should delay our trip to Hartford Hall."

Her mouth fell open, and she clutched her chest. "Y-you don't want to question Melissa?" Her tone held a thread of unease. "We must face her at some point."

And when they did, he feared Melissa would pull a dreaded ace from her sleeve. She could do nothing to hurt him directly. He would thrust his arm into a lit brazier to save Naomi. But the thought of what she might do to his wife chilled him to the bone.

"We should deal with the most pressing matters today and visit Hartford Hall tomorrow. We cannot rely on your sister for help." Chivers had made it clear he did not want Lydia embroiled in a scandal. Not if he meant to marry her and keep his yearly income. "Solving the murder must be our priority."

"You weren't to know a fiend would murder Budworth and attempt to blame you." In a move that was quite unlike him, he reached for her and pulled her onto his lap. "Trouble is nothing new to me. And in case you're in any doubt, I'd fight an army to clear your name and secure your inheritance."

She threaded her arms around his neck. "I pray you get

retribution. I want Melissa to know she doesn't deserve you."

They kissed. A deep, passionate kiss that had her thrusting her hands into his hair and wiggling her bottom against his growing erection.

He would have tugged down the blinds and given life to his wicked thoughts had he not been forced to tell Gibbs to take a detour to Covent Garden.

"We will feed our voracious appetite for each other tonight," he said, longing to sink into her warmth. The case was proving to be an annoying distraction, as were his responsibilities at Fortune's Den. "We'll hire a room at a coaching inn and put our troubles aside for a few hours."

"You've the stamina to last a few hours?" she teased.

"You know damn well I have."

"Then let's pray nothing happens to scupper our plans." She slid her hand inside his coat, her palm resting on his chest. "Judging by Aaron's sour mood at breakfast this morning, I fear he'll invent a reason to keep us apart."

Aaron had done his best to keep him in the club last night. "Should that be the case, you'll have to wage war."

"You expect me to fight with your brother?"

He brushed his mouth over hers and smiled. "There's no need for fists. Threaten him with the thing he fears most. Invite Miss Scrumptious to tea."

The Dog and Duck was a small red-bricked tavern on Maiden Lane, a stone's throw from the Belldrake theatre, and the drinking den of wealthy scoundrels hunting their next mistress.

Even at midday, preened actresses sat at the long, narrow tables while men plied them with food, ale and empty compliments. It came as no surprise to find Miss Gray and the banyan-wielding Kendrick supping from tankards, their heads buried in a script.

Aramis kept his back to the pair and led Naomi to the crude oak bar, where he summoned the landlord.

A thin man with sunken eyes dried his hands on a rag and came to greet them. "What's your fancy, gov'nor?"

"Two glasses of ale and a piece of information." Aramis placed three gold sovereigns on the counter. "Regarding an incident that occurred here the night someone murdered the manager of the Belldrake." The trick to getting the truth was to pretend you knew more than you were willing to reveal.

"What makes you think we had trouble here?" The landlord looked Aramis keenly in the eyes before his gaze betrayed him and he glanced at Kendrick. "We're always quiet when the playhouses are full."

Aramis wore the stern mask he used when hounding debt-ridden lords. "Let's just say I know Kendrick has a secret that might see him hauled before the magistrate. A secret that might incriminate him and any witnesses who would turn a blind eye." He hardened his tone. "Accept the coins, or I'll tear this place apart in a bid for answers."

The landlord gulped. He stared at Naomi, perhaps

wondering why an angel would keep company with the devil.

"I advise you to heed my husband's warning, sir."

"Husband?" Suspicion clouded his dull eyes. "Are you in some kind of trouble, Miss Fontaine? Lord Bedlow came in last night asking the punters if they'd seen you. He said you'd vanished. He had Kendrick by the throat, wanting to know if you'd made him a cuckold."

Naomi was quick to correct the man's misconceptions. "You've mistaken me for someone else. Miss Fontaine is my sister. She went missing from the theatre, and we're trying to determine her whereabouts." Along with the lie, Naomi offered a smile that could steal a man's breath. "We would appreciate your help."

The fellow frowned. "But you look just like her."

"They're nothing alike," Aramis countered. The sisters had the same golden hair and pale complexions, but that's where the similarities ended. "But you could assist us by giving your version of what happened between Kendrick and Miss Gray on the night of the murder."

The landlord took the coins and slipped them into his apron pocket. "There's nothing much to tell." As he leaned closer, the stench of sweat assaulted Aramis' nostrils. "A man joined them at the table. They argued, and then all three of 'em left. Must be gone midnight when a punter said he'd seen the coroner outside the Belldrake."

It couldn't be a coincidence.

In all likelihood, Kendrick knew Budworth's killer.

"And it wasn't Lord Bedlow?" Naomi asked.

The landlord shook his head. "I don't know his name, but he's been in here a few times. Happen he had something to hide because he kept his hat pulled low. There's nothing more I can tell you."

Aramis thanked the man. He grabbed their drinks and led Naomi to Kendrick's table. The keen thespians were so engrossed in conversation they didn't notice Aramis until he plonked the tankards on the table and pulled out a chair for Naomi.

"Mr Chance." Kendrick blinked and almost choked on his own spittle. "Good heavens. You gave me a fright."

"From what I hear, you have every reason to be nervous." Aramis dragged a chair from the adjacent table and reluctantly sat beside Miss Gray. "I'm sure you won't mind if we join you."

The actress—a term she embodied—ran her tongue over her bottom lip and shuffled closer. "How good it is to see you again, Mr Chance. I had a sense our paths would cross."

"Did you? I had no intention of seeing either of you again."

Unaffected by his abrupt manner, Miss Gray slipped her hand beneath the round oak table, her fingers settling on his knee. "And yet here you are, sir, unable to stay away."

He jerked his leg from Miss Gray's reach and would have told the woman to keep her damn hands to herself had Naomi not intervened.

"We're merely following the evidence." Naomi's voice was as cold as a winter's frost. Her icy glare could freeze the Thames. "Touch my husband again, Matilda, and you will find me in the pit tonight, ready to pelt you with rotten tomatoes."

Warmth filled Aramis' chest.

He liked this unexpected flash of jealousy.

Miss Gray tutted as if life were unfair. "It may surprise you to learn everyone enjoyed my performance last night."

Naomi snorted. "If they want to see you perform again, they'll have to visit you in Newgate. I wonder if you'll lose the bravado when the hangman escorts you to the scaffold."

Kendrick's hand shook as he reached for his tankard. "The scaffold? I can vouch for Miss Gray and say with the utmost certainty that she did not kill Mr Budworth."

"And I believe you," Aramis said, shocking the fellow.

"Then what is this about?"

"It's about the person you met here on the night of Budworth's murder." He recalled Mrs Boyle's statement about the menacing man she saw in the alley. "Do you want to make this easy and tell us his name, or would you prefer I drag the truth from your lying lips?"

Miss Gray looked at Kendrick and shook her head by way of a warning. "We spent the night alone, reading the script."

"We've a meeting at Bow Street this afternoon and intend to put your names forward as potential suspects," Naomi said, applying a little more pressure. "Sergeant Maitland is incompetent and desperate to punish someone for the crime. Unless you can provide us with additional evidence, we'll have no choice but to make a case against you."

Kendrick shifted in the seat. After a wrestle with his conscience, he sighed and turned to Miss Gray. "This is all your fault."

"Mine?" Miss Gray snarled indignantly. "I don't see how. You gave him the key. I simply had the misfortune of sitting at the same table."

"You told him I had the key. All because you dreamed of rising up the ranks. If anyone is to blame for this sorry situation—"

"I want his name," Aramis interjected, tired of this Punch and Judy show. "And I want it now, else you'll wish you were never born."

Kendrick froze. "If I do that, we'll all be thrown to the gutter. Do you know how hard I've worked to build a reputation? No man in London can play Leonato with my skill."

Miss Gray added her tuppence worth. "We can't tell you his name. He's the only hope we have of saving the theatre. We'll struggle to find work elsewhere. No one will hire us while there's a murderer on the loose."

Kendrick slapped his palm to his forehead. "For the love of God, Matilda. An imbecile could determine the rest. You've as good as told them."

The man was right. Who else but Edwin Budworth could have met them in the Dog and Duck that night? "Yet you didn't give Edwin Budworth the key. You accompanied him to the Belldrake."

"On my sweet mother's grave, we didn't enter the building," Miss Gray blurted. "We opened the side door and left the man in the alley."

As Miss Gray had a tongue as loose as a bawd's drawers, Aramis pressed harder. "If Edwin killed his brother, that makes you an accessory to murder. You heard the manager make advances towards my wife and decided to punish your lover. You wanted the role of Hero and sought to eliminate the competition by casting the blame elsewhere."

"What? No!"

"You told us Edwin wanted to sell the theatre. Now you tell a different tale. You're a liar, Miss Gray. A jury will see through your facade and declare you guilty."

The lady choked on a sob. Much to Aramis' chagrin, she grabbed his coat sleeve. "Miss Fontaine told me Edwin wanted to sell the theatre. She was trying to persuade him otherwise, using her womanly wiles to win his favour. That's what he was doing in her private dressing room. That's the excuse she gave for his frequent visits." Miss Gray slapped her hand to her heart. "Good Lord! What if Lydia isn't missing and Edwin has murdered her too?"

Before Naomi could speak, Kendrick gritted his teeth and whispered, "For God's sake, be quiet. You know how people like to twist a story. I'm certain Miss Fontaine found a better offer elsewhere and will be in touch soon."

"I pray you're right," Naomi said, keeping the truth about her sister's whereabouts from this devious pair. At present, they were suspects in a murder investigation. "Though I find it hard to believe your tale about Edwin Budworth. I've never seen him at the theatre, let alone cavorting with Lydia in her dressing room."

Miss Gray quickly dispensed with her tears, her thin lips curling into a smug grin. "Perhaps she wished to keep it from you. I've seen her climb into his carriage a few times while you cleaned her mess and folded her clothes."

Aramis silently cursed. The comment only fuelled his

anger towards Lydia Fontaine. His wife was no one's slave.

"Why should I believe either of you?" Naomi said, dismay evident in her tone. The more they learned about her sister's antics, the more disheartened she became. "Your stories change with the wind. How did you come by the key, Mr Kendrick, when Mr Budworth kept the only spare? Or was that a wicked lie, too?"

Kendrick paled. He glanced nervously around the taproom. "Maddock gave me a key because he had plans to visit his sister. He keeps one for Edwin Budworth to use during the odd times he visits town. Edwin likes to check on the theatre when there's no one about."

Aramis thumped the table with his clenched fist, almost sending the tankards flying. "You should have told us about this before. Lie to us again, and I'll ensure no playhouse in England will hire you."

People were staring, but he didn't give a damn.

"We were trying to save the theatre." Kendrick kept his voice low. "If Edwin did murder his brother, we're doomed."

"As that's becoming increasingly likely, I suggest you start looking for work elsewhere." He was about to demand they visit Bow Street but feared what this devious pair would say about Naomi. "You said Maddock went to visit his sister. So why has he not returned?"

Miss Gray exchanged nervous glances with Kendrick. "I can only think that Maddock is involved. I know he spies for Edwin Budworth."

"It makes no sense." Kendrick shook his head and stared into his tankard. "Why would Maddock give me

Edwin's secret key if he wasn't planning to visit his sister until the next day?"

Why would the owner of a theatre not have his own key?

Only one person knew the answer, and he was nowhere to be found. "Do you know where in Hounslow his sister lives?"

They would pay Maddock a visit before moving to Uxbridge and the home of Edwin Budworth. Yet a terrible feeling in Aramis' gut said he should leave Naomi at Fortune's Den and take his brother Theo instead.

"His sister lives in a cottage on the road to Whitton Park." Miss Gray's attention strayed to the tavern door as she eyed the two men who'd just entered. "He told me she helped a wealthy lord whose coach overturned in a ditch. He gave her five pounds for her trouble."

Aramis glanced at the newcomers, surprised to see Aaron and Theo, necks craned, scanning the busy taproom. He brought the conversation to a swift end when he met Aaron's gaze and was beckoned outside.

"We will want to question you again on our return," he informed both suspects while drawing out Naomi's chair. "Be warned. If you run, we will find you."

They left Kendrick and Miss Gray squabbling and joined his brothers outside on the narrow lane.

"I meant to catch you before you left for Northwood." Theo thrust a note into Aramis' hand. "It's the evidence I gathered this morning from Mr Grant's will at Doctors' Commons. I saw Gibbs leaving as I returned to the mews. Luckily, Aaron had summoned his carriage, and we were able to follow you."

Aramis peeled back the folds to reveal a list of names.

"Jeremiah Grant was the sole executor," Aaron said, his tone frosty.

"Yes, my uncle was named executor on the copy my father gave to me. I doubt the same can be said for the witnesses." Naomi took the note and read out the names.

Aramis picked two from the three mentioned. "Do you know Mr and Mrs Houseman of Stanhope Manor?"

"Yes, they own the neighbouring estate and signed the original copy." She pursed her lips, evidently confused. "But why would they put their names to a forgery?"

Aaron's dark eyes grew heavy with suspicion. When he spoke, he had the decency to soften his tone. "Perhaps your father lacked clarity in the weeks before his death. It seems odd he would give you a copy of his will and not your elder sister."

Naomi did not falter under the weight of Aaron's gaze. "He trusted me, and I was raised never to question his word. He wanted me to know I would be cared for in his absence."

Aramis inwardly cursed.

Melissa had fed her to the wolves.

"The will states you would always have a home at Hartford Hall," Aaron countered.

"Only until she married," Theo corrected. "Then her uncle and stepmother are under no obligation to care for her."

Aaron raised his hands in mock surrender. "I mean no offence when I say this, madam, but perhaps you should return to Fortune's Den and allow me to accompany Aramis to Northwood."

It was the act of subterfuge Aramis had been expecting.

A means to separate him from his wife.

While the suggestion of Aaron fighting beside him had merit, he wished to be the man who floored their opponents. Protecting his wife was his responsibility. Yet he knew Aaron's conscience plagued him, and the desire to heal his brother's wounds was great indeed.

He could leave the decision to Naomi, but he was no coward. "I'll not deprive my wife of an opportunity to avenge her father, but there are things you can do to help." They needed Lord Bedlow's statement.

Someone had to watch Lydia and her lover Chivers.

And they had to locate the solicitor's clerk Mr Piggot.

Aramis mentioned the tasks to his brothers. "With your help, we might solve the case sooner rather than later."

He knew the statement would appease Aaron. His brother sought normality. He wanted Aramis to return to the fold, to stop gallivanting about town with the woman he'd married.

But Naomi was more than his wife.

She was his friend, his confidant, his lover.

All the things he never wanted.

All the things that never mattered.

All the things he couldn't live without.

Chapter Fourteen

Hounslow, Middlesex.

There were many cottages dotted along the road leading to Whitton Park. It might have taken hours to knock on every door and enquire after Mr Maddock—assuming that was his real name. But, not for the first time during the investigation, fate granted Naomi a boon.

"Wait! Have Mr Gibbs stop the vehicle." Naomi pressed her nose to the window and peered at the man tending the garden of the thatched cottage they'd just passed. "I'm quite certain that was Mr Maddock digging the overgrown beds."

Aramis rapped on the roof to alert Gibbs. "If the investigation had gone this smoothly in the beginning, we'd have the murdering blackguard behind bars now."

Though she nodded, she was glad the villain had led them astray. The thought of solving the case filled her with dread. While she wished to avoid a trip to the scaffold, the days spent with Aramis were amongst her happiest.

Her husband did not share her reservations. "Let's pray Maddock has information that will lead to an arrest. Then we can put this sorry business behind us."

Mr Gibbs brought the carriage to a halt on the roadside, and they alighted. If Mr Maddock noticed them, he gave no clue and remained hunched over his spade, working the tool into the soil.

"What if he uses the spade as a weapon?" she whispered as horrid images flashed into her mind. Mr Maddock had the strength to beat a man with a marble bust. Would he put up a fight if they were forced to take him into custody?

Aramis snorted. "I hope he does. He'll struggle to keep his balance when wielding a weapon of that size."

Mr Maddock did not curse, threaten them or raise the tool to warn them away. He didn't throw it to the ground in a panic or vault the stone wall and sprint through the open fields. The instant their gazes met, his shoulders sagged. He thrust the spade into the ground and left it standing, brushed dirt from his hands and stood waiting at the garden gate with a glum expression.

"I'm glad it's you what's come, Miss Grant," he said, his voice brimming with regret, though he observed Aramis with an edge of unease.

"And why is that, Mr Maddock?"

"Cause you ain't one to judge. Cause you won't use fancy words to tie me in knots and make me say things I don't mean."

She wasn't sure who he was referring to, but Lydia often belittled the man for his poor use of the King's English.

"You know why we're here. May we come inside?"

He glanced at the quaint cottage and released a soul-deep sigh. "I'll not burden Sarah with my troubles. Happen you want me to return to London and speak to the sergeant. Tell him what I know."

"Once we've heard your account, we can decide how best to proceed."

Aramis was not so calm or understanding. "If you have information that may prevent my wife hanging for murder, why the hell haven't you come forward sooner?"

Mr Maddock appeared confused. "Who's your wife, sir?"

Naomi told the story she had repeated to all those shocked to hear of her nuptials. "Forgive my husband's gruff temperament, but he is merely trying to clear my name."

"Then he's a better man than me. I'd be lying stiff on a cold slab if I'd stayed in town."

With his impatience for answers evident, Aramis came straight to the point. "Do you know who killed George Budworth?"

Mr Maddock glanced along the lane. "I never seen it with my own eyes, but I'd swear on my mother's grave I saw Edwin running from the alley. The whole world knows when he's in a temper. Happen it got the better of him."

"Because he wants to sell the theatre?" Aramis pressed.

"No one knows what goes on in that man's mind. He paid me to do his dirty deeds. The night of the murder, he came for the key. He threatened me with a blade when I

205

told him I'd given it to Kendrick. Said if he saw me again, he'd slit me throat."

While she was keen to learn more about these nefarious deeds, Aramis asked practical questions. "How long have the brothers owned the Belldrake? How did you come to work for them, and why did Edwin permit George to take the reins?"

Mr Maddock shrugged. "Edwin hired me last year. He saw me cleaning Mrs Boyle's windows and offered me a job. He don't like coming to town and wanted me to keep an eye on things. Kendrick has worked there since George Budworth bought the place two years ago."

"Are Edwin Budworth and my sister lovers?" She didn't want to embarrass the man, but the answer might explain Lydia's need to hide.

"That ain't for me to say."

"But you've seen them together?"

"Miss Fontaine keeps company with lots of men. It's hard to know what's true and what ain't, but I heard it's to bring punters into the theatre." He turned to Aramis and lowered his voice. "She lets them think they have a chance but never does the deed, if you take me meaning."

It was obvious what *the deed* meant. It sounded sordid and crude, nothing like the beautiful experience she had shared with Aramis in bed. An experience they would repeat tonight.

"Miss Gray said Edwin visits my sister in her dressing room." The fact Naomi had never seen them together proved puzzling. Perhaps Lydia was embarrassed to have set her sights on a man without a title.

Mr Maddock nodded. "Sometimes he comes when the

Belldrake is open but keeps out of sight. Sometimes he asks for the key in the dead of night. I've heard him threatening to kill his brother before leaving with the day's takings."

Naomi fell silent. It was no secret that ticket sales barely covered the Belldrake's running costs. Maybe Edwin cared about nothing but his share of the proceeds. As siblings went, Edwin Budworth made Lydia look like a saint.

"Mr Kendrick said you gave him the key to the Belldrake on the night of the murder." Perhaps he'd left a door open, crept back inside and bludgeoned the manager to death. "Why not give it to him the following day before you left for Hounslow?"

Aramis answered for Mr Maddock. "Because he knew Edwin Budworth would come asking for the key. He knew tensions were running high between the brothers and didn't want to implicate himself in a murder."

Mr Maddock bowed his head. "I knew things were bad when Edwin told me to scarper. He had a hard look in his eyes, like he was born to the devil."

A memory of Mr Ingram flashed into her mind, as jarring as a violent streak of lightning. "Don't make the mistake of thinking you're safe here." She would never feel safe at Hartford Hall with Melissa in residence. "Edwin Budworth cannot afford to let you live." She gestured to the quaint cottage that looked in desperate need of repair. "Think of Sarah. In being here, you place her at risk, too."

Tears filled Mr Maddock's eyes. "I shouldn't have

come. I ain't been the best of brothers, but I'll not bring trouble to her door."

"It's too late for regrets." Though Aramis spoke with a hint of compassion, he came straight to the point. "You will return to London and tell Sergeant Maitland the truth."

Naomi considered clasping her husband's hand and urging him to follow his own advice. He would be forever imprisoned in his nightmares if he didn't speak openly to Aaron.

With a stern shake of the head, Mr Maddock said, "I can't leave Sarah here alone. What if Edwin comes knocking? What should I do?"

"I'm not the best man to help you in this matter." Aramis cast her a sidelong glance. The dark, sinister veil that kept everyone out slipped to reveal the man who had made love to her with surprising tenderness. "I care about no one's welfare but my wife's."

Her heart swelled. There were things she wanted to say, kind things, loving things, words that would leave her exposed.

You're everything a man should be, Aramis.

He was loyal, honest and fiercely protective.

Someone other than your kin loves you.

She loved him.

What chance did she have when his touch weakened defences?

She avoided looking into his eyes, afraid he might catch a glimmer of the love blossoming in her heart. "I have you to protect me. Sarah needs someone to keep the wolf at bay."

He stood firm, unshakeable in his determination to

save her life. "Maddock's testimony will help to prove your innocence. I cannot permit him to remain here. For all we know, Sergeant Maitland is building an iron-clad case against you. You'll not pay for someone else's mistake."

Mr Maddock was keen to defend her, too. "Anyone who knows Miss Grant knows she ain't guilty. It's why I took the note."

Aramis drew back. "The note?"

"The note shoved in the manager's pocket."

"Do you still have it?"

"It's in the house." Upon their orders, Mr Maddock hurried inside and returned with the letter. "I'll take the blame for being weak, but I'll not have a bad word said about Miss Grant."

"Mrs Chance," Aramis snapped possessively. He snatched the note, gazed at the bloody fingerprint, and then read the missive. A muscle in his jaw twitched. "This makes for an interesting tale. The villain is determined to lay the blame at your door."

Her heart skipped a beat when she took the note and saw her name scrawled at the bottom of the page. Her thoughts whirled in disbelief as she read every sordid line. It spoke of a passionate affair with the manager. A suspicion he'd grown tired of her. A threat he would pay for his deceit.

Days ago, she might have panicked, but if Aramis didn't trust her now, he never would. "The fingerprint is too large to be mine," she said, keeping calm as she measured her thumb against the mark. "The choice of words suggests a man is trying to frame me for murder. Everything written here is a lie."

Aramis' mouth curled into a knowing smile. "I didn't for one moment think there was any truth to the claim. If anything, the need to blame you suggests your uncle may have had a hand in the deception. Perhaps your sister did see him in the audience. Someone wants rid of you, and I'll not rest until I know who."

Perhaps Lydia was right to hide, though it would be safer if she left London. It wouldn't take the villain long to discover Mr Chivers' new Mayfair address.

Still, instinct said they were missing a vital piece of the puzzle. "Edwin Budworth sounds like a dangerous man. Witnesses place him at the Belldrake at the time of the murder. How is my uncle connected?"

"The only way to know is to ask Edwin Budworth," Aramis said.

"He don't take kindly to men prying into his business." Judging by the tense look on Mr Maddock's face, he spoke from experience.

"I have no intention of prying." Aramis' sinister chuckle raised the hairs on her nape. "I mean to tear the man limb from limb to get to the truth."

Naomi's breath caught in her throat. Men like Edwin Budworth and Uncle Jeremiah didn't care who they hurt in their quest for power. They paid other men to do their wicked deeds. From this point, they should trust no one but each other.

"I suggest you and your sister return to London." If she had found Mr Maddock so easily, so could Edwin Budworth. "You're to go straight to the office of the Order in Hart Street, Covent Garden. Ask for Mr Daventry. Tell him everything you know, and he will find you a safe place to stay."

Showing he supported her suggestion, Aramis reached into his pocket and thrust a few gold coins into Mr Maddock's grubby hand. "Our coachman will return for you tonight and take you to Hart Street. We can't have you getting lost in the metropolis."

"It's the only way to guarantee your sister's safety." Naomi felt a measure of guilt for not telling Lydia to seek Mr Daventry's help, too. "It's the only sensible solution to your dilemma."

Knowing he had no option, Mr Maddock agreed. "It will mean telling Sarah the truth. I don't like to disappoint her. She's all I have."

Naomi's heart sank. If only Lydia shared the same sentiment. "Lies are the devil's poison. Trust me. She will be grateful for your honesty."

The case had tested her faith in Lydia to the limit. While she hoped her sister's endless secrets amounted to nothing more than a need for control, she had to face facts.

Lydia had changed.

She'd always been selfish and vain but never a liar.

Perhaps her motive for taking Edwin as a lover was to save the Belldrake. Perhaps she'd fled because she knew Edwin planned to kill his brother. Did it explain why Lydia had left her behind? Possibly. That was the question uppermost in her mind as they returned to the carriage.

"We'll travel the ten miles to Uxbridge and find an inn," Aramis said, having given Mr Gibbs instructions. He settled into the seat and rapped on the roof. "Gibbs will return to take Maddock to London. It's imperative Daventry takes his statement."

The carriage lurched forward and picked up speed.

Aramis frowned. "You look pensive. Are you afraid Maddock will run? He cares about his sister too much to place her in jeopardy. Now we've planted a seed of doubt in his mind he won't risk leaving Sarah here alone."

She appreciated his efforts to soothe her. "It's not that."

"What, then?" When she failed to speak, he said, "Whatever it is, you can tell me. We keep no secrets."

"I have a thought I'm too scared to vocalise."

His frown deepened. "A thought about us?"

"No," she said, though worrying thoughts of the future were always prevalent in her mind. "About my chemise. The pretty one found in George Budworth's bedchamber."

He narrowed his gaze. "I remember."

"I've spent endless hours wondering how it got there." Had she left it in Lydia's dressing room? Had someone taken it from her apartment? "Sadly, I keep coming to the same troubling conclusion."

He pursed his lips, pity evident in his dark eyes. "Lydia staged the scene, or Edwin Budworth used her to frame you for murder."

From the strength of his conviction, he'd arrived at that conclusion some time ago. Had he mentioned it, she would have found every reason to excuse Lydia's behaviour.

"Yes. It would explain her lack of interest in the fraudulent will. I can only assume she's desperate to marry Mr Chivers before she's implicated in George Budworth's death."

He fell silent, the expression on his handsome face unreadable.

"It's unlike you not to have an opinion," she said.

"I don't want to hurt you."

Those words alone sent her heart sinking to her stomach. "You think I'm naive and foolish. Don't you?"

"I would never think that. You're the most exceptional woman I've ever met. There's a simple explanation. Your kind heart has blinded you to what is obvious to most."

Tears gathered behind her eyes; the joy of knowing he could see her worth and grief for the loss of a sister who had never given a damn.

"I am a fool. I make excuses for Lydia because I'm afraid to admit she doesn't care." One only had to dine with the Chance brothers to understand the value of love and kinship. "Your family would never forsake you."

He did not disagree. "Even when battling his demons, Aaron puts my welfare above his own. It's why I cannot forgive Lydia for leaving you, regardless of why she ran."

Naomi bowed her head. A tear landed on her lap. "I'm alone in the world. It's quite a daunting prospect." Her throat constricted. Not because she mourned the loss of a loving sibling. In truth, Lydia's idea of affection was to belittle those with blood ties. No. She was mourning a husband who was never hers to begin with.

"You're not alone. You might not want four disagreeable men in your life, or a woman who will insist on dressing you at every given opportunity, but my family is your family. They'll protect you in the same way I have sworn to do."

His kind words tugged at her heart. But the picture he

painted would alter in the coming days. When necessity no longer forced them to spend time together, would they drift apart? Become nothing more than friends? Heaven forbid she had to sit around the family dining table and hear tales of his amorous exploits.

"Thank you." She should have stopped there, but her insecurities insisted on having a voice. "Though I'm sure you don't need another sister."

Aramis laughed. "Perhaps you should spend more time with my family. Instead of hinting at a problem, you might attack it directly."

"A problem?"

"Must I spell it out?"

She couldn't quite muster the words to explain this bout of anxiety. There was no other way to say that she wanted him to care for her, to always be her husband.

He knew exactly what to say. "I've learnt to live in the moment. I never plan for the future. Life has shown how quickly one's fate can change."

"I understand." When one lost everything, one learnt to adapt.

"Do you? Then tell me what you want now, in this moment, when there's no one here but us."

She sat quietly, at one with her feelings not her thoughts, searching for the courage to admit to the only thing she craved. "I want to feel close to you."

"We are close. There's nothing more intimate than two people engaging in an honest conversation."

He was determined to wring a confession from her lips. "I want to feel physically close to you. I want you to hold me in your strong arms and tell me there's nothing to fear."

His gaze slid slowly over her body. "Perhaps you would like to make this a ride to remember."

Her sex pulsed in response, anticipating the moment he entered her body and filled her full. She wanted days, months, years to remember. Beautiful dawns. Hot summers. Cosy winter nights. She wanted this man in every imaginable scenario.

"What do *you* want, Aramis?"

He ran his thumb over his bottom lip and grinned. "Would you like the truth or a tamer version?"

"Always the truth."

A sensual hum vibrated in his throat. "I want your hands on my body. I want your tongue in my mouth. I want you hugging my cock as we bounce through every rut in the road."

Heat flooded every part of her, the needy ache urging her to act. In Lydia's shadow, she always felt inadequate. Aramis Chance made her feel like the most desirable woman alive.

She reached forward and let down the blind. "How fortunate that our thoughts should be aligned."

His hungry eyes remained fixed on her. "Come here. Raise your skirts and sit astride me. You can ride me all the way to Uxbridge."

It was an invitation she could not resist.

While he freed his engorged manhood, she gathered her skirts to her waist, then lost her balance and tumbled into his lap.

"I'm sorry." She gripped his shoulders and braced her knees either side of his thighs. "This is much more difficult than I anticipated."

"I need to anchor you down," he teased, guiding her over his erection. "Once I'm inside you, every bump in the road will heighten our pleasure. Let's play a game."

"A game?"

"You must take an inch at a time, no more."

Though she was a novice in the art of lovemaking, she suspected he would struggle to abide by the rules. "Very well."

"Kiss me. Kiss me while I touch you." He began stroking her sex with the head of his erection, the movements gentle, satisfying, but the sweetest kind of torture. "Kiss me softly, slowly. Build the momentum."

She pushed her hands into his hair, holding him as their open mouths met. She tried not to hurry but her sex pulsed, and the need to feel full had her slipping her tongue into the warm, wet depths.

He did not reciprocate.

She tried to tempt him with the sensual moans he liked. But he was steadfast in his ambition to win the game.

"I'll be inside you soon." It was like he knew she needed to feel the wild plunge of his tongue, needed his manhood pumping hard to banish the emptiness. "You're so wet for me."

He was doing it on purpose—saying arousing things, tormenting her, drawing her to the edge of her climax and holding her there.

But this was a game of two players. She might be a novice but she wouldn't make winning easy for him.

She pressed her mouth to his ear, her tongue tracing the shell. "Tonight, I want to be your dinner and your dessert."

He quivered against her, bolstering her confidence.

"I want you to taste me, Aramis. I want your hot mouth feasting on my flesh. I want to shudder against your lips."

A guttural groan rumbled in his throat. He pushed slowly into her entrance, though she came up on her knees, denying him the pleasure.

"You're good at this game," he growled.

She looked into his eyes, resisting the urge to surrender. "I'm aching and wet and want to feel you moving inside me, but perhaps we should wait until tonight."

"Like hell we will." He entered her in one long thrust, burying himself so deep they both moaned in pleasure. "Sweet mercy! We were made for each other, love."

He claimed her mouth in fierce possession. There was nothing soft and slow about the way he owned her. Every powerful thrust said he was the victor. But it was the way he watched her that tightened every muscle in her core. It was the light in his eyes, the lingering smile on his lips as she came apart around him.

It was words he used. "God, you're magnificent."

Not useless. No one's burden.

He was magnificent—kind, strong, considerate, so desirable she could hardly breathe. As the swell of emotion in her chest gathered behind her eyes, one thought entered her head.

Was this what it felt like to be in love?

Chapter Fifteen

The Fox and Crown
Uxbridge

After a night spent drinking with the locals in the taproom of a coaching inn on the outskirts of Uxbridge, it was evident Miss Gray had lied or made a mistake.

No one had heard of Edwin Budworth.

No one knew a man with connections to the Belldrake theatre.

Aramis had been forced to curb his temper when a farmer insisted on naming those who'd lived in the area since the eighteen hundreds. At one point, the fellow confused his prized cow with his great-aunt Bella. Aramis must have nodded off because he woke to Naomi giving him a covert nudge. It was midnight when they dragged themselves away, though that didn't stop them stripping off each other's clothes and indulging in every wicked pleasure.

"I wish I could say I'm disappointed," Naomi said,

buttering her toast while seated at the table in the private parlour. Her face had a radiant glow that held his attention. "We may not have found Edwin Budworth, but we've made the most of our time together."

Though they had made love twice before dressing for breakfast, he would take her on the table, amid the clattering china, if he'd had the foresight to lock the damn door.

He was obsessed. Tormented by an insatiable hunger. With it came profound fear. He'd thought himself numb to pain until he imagined losing the one thing that mattered.

Her.

"We'll stay at an inn near Northwood tonight." While he knew they would spend endless hours lying naked in each other's arms, he didn't know how they would tackle Melissa and Jeremiah Grant. "Perhaps we might find an excuse to delay our return to town. We could always tour the south coast."

Naomi looked up and smiled before sucking jam off her finger. There wasn't a woman alive who could affect him so deeply.

"I'm sure you'd tire of me before we reached Brighton."

Though she chuckled, he said, "Don't do that."

She blinked in surprise. "Do what?"

"Imply you're in some way lacking."

She shrugged, holding her toast in midair. "Aramis, we agreed to part once we prove Melissa lied. You made it clear this is a temporary arrangement. I was merely referring to that."

"There's nothing temporary about what's happening

here." He downed his coffee, wishing it was brandy so it might numb his senses. "Do you think I make a habit of discussing my thoughts and feelings? Do you think this is in any way normal for me?"

"How would I know if you don't tell me?"

"You're an intelligent woman. When one considers the concessions I've made, it's obvious I'm in no rush for this to end." Was it not there in his desire to hold her close? Was it not evident when he lay beside her, stroking her hair? "We make love, Naomi. For the first time in my life, I understand the difference."

Her curious gaze swept over him. "I lack your experience and have no means to compare. Surely you made love to Melissa."

The sound of the woman's name grated like grinding metal. His wife had made an assumption. One he was quick to correct.

"I never had sex with Melissa."

Naomi's eyes grew wide in disbelief. "Never?"

It sounded so ludicrous, he'd not told another soul. Not even Aaron. Melissa had no interest in a young man ten years her junior. She'd permitted certain liberties. She'd used him, manipulated him, messed with his mind. He'd wanted to believe someone could love him. Instead, he'd been left with a scar as hideous as the man he was inside. A permanent reminder of his mistake.

"Never," he reiterated. "I've made love to no one but you."

Water filled her eyes. "And I've made love to no one but you."

Their gazes remained locked.

If one look could tell a story, theirs was a tale of hope.

Emotion bubbled in his chest, but a loud knock on the door brought an end to their intimate conversation.

The ageing innkeeper, Mr Talbot, entered the parlour. "Beggin' your pardon, sir, but you asked me to tell your coachman to be ready to leave at midday. Only he never arrived last night. There ain't no sign of your man or your coach."

Aramis sat bolt upright. "You're certain?" Disturbing questions flooded his mind. Had Maddock absconded? Had Edwin Budworth caught up with them on the road and silenced his lackey?

"I've been out to the yard and coach house myself."

Gibbs could be trusted and would not leave them stranded. "I suspect he's delayed in town." He didn't want to worry Naomi, but surely Daventry would have sent an agent to inform them of any problems. "We'll finish our breakfast and consider our options while we wait."

Their options were limited. Did they send for Aaron and entertain themselves in the meantime? Did they hire horses or take the mail coach to London?

"I'll send word as soon as he arrives." Mr Talbot lingered at the door, keen to relay other news. "About the gentleman you mentioned last night. The one you thought lived around here."

"Edwin Budworth?" Naomi said, her interest piqued.

Mr Talbot nodded. "My wife thinks the man living at the old Croft Manor makes regular trips to London. He ain't no gentleman. He's been the caretaker there since Mr Holland went to visit his sister in Madras last year."

"What makes you think his name is Budworth?" Aramis said.

"It ain't. He goes by the name Edward Worth. Seems like an odd coincidence if you ask me. I ain't never spoken to him myself. He's not one for social gatherings. No one has seen the housekeeper, Mrs Fisher, for nigh on six months."

"Is it far to the manor?" Naomi asked, clearly hoping to make a house call.

"A mile north on the road to Ruislip." Talbot pointed to the dirty window. "Left at the first crossroads. It's a fine day. I can have Mrs Talbot make you a basket."

Despite every effort, Aramis could not envisage sitting beneath an oak tree with his wife, sharing more than a picnic. Every muscle in his body tensed. A warning they should wait for Gibbs before venturing to Croft Manor.

"Don't trouble your wife. We'll wait for our coachman."

"As you wish. I'll be in the taproom if you change your mind."

The instant Talbot left, Naomi questioned the decision. "Should we not visit Croft Manor and establish if Edward Worth is the man we seek?"

"Indeed. Though we have a slight problem."

She arched a brow. "Me?"

"I can protect myself against the likes of Edwin Budworth. But the man need only put a blade to your throat, and I'm as helpless as a lame beggar."

She would always be his weakness. A pawn the dissolute lords of the *ton* might use against him. Debt-ridden men were desperate. Desperate enough to take a woman hostage to save their necks. It was why Aaron urged them to avoid romantic entanglements.

"I can defend myself. We're close to uncovering the truth." She spoke like a barrister, confident in her conviction. "There's too much at stake to sit idly. We need to discover if Edwin Budworth is guilty. If we don't, and the evidence we've hidden comes to light, I'll hang."

The last word hit him hard, cleaving his heart in two. Horrid visions burst into his mind. The hooded hangman. The rope pulled tight, burning her porcelain skin. The gruesome nightmares would plague his waking hours like malevolent spirits. He'd be fit for nothing but Bedlam.

"I'll take you to France before I let Maitland get his hands on you." The vehemence in his tone made her gasp. Or perhaps she was shocked he would go to great lengths to save her.

"But you can't leave your family."

"You're my family, too."

A tense silence descended.

The innkeeper returned, knocking persistently.

"What is it, Talbot?" He was ready to tell the man what he could do with his basket. "I hired the private parlour for a reason."

The fellow placed a note next to the coffee pot on the table before returning to stand by the door. "This came for you an hour ago. A man rode into the stables and asked Samuel to check you were here. He said not to bring the letter inside until another hour passed."

Aramis snatched the grubby note. He tried to keep calm for Naomi's sake, but as he scanned the message, he had every reason to be alarmed. "Thank you, Talbot. That will be all."

"Can I get you anything while I'm here, sir?"

Naomi smiled. "I'll have a fresh pot of tea."

Talbot withdrew, leaving them alone to discuss the message that chilled his blood. He scrubbed his face with his hand, but it did nothing to quell his fears.

"It's from Lucius Daventry." He gazed into her blue eyes, aware she was about to slump in the chair and sob till there were no more tears left to shed. "Gibbs cannot return for fear he will lead the men from Bow Street here. We're on our own. No one can risk coming to our aid. Daventry cautions us against returning to London."

Her smile died. "Bow Street? Did something happen to Mr Maddock? What of his sister Sarah?"

Aramis swallowed past the lump in his throat. "They're safe. Daventry took them to his country estate. Maddock gave a detailed statement naming Edwin Budworth the prime suspect."

She clasped her chest. "Then all is well."

"Not quite." He steeled himself against a pang of despair. "Mrs Wendon gave a statement. She claims she saw blood on your cloak and beneath your fingernails." He'd always known that woman was trouble.

Naomi stared in disbelief. "But I wore gloves that night."

"She said you were in a hurry to flee the Belldrake and placed you at the theatre at midnight." He released a weary sigh. He should have followed his instincts. He should have left Mrs Wendon on the pavement. "According to Mrs Wendon, I was there under duress. She said she saw a pistol in your carpet bag and believes you forced me to marry you."

As predicted, she sagged in the chair. "There's little point wondering why she would lie. If I hang, you're free to remarry. But I kept my bag closed. She couldn't have known about the pistol, and only a handful of people know we're married."

Aramis cursed beneath his breath. "According to Daventry, Mrs Wendon turned detective and overheard Miss Gray gossiping in the Dog and Duck."

Naomi's face turned ashen. "Mrs Wendon will force Hester to make the same statement. The evidence of three people will be enough to convince a jury I'm guilty of the crime."

"Unless we can prove Edwin Budworth is the killer." Despite his misgivings, there was only one way forward, though he would give her the option to run. "We can tackle this my way, like dangerous bastards out for blood. Or we leave for Portsmouth or Dover and I hide you somewhere abroad." Aaron could cope without him, and his brothers would hold the fort.

She blinked back tears and raised her chin in defiance. "This is a fight for the truth and for my liberty. I ran from Hartford Hall. Fled my family home like a thief in the night. I won't run from this. I suggest we dispense with tea and gather weapons."

Amid his despair, heat warmed his chest, a deep respect for her tenacity. "You sound like a Viking shield maiden preparing for battle."

"People often confuse kindness with weakness. I can be strong when it matters."

The blend of sweetness and strength had impressed him the night they met. "I applaud your ability to take control of a situation. I have every faith you will win this battle, too."

Her tender gaze caressed him. "You're the only person who believes in me, Aramis. The only person I trust."

I'm in love with you.

The words stole into his mind. The physical sensations flooded his body. He fought the rush of euphoria, breathed to settle his racing pulse, to suppress the intense yearning.

He stood, keen to speak from the heart. But one wore armour to face their foes. Sentiment was as useful as a shield of sand. Still, he was compelled to offer a token of his affection before preparing to tackle the dangers ahead.

He clasped her hand and drew her from the chair. "My life changed the day you invaded my carriage. There's no woman on this earth I admire more than you."

She wrapped her arms around him. Her embrace had the power to transcend words. She was his strength and his solace. A beacon of light, drawing him from the shadows. An angel sent to prove everyone deserved to be loved.

Weeds littered the gravel drive leading to the Elizabethan Manor. Weeds swamped the raised beds, strangling the forgotten flowers. Dirt clung to the manor's facade like a choking vine. Like the rancid air in the rookeries, one could taste the stench of neglect.

Aramis tugged the iron bell pull, his heartbeat pounding in his throat as he waited. "I shall ask for Edwin Budworth. Say we're here to deliver the sad news of his brother's death. That Miss Gray gave us this address."

Naomi exhaled deeply. She reached for his hand and gave it a reassuring squeeze. "I couldn't do this without you. I know you're used to fighting battles, but this wasn't part of our agreement."

He hadn't considered his list of demands since signing his name on the page. "I swore to protect you, and I never break a vow." He'd vowed to love and cherish her. Words fate had decreed would become a self-fulfilling prophecy.

"Then the least I can do is tend to your wounds."

A mocking snort escaped him, and he tugged the bell for the second time. "Be assured. I shall emerge from this war unscathed."

Her voice turned coy. "You don't want me to pour Frankincense oil over your tight shoulders and massage the tense knots?"

The sinful train of her thoughts made him smile. "My muscles are as hard as stones. You'll need more than one bottle and may need to repeat the process every night for a week."

Her blue eyes softened. "After all you've suffered at my expense, I shall be forever in your debt."

Forever.

He liked the way the word rolled off her tongue.

The sudden clip of footsteps in the hall beyond preceded the grinding of rusty metal. The door creaked open. A dark-haired woman, no older than thirty, peered around the jamb.

"Can I help you?" She looked nervous as she scanned the breadth of his shoulders. Her frown softened as her gaze settled on Naomi's angelic face.

"Mrs Fisher?" Aramis asked.

"Mrs Fisher left six months ago. She went to live with her sister in Sheffield. I'm her replacement Miss Cooper. I have her forwarding address somewhere if you'd care to wait."

Aramis explained they were looking for Edwin Budworth. "We've been tasked with delivering news of his brother George."

Miss Cooper's mouth thinned. She gripped the jamb tightly, her knuckles turning white. "There's no one here of that name. You should ask at the inn. They know most people in these parts."

Having spent many nights at the card tables, watching men trick their opponents with blank faces and fake grins, he knew Miss Cooper had something to hide. "May we speak to the caretaker Edward Worth?"

A shadow of alarm touched Miss Cooper's face. "He's taken the cart to town to fetch supplies. He'll be back tomorrow after dark. Call back then."

She tried to close the door, but he wedged his boot in the narrow gap and hardened his expression. "Do you know when Mr Holland might return from Madras? Surely he writes regularly."

Miss Cooper frowned. "Madras? Mr Holland returned a few months ago." She struggled to look him in the eye. "He took ill on the ship and died of consumption. His sister plans to relocate back to England with her husband."

The last comment proved she was lying.

Naomi was quick to notice, too. "A letter was sent to Madras, and you received a reply in the space of three months?"

Miss Cooper quickly scrambled to defend her error. "Mr Holland told us his sister planned to return. Mr Worth wrote to her but is still waiting for a reply."

Again, she tried to shut the door but couldn't.

"If Holland died at home, why is there no record in the parish register?" he lied. "There's no headstone in the graveyard. There's no record of him on the passenger lists for ships returning from India these past twelve months. We know because we've been hired to investigate his disappearance."

The woman blinked in confusion but then jumped, remembering something important. "Mr Holland is buried on the grounds. In the old family crypt on the path near the woods. Come back tomorrow. Mr Worth will take you there."

They couldn't wait until tomorrow. Sergeant Maitland needed to hang someone for murder and didn't care if they were guilty or not. The local magistrate could arrive at any moment with a warrant for Naomi's arrest.

"Point us in the right direction, and we'll find the crypt ourselves." If he could prove the housekeeper was lying, he would return to the house and demand answers.

The housekeeper danced around the decision, her anxious gaze revealing every faltered step. "Follow the path through the gate in the herb garden." With a shaky hand, she pointed to the left of the house. "I—I wouldn't go down there. There's all manner of ghosts haunting that place. Best you return tomorrow."

Experience had taught him to be wary of people not shadows in the darkness. He stepped back from the door. "For your sake, I pray you've spoken the truth."

The housekeeper repeated the need for them to leave and seek out Mr Worth, but Aramis gripped Naomi's hand and headed off in search of the herb garden.

They paused at the kitchen window. There was no sign of a cook or maid, no fire in the hearth. A hunk of bread and a measly slab of butter were the only edible items gracing the wooden table.

The stables were empty.

"Miss Cooper is here alone." He'd been expecting the grooms to attack them with pitchforks but the place was deserted.

"She wasn't dressed like a housekeeper and seemed quite young to bear the responsibility. Perhaps she's Mr Worth's sister, and they're taking advantage of the owner's absence."

"By owner, do you mean Mr Holland's sister?" He scanned the herbs growing amid grass and weeds in the borders before opening the wooden gate. "I'm quite certain Mr Holland is dead. What I'm unsure about is how he died and where he's buried."

"Or why Miss Cooper would invent aspects of the story."

They fell silent while following the path to the crypt. The grey stone mausoleum stood on the edge of the woods like it had been born of the earth, a doorway to the underworld.

Naomi clasped his hand tightly as they moved closer to the wrought-iron gate. "Do you think shield maidens admitted they were scared? How does one approach dangerous situations and not feel a tremor of fear?"

He peered through the bars at the stone steps leading down into an eerie blackness. "The rational mind plays tricks. There's nothing frightening about the dead or the darkness. Fear stems from a story we've invented in our minds."

She faced him, her curious gaze searching his. "Like the story you've told yourself about Aaron? You called out to him in your sleep last night. You said you were sorry for being so weak."

He felt the dull ache of inadequacy. He was skilled at playing a hard-faced devil. Made sure no man thought him lacking. "It's not the same. My opinion is based on actual events."

"Events that happened when you let fear overwhelm you." She placed her hand on his chest, covering his heart. "You're not that boy anymore. You're the most impressive man I have ever met. I've no doubt Aaron thinks so, too."

He tried to make light of her compliment. "You're biased, swayed by the way I make you feel in bed."

A twinkle of desire danced in her eyes. "What happens between us in bed is magical. I'm referring to those qualities that make you the man I admire."

He cupped her nape and kissed her deeply. "I don't deserve you."

"Yes, you do."

They kissed again. The profound tenderness in each stroke of her tongue was a balm to heal his wounds. Though he longed to discuss the future, he needed to wait to see how she felt once the case was solved and she was free.

"Would you prefer to wait here while I inspect the tomb?" He brushed a strand of hair off her cheek. "I'll be a minute, no more."

She glanced at the dense thicket of trees looming behind them. "I want to stay with you. Though we forgot to ask for the key."

Aramis tried the gate and found it open. Inhaling deeply, he led Naomi down the moss-covered steps into a dim room. Stone plaques lined the damp walls. The solemn air carried the heaviness of grief.

His attention moved to the crude wooden coffin, dumped on the floor like the poor souls in the rookeries, abandoned to suffer the cold.

Naomi sidled up to him. "Are those bloodstains on the lid? Might that be dried blood on the floor?"

He decided to investigate, hoping to use the blade he had strapped to his shin to prise open the lid, but the creak of the rusty iron gate sent his heart galloping.

Naomi grabbed his arm. "Aramis! Quick! She's locking the gate."

He mounted the steps three at a time to find a terrified Miss Cooper slipping the key into her pocket.

"You should have listened to me. You should have left while you had the chance. Mr Worth will want to see you the minute he returns."

He gripped the bars, shaking them violently. "Open the damn door!"

But he was too late. Miss Cooper took to her heels, leaving them prisoners inside the eerie crypt.

Chapter Sixteen

It was dark outside, though the moon cast a silvery sheen over the crypt's iron gate. Miss Cooper had not returned to set them free. No one had ventured along the woodland path. The only sounds heard were the distant hoots of an owl and the rustle of nocturnal creatures foraging in the undergrowth.

Aramis had stripped off his cravat and coat and was busy chiselling the stone doorframe with his blade. "Another half an hour, and I should free the latch."

Most women would sit and stare at his muscular physique, their mouths watering and heat pooling in their loins. While Naomi did indeed feel the lick of lust's fire as she watched him work, she admired his steely determination. He was tired and thirsty but refused to admit defeat.

She stood shivering on the cold steps, arms folded tightly across her chest, praising his efforts and reassuring him they would not perish like the couple in the coffin. The coffin she was trying her damnedest to ignore. The stench of death had hit them as soon as Aramis lifted the lid. The smell of decay lingered despite the chill wind breezing through the iron railings.

They had found a silver case in the dead man's pocket, the calling cards bearing Mr Holland's name. Aramis was convinced the man had been dead for a year. Based on the woman's plain grey dress, she was the old housekeeper who never left for Sheffield.

"Is there anything I can do?" she asked for the tenth time. "Something that might distract me from thoughts of what lies in that coffin."

Aramis glanced over his shoulder and smiled. "You can mop my brow. Talk to me. Tell me what you mean to do with your inheritance."

She joined him on the top step, rubbing her hands together to banish the cold from her bones. "We've been so preoccupied with finding Edwin Budworth, I've not thought beyond clearing my name." How could she think about money when in the throes of a passionate love affair?

"Whatever happens, I can't imagine you living with Lydia at Hartford Hall. You're not the same woman she abandoned at the playhouse."

She smiled as she brushed a lock of hair from his damp brow. "You're to blame. You have such a profound effect on women."

He bent his head and kissed her, his mouth moving with the promise of something wicked, his tongue sliding over hers, tightening the muscles in her core. "Neither of us are the same people we were the night our paths crossed."

Sadness loomed. Soon they would reach a crossroads, their paths veering in opposite directions. The thought made it difficult to breathe. "You're right. Although Lydia saved me, her selfish actions have ruined any trust between us. It would be impossible for me to live with her at Hartford Hall."

But I could live with you, Aramis.

She could wake next to him in bed each morning, inhaling his earthy essence, staring at his tight buttocks as he crossed the room to the washstand. She knew what sort of life it would be—one filled with lust and love and laughter.

"Lydia won't settle in the country, not now she's spent time in the metropolis. Perhaps you might purchase her share."

She fought a crush of disappointment. Had he not considered she might want to live with him? Did he still think this was a marriage of convenience? A vision of a bleak future entered her head, the pain of unrequited love crippling.

"I don't have the means to raise the capital."

"I could give you the money."

She shook her head. It was a generous offer. An opportunity for him to walk away with a clear conscience. "You've worked hard for what you have. You've done enough for me already."

Confusion reigned. He was renowned for his blunt manner and direct approach, yet waltzed around the only question that mattered: would they part ways when the war was over?

A shadow of uncertainty passed over his handsome

features. Was he searching for answers, too? Was he thinking about the question they were keen to avoid?

"I want you to have the freedom to make honest choices." He faced the wall and began hacking at the hunk of grey stone, shutting her out. "Money shouldn't be a factor in any decisions you make."

Desperate to feel close to him, she smoothed her hand over the bulging muscles filling his shirt sleeves. "I don't care about money. I care about the things that matter most. I care about you."

He inhaled sharply and met her gaze. "And I care about you. It's why I offered to make your life a damn sight easier."

He had missed the point. She would live above Mrs Maloney's bookshop if it meant spending her days and nights with him. Was she expecting too much from a man most people considered heartless?

Perhaps he was distracted by thoughts of freedom and vengeance. He threw the blade to the floor, wrapped his fingers around the iron bars and shook the gate so violently the stone securing the latch crumbled away.

They both breathed a sigh when the gate flew open.

"Now to find that witch of a woman who locked us in here." He snatched his coat and cravat from the floor and dressed. His blade was blunt, but he slipped it into the sheath inside his boot. "I'm not leaving without answers." When she shivered, he pulled her cloak tightly around her shoulders and kissed her like it might be their last. "We've much to discuss when this is over. We need to stop dancing around the truth."

Aramis took her hand and led her back to the manor,

though she had trouble keeping up with his lengthy strides. The house stood in darkness. That didn't stop him kicking the servants' door until the impact splintered the frame.

Inside, the rooms smelled damp and dusty. The once plush drawing room was now a makeshift bedchamber with blankets and cushions strewn over the floor. They stepped over dirty plates and apple cores, examined the cold embers in the grate. After inspecting every room, they found a note from Miss Cooper on the cluttered desk in the study.

Naomi attempted to decipher the poor handwriting. "It's addressed to Edwin. Miss Cooper said we came looking for him, and she was forced to take matters into her own hands." The tone suggested the woman was more than his servant.

"Where the hell is she?" Aramis barked.

"She says no amount of money is worth hanging for and has left for good this time." Naomi turned the letter over in her hand. "There's no mention of where she's gone."

Aramis punched the air. "What in God's name is going on here?"

She tried to piece the puzzle together. "So, Edwin Budworth is posing as the caretaker. Hence the reference to the man with many faces in the journal. What if his brother discovered he'd assumed another identity and had killed Mr Holland? Perhaps Edwin hit his brother with the bust of Julius Caesar to silence him."

Aramis yanked the desk drawer open and rummaged inside. "Perhaps Lydia discovered her lover was a lying murderer. That's what caused her to leave the theatre halfway through the performance."

"It would explain why she abandoned me." Naomi regretted the words as soon as they left her lips. "Strike that from the record. I lapsed into the fool who wants my sister to care."

Aramis looked up, his gaze warming her. "It's natural to make excuses for her. You have a kind and loving heart. Why wouldn't you expect the best from others?"

The sudden creak of the boards in the hall made them both freeze.

Aramis crept around the desk, snatching the marble paperweight. "If things become ugly, you must run," he mouthed.

"I'll not leave you," she whispered, her heart slamming against her ribcage.

I'll never leave you by choice.

He stepped in front to shield her from the intruder.

The door handle rattled.

Silence.

Seconds passed as she listened for retreating footsteps.

Then the door burst open.

A dark figure filled the doorway.

Sheer terror held her rigid. She couldn't move or speak. Her only thought was finding the strength to save Aramis.

"Aaron?" Aramis' shoulders sagged in relief. "What the hell are you doing here? Did Daventry not tell you it was too dangerous to follow? Sergeant Maitland is looking for Naomi."

Aaron Chance stepped into the room, exuding a raw

masculine energy that would have most people fleeing for cover. "I'm quite capable of evading a fool like Maitland. Do you think I'd leave you here without protection?"

The men did not embrace, but love flowed between them, an unstoppable molten river capable of destroying anyone who stepped in their path.

"We're extremely pleased to see you, Mr Chance."

Aaron looked at her with a disapproving eye. "I had every reason to fear the worst. The innkeeper in town said you left for the manor at midday and failed to return. I called at the house, but no one answered. I've spent hours searching the woods and scouring every deep ditch."

Another woman might cower beneath the force of his growing temper, but she knew his annoyance stemmed from fear. Who comforted him in the darkness?

Much to the man's shock, she hurried forward and hugged him. "I'm sorry if we worried you. Please know I'd rather die than let anything happen to Aramis."

Aaron stood stiffly, his body as hard as granite. "Based on the facts, it's only natural a man would be concerned."

Silent words must have passed between the brothers because Aramis came to Aaron's aid. "If you don't release him, we'll have another body to contend with. He's not drawn a breath since you pressed your cheek to his chest."

She stepped back into the comfort of her husband's embrace. "Forgive me. My emotions often get the better of me." And it was evident from Aaron's stony expression he did not welcome this show of affection.

Aaron brushed his hand down his black waistcoat. "Would you mind telling me why you're creeping about in the dark?"

Aramis explained all that had happened since they'd left London, omitting to mention they could barely keep their hands to themselves. "We think Lydia discovered the truth about Edwin Budworth. That's why she's agreed to hide at Chivers' apartment."

"No woman in her right mind would want Chivers for a husband," Aaron agreed. "The man's terrified of his own shadow. Though I have news that may cast doubt on your theory."

"Oh?" Nothing Lydia did would surprise Naomi now.

"Miss Fontaine has disappeared again along with her clothes and Chivers' diamond cuff links." Aaron's raised hand prevented them from interrupting. "We found the solicitor's clerk. Miss Fontaine paid him a visit along with a man fitting Edwin Budworth's description."

"Edwin?" The news hurt like a blade to the heart. Lydia was attempting to find evidence of fraud. "Have any letters arrived for me?" Had guilt pricked Lydia's conscience? Was she trying to help solve the case? Did she even know her lover was a cold-blooded killer?

"Not to my knowledge," Aaron said.

"Did the clerk say what Miss Fontaine wanted?"

"The clerk admitted his employer was paid to forge the will. He insists he played no part other than remaining silent. Miss Fontaine made him pen a confession. Daventry has the man in custody."

"Does he have his employer's new address?" she said.

"No. He's not seen or heard from the solicitor since the reading of your father's will. There's every chance he's dead."

Sadness hung like a heavy weight in her chest.

Greed was indeed one of the deadliest sins.

"Had my sister visited the clerk with Mr Chivers, I might have faith in her motives." She glanced at Aramis. The tower of strength she couldn't live without. "She has chosen Edwin Budworth over me. They mean to frame me for murder and claim my share of the inheritance."

Aramis captured her hand and pressed a lingering kiss to her knuckles. "You have my word they won't succeed."

"Every instinct says you're right," Aaron said, observing his brother keenly. "Lord Bedlow told me he offered to marry your sister, but she refused him. He said regardless of the gossip, he was not her lover. She insisted he was too good for her, so he showered her with gifts to win her favour."

Naomi hung her head in shame.

It was her fault Lydia was cavorting with a criminal. Had they remained at Hartford Hall, things might have been different. "I knew Lydia Grant. I don't know Lydia Fontaine. My sister was patronising but always caring. The actress is everything I despise."

Aramis gathered her in his arms. Despite the uncomfortable silence, he stroked her hair. "Nothing I can say will ease your pain, but you're not alone, Naomi. You're part of my family. Delphine will be a good friend to you."

"Difficult decisions lie ahead." Aaron's stern tone said he thought she would stumble at the first hurdle. "No one wants to see their sibling hanged. Miss Fontaine's actions will lead to nowhere but the scaffold."

It hurt to hear the truth, but she couldn't worry about Lydia anymore. Not when she risked losing the one thing she held dear.

She kissed Aramis on the cheek and then straightened. "I mean to save my own neck, Mr Chance. Let us search the house for clues before departing for Northwood. I suspect we will find Lydia and Edwin Budworth there."

Hartford Hall
Northwood, Middlesex

The house looked just as Naomi remembered. The rose bushes were blooming. The wisteria was in its second blush, the sweet scent from the purple pendants carried on a gentle breeze. The rays of the midday sun bathed the grounds in a golden glow. She could picture her parents strolling arm in arm through the verdant walkways, talking and smiling, a vision of heavenly bliss.

It was a mirage.

A heartbreaking illusion.

Hartford Hall was the devil's den. A shelter for criminals. Villains out to soil her sacred memories. Despite her father's hopes, Melissa was not the ointment to heal grief's wounds. Spiteful by nature, she'd rubbed salt into every lesion. Now Edwin Budworth professed to be the bandage Lydia needed. The mistake would be her sister's downfall, too.

"Remember what I said." Aramis addressed his brother. It was the first time he'd spoken since leaving

Aaron's hired carriage and marching past the gatehouse. "You'll hold your tongue and permit us to deal with this matter."

Aaron made no objection. "You've waited ten years for retribution. I'm merely here to witness the end of your nightmare."

Naomi glanced at Aaron, wondering if he knew the guilt Aramis lugged around like a sack of broken bricks. "If Aramis had to pick anyone to stand beside him, he would always choose you."

Aaron swallowed hard but said nothing.

She stepped forward. "Allow me to announce our arrival. Wilson will be less inclined to turn us away." Nausea roiled in her stomach as she tugged the bell. The ringing echoed through the hall like a death knell.

Wilson opened the door. Their eyes met, his brightening as he inhaled like a prisoner in need of clean air. "Miss Grant! Bless my soul! Why did you not let yourself in?"

She smiled. It was so good to see a familiar face. "Hartford Hall is no longer my home. I wouldn't dare be so presumptuous."

Wilson observed the men flanking her like soldiers of the King's Guard. As agreed, she didn't introduce Aramis as her husband.

"I'm here with friends to see Melissa and Uncle Jeremiah."

The butler leaned closer. "Tell me you mean to overthrow them. If you do, you'll have an army of servants at your disposal."

She patted the man's upper arm as her mother did

whenever he found her misplaced books. "That's good to know. But I mean to rely on the might of the law, not the power of our fists."

Wilson gave a knowing grin, unaware of the chaos about to erupt. "If you'd care to follow me, Miss Grant, I shall announce you at once."

"Don't announce my friends. I insist on a private audience first."

They entered the house that was no longer her home.

Stale pipe smoke clung to the air. Her mother always kept a vase of hothouse flowers on the console table. Now it was a stuffed stoat.

Naomi's gaze moved to the grand staircase. Six months had passed since Lydia gripped her hand and pulled her down the dark steps, urging her to hurry. Lydia was every woman's hero. A lady's saviour in a time of trouble. Yet it was an act she had failed to repeat.

Wilson knocked on the drawing room door.

With her usual lazy drawl, Melissa called, "Enter!"

Aaron gripped Aramis' shoulder in a firm gesture of brotherly affection. The men shared glances that said no matter the outcome, they would always have each other.

"You have a visitor, ma'am."

"A visitor? Here? Well, don't stand there gawping. Who is it?"

"Miss Grant requests an audience."

Melissa snorted like a pig. She always snorted when unsettled. "Lydia is here? That girl has the devil's cheek. Nary a word sent these last six months, and she thinks she can just appear like a phantom in the night. I have a mind to throw her out and bar the door."

The rustle of a newspaper preceded Uncle Jeremiah's frustrated grumble. "Doubtless the chit has run out of funds. Perhaps it's a blessing in disguise. Ingram will marry her. He's always been besotted. Once she's wed, we'll be rid of her for good."

Clearly they had no idea Naomi was at the drawing room door.

"Show her in, Wilson." Melissa sounded smug now. There'd be empty hugs and vacant kisses. "We could do with a little entertainment to brighten the day."

Wilson appeared to escort her into the drawing room.

Though every muscle in her body urged her to flee, she said a silent prayer to her father, begging for the strength to avenge him.

Aramis wrapped his fingers around her wrist to stall her. He pressed his mouth to her ear. "I'm in love with you. I love you, no one else. Don't lose sight of that in this game of charades."

She turned her head, shocked he'd chosen this moment to make a declaration, ecstatic because she was in love with him too.

He read her mind. "I couldn't let you face Melissa without knowing the truth. Don't let her convince you otherwise."

Tears gathered behind her eyes, tears of joy. Heavens! Sentiment was a warrior's curse. "I love you." She could barely catch her breath. "When this is over, I shall spend a lifetime reminding you why."

He inhaled deeply, as if capturing the words before they dispersed into the ether. "If I could go back to that night at the Belldrake, I wouldn't change a thing."

"There's no need to look back, only forward."

She saw it then. The twist of unease, the flicker of uncertainty marring his handsome features. He was preparing for the worst possible outcome. The deep sense of trepidation that consumed her plagued him, too.

"Wilson!" Melissa called.

The sudden clang of a handbell echoed through the hall.

Naomi cupped Aramis' cheek and whispered, "I should go, or we will ruin the surprise."

"Be careful." With some reluctance, he relinquished his grip.

Her nerves were in tatters when she followed Wilson into the drawing room. She didn't care about money or vengeance. Running away with Aramis was the only thought in her mind. But where would they go? He had responsibilities in town, and strong family bonds that meant everything to him.

"Naomi? What are *you* doing here?" Melissa looked like she'd won a prize at the fair, only to discover it was a rotten apple. "Where is Lydia?"

"In London, the last I heard." Wherever Lydia was, trouble wasn't far from her door. "I wondered if she might be here."

Melissa patted her perfect black curls as she sneered at Naomi's creased cloak and dusty boots. "It's clear you regret racing away in the dead of night. If you've come back expecting us to feed you, think again. After the diabolical way you've behaved, you'll need to earn your keep."

She glanced at her uncle, who had taken up his newspaper. His clenched jaw said he did not care for the disturbance. "My father's will states you must provide every comfort."

Jeremiah met her gaze, his grey eyes as hostile as a storm cloud. He always roused a tempest when trying to unsettle her. "You'll be grateful for what you're given. Your papa isn't here to pander to you now."

When one had dined with the Chance brothers, Uncle Jeremiah was as intimidating as a kitten chasing a ribbon. "No, but I'm sure he'll watch from heaven's plains as you walk to the scaffold."

Her comment stumped the man who'd stolen her inheritance.

Melissa's laugh was more like a cackle. "You seem to have found a sense of humour during your absence. Though I wouldn't test your uncle's patience. He'll not think twice about throwing you out."

"Oh, I'm not leaving," she said, determined to fight her corner. Aramis' passionate kisses had curled her toes and left her empowered. "I shall remain here until the magistrate arrives. While you have been idling your days away here, I have gathered evidence of fraud. The solicitor's clerk gave his testimony, as did the Hendersons."

She was sure the sweet old Hendersons were tricked into signing the papers. Indeed, her uncle's reaction confirmed as much.

"John Henderson can't remember what day it is, let alone what happened over a year ago. His testimony will be worthless in court."

Melissa gritted her teeth. "Be quiet, Jeremiah."

"Yes, Uncle. You wouldn't want it known Mr

Henderson was not in his right mind when he signed the forged will."

Jeremiah leapt from the chair amid a tussle with his broadsheet. "Don't threaten me, girl. You're in my house now. Don't you forget it."

She might have lacked the confidence to proceed were it not for Aramis waiting in the hall. "You're in my house, Uncle. The courts will convict you both of fraud. It's still a capital offence."

Jeremiah's cheeks burned with fiery intensity.

Melissa intervened before he exploded. "You're just a girl on her own. You lack the strength of your convictions. No wonder Lydia has forsaken you. Stop this nonsense. No court in the land will side with a homeless waif over a man with your uncle's good standing."

Naomi breathed deeply. She couldn't wait to put Melissa in her place, yet dreaded witnessing a reunion between Aramis and the woman he once thought he loved.

I love you. No one else.

His declaration entered her mind, a silent reminder his loyalties lay with her. They could not move forward with their lives until the ghosts of the past were laid to rest.

"I'm not on my own. I'm here with my husband and his brother to ensure the truth prevails."

Melissa's eyes widened. Her hand shook as it came to rest on her bulging bosom. "Husband? What fool married you?"

Naomi smiled. "Mr Chance. Mr Aramis Chance."

Chapter Seventeen

Aramis listened to the verbal exchange. The need to protect his wife had his blood charging through his veins. Twice, Aaron gripped his arm to stop him storming into the drawing room and knocking Jeremiah out cold.

The instant Naomi spoke his name, he burst into the elegant room, his fists balled at his sides, his jaw clenched so tightly he was liable to snap a tooth.

He did not stare at Melissa to determine why he'd once believed every lie that left her lips. Nor did he study her sly face to see how well she had aged. The hatred twisting in his gut did not detract from the only thing that mattered.

He captured Naomi's hand and pressed a tender kiss to her knuckles. "You'll never have to face them alone again. You'll never have to endure their censure." He turned to the slender man, whose sharp features made him look like a weasel. "You're a trespasser here. A swindler. A thief."

The subtle tremor in Jeremiah's thin lips confirmed he was everything Aramis claimed. "I assure you, the will is legally binding. I don't know what my niece has told you about her father's dying wish, but he feared his daughters would fritter away every penny."

"That's a lie," Naomi countered.

Indeed, who would believe the word of a man dressed in a mustard coat?

"They're frivolous girls. Girls ruined by a father who was too kind for his own good. Girls who—"

"My wife is every bit a woman." Aramis glared at the devil. "You stole what is rightfully hers, and I mean to make you both pay."

Melissa approached, the confident sway of her hips meant to draw his eye. The low-cut bodice served to make every man drool but him. "You're more handsome than I remember, Aramis. I always knew you'd grow to be a perfect specimen of masculinity. Poor Naomi. I doubt she knows what to do with you." Deceitful brown eyes roamed over his chest before dipping to his forearm. "Fate has granted me an opportunity to seek forgiveness. I had no idea Jacob could be so cruel. If it's any consolation, I'm sure he's picking the scraps off Lucifer's table."

Jeremiah's confused gaze shifted between them. "You're acquainted with this gentleman?" Jealousy coated every syllable.

"We were friends many years ago."

"We were never friends." Keen to refute her claim, he delivered a blunt assessment of their relationship. "She used me because she hoped I would kill her husband. I was nineteen when Jacob Adams held my arm over a brazier because he thought I'd made him a cuckold." With a sharp tug, he pulled up his coat sleeve, revealing the marred flesh hidden beneath. "So you see, nothing you can say will convince me she's anything but a scheming harlot."

Aaron stepped into the room, and the temperature plummeted. He sauntered over to Melissa, who grappled with the air behind her, seeking stable support. "I would have killed you for what you did to him. The sands of time haven't cooled my temper. But this is my brother's fight. You're lucky I'm here as a spectator."

Aaron strode to the drinks table, poured himself a brandy and sat in the leather wing chair like Satan surveying his minions.

As the silence stretched, Melissa and Jeremiah traded nervous glances.

"My father trusted you, and you betrayed him." Naomi jabbed her finger at her uncle. "When did Melissa persuade you to turn traitor? Surely you know it's only a matter of time before you're in the grave and she inherits your share."

Jeremiah must have had the same suspicions. He turned on Melissa. "Is that why you've been pestering me to visit a solicitor?"

Melissa gave a nonchalant shrug. "There's nothing wrong with putting one's affairs in order. I agreed to leave you my share of the estate. Naomi is trying to cause problems between us."

Aramis couldn't help but chuckle. It was a means to disguise his shame. Only a fool would fall for this woman's tricks. "I wouldn't believe a word from her lying lips. She had her lover kill her first husband. Doubtless she found a way to kill Mr Grant. Be warned. There's always a man waiting in the wings, keen to do her bidding."

Who had killed Jacob Adams?

He'd first heard of the rogue's demise two years ago. Stories were rife and often conflicting. Some said a military man had driven a blade through his black heart. Some said he'd been beaten over the head by a French sailor Melissa was bedding. That his body had been dumped like fish guts into the Thames.

"You would know, Aramis." Melissa stroked her throat, the heat in her eyes a ploy to suggest she knew a titillating secret. "I recall you'd have done anything to win my favour."

"I was naive, barely a man." He'd been seeking sanctuary. A safe place where Aaron did not need to fight his corner. Somewhere he could be the master of his own domain. "Sadly, it took the burn from a lit brazier to reveal the true nature of your character." She had gone crawling to her husband and not given him a second thought.

Aaron pursed his lips and swirled the brandy in the glass.

"I was attracted to you because we're like-minded." Melissa pasted the seductive smile that made her seem ugly to him now. "You use people for your own gain. It's called surviving. But while I have found peace with Jeremiah, you have married my stepdaughter to exact revenge." She stared at Naomi as if she were a fawn caught in a poacher's trap. "Stupid girl. Do you honestly think he gives a damn about what happens to you? Sad little Naomi. Fooled by a heartless beast."

He reached for Naomi's hand and clasped it tightly, but Aaron intervened before he could put Melissa in her place.

"Aramis is in love with her." Aaron's indifferent tone

masked any personal feelings on the subject. "He's never been the cold man the gossips claim."

Melissa tutted. "Aramis is still in love with me. Regardless of what he's told you, he wouldn't be here if he didn't feel something."

Aaron's humourless laugh added to the tension. "I know my brother better than anyone. He never loved you. He loved the idea of being wanted. He loved the thought of being someone's protector. But he would die for Naomi. That tells me all I need to know."

Aramis stared at his brother, feeling a rush of pride. His hero had never disappointed him. Now was not the time to make grand statements, but he might not get another opportunity.

"I'm sorry if I failed you. You've dedicated your life to supporting our family. I know I've let you down at times." It was tough to say, but he felt better for it.

Aaron remained seated, a fleeting glimpse of sadness dulling his dark eyes. "You've never let me down. I couldn't be more proud of you than I am at this moment. Let's say no more on the matter now."

"Good," Jeremiah said, a bite of anger in his tone. "Now take your empty threats and get the hell out of my house."

"Our house," Melissa reminded him.

Being nothing like the poor fool Melissa suggested, Naomi pressed her case. "It's my house. The Prerogative Court is currently examining evidence of your fraudulent claim. If you mean to save your necks, I suggest you pack a valise and flee for your lives. Much like I was forced to do the night you paid Mr Ingram to ruin me."

Failing to take the threat seriously, Jeremiah asked the only question that seemed to matter. "Ingram? What has he to do with this? I assure you, he'll not take kindly to slander."

Naomi's hand trembled in his. "Don't pretend you don't know. He attacked me in my bedchamber. Lydia saved me. That's why we fled."

Melissa frowned. "Why on earth would he do that? I assure you, Mr Ingram is loyal to this family. I suspect this is another lie to add to the growing list."

Aramis watched the couple's reactions with hawk-like intensity, a skill he'd honed in the card rooms. Both appeared to be telling the truth.

A flicker of suspicion roused another thought. One so outlandish he'd be a fool to give it merit. Might Ingram have come looking for Naomi? Was he the person seen fleeing the alley?

"Describe Ingram." A feeling in his gut said he knew the answer before anyone opened their mouths.

Jeremiah's expression tightened. "What does it matter? If you have sufficient evidence to overturn the will, take it up with the relevant office. In the meantime, leave my house before I send for the magistrate. And be warned. People in these parts have no tolerance for outsiders."

Tired of this weasel's chirping—and needing Jeremiah to understand the severity of the situation—Aramis lunged at the buffoon. He grabbed him by his coat lapels and slammed him into the chair.

"One more word, and I shall show you why men fear me." He clenched his fists. How he longed to teach this pillock a lesson. "I want a description of Ingram. How long have you known him, and in what capacity?"

Jeremiah turned ashen and struggled to speak.

"Mr Ingram is tall and broad and has dark brown hair." Naomi's voice held a tremor of fear. "He has the strength to subdue two women, yet he returned to his room when confronted by Lydia."

"Oh, for goodness' sake, Mr Ingram is harmless," Melissa countered. "Jeremiah knew his older brother at boarding school. They've been friends for years."

While grappling for the clue that would tie the loose ends together, Aramis' mind ran amok. They had Edwin Budworth, the man with many faces who'd murdered at least three people. He'd used Lydia and tried to frame Naomi for killing his brother. But why?

There was Melissa and Jeremiah.

Two greedy fools guilty of fraud and deception.

They were separate cases, yet a sinking feeling in his gut said they were connected. Lydia was the linchpin. The person who had encouraged Naomi to flee. The person who'd left her at the mercy of Bow Street. Lydia kept company with a murderer. Lydia was sneaking about trying to gain evidence of fraud.

Now he was forced to ask the question that would cause his wife some distress. "Might Lydia have encouraged Ingram to attack Naomi? Might she have used him to frighten Naomi into leaving her home?"

Naomi's pained gasp tore through him. "No. Lydia wouldn't do that to me. We've both suffered greatly since leaving Hartford Hall."

He met her gaze, wishing he could spare her the truth.

"Lydia has hardly suffered. She's been free to pursue her own goals, always at your expense."

Melissa was quick to cast the blame elsewhere, too. "I saw Lydia and Ingram talking in the garden. It was during the party I held to celebrate the new year. They had their heads together, whispering like a pair of conspirators. He's always admired her, but Jeremiah wanted her to marry for money."

Naomi scowled at Melissa. "You would say that. I remember you being too drunk to stand. I'm surprised you can recall the details. You were supposed to be in widow's weeds, yet wore that garish red dress."

Aaron brought a measure of calm to the situation. "You're an intelligent woman, Naomi. You've proven that during the investigation. I know it's painful to acknowledge the truth, but the sooner you do, the sooner you can move on with your life."

Praise was for the weak.

That had always been Aaron's philosophy.

Yet these rare glimpses of compassion were an encouraging sign.

"Thank you, Mr Chance." Naomi sounded a little astonished. "Your faith in me means more than I can—"

The sudden knock on the door stole everyone's attention.

Wilson entered when summoned. He coughed before saying, "Miss Grant, your sister wishes to speak to you privately. She arrived a moment ago. I mentioned you were visiting, and she—"

"Lydia is here?"

Aramis wished he could say he was surprised, but it

256

was obvious Lydia had every intention of confronting her stepmother. The chit was no threat. Not unless she had Budworth in tow. "Does the lady have company?"

Wilson stared blankly. "It appears she arrived alone in an unmarked carriage, sir."

Whose carriage? Had she returned to Chivers' Mayfair abode and begged to use his vehicle? Had she sold more of her mother's jewels and hired a conveyance?

"This isn't a refuge for waifs and strays," Melissa grumbled. "I shan't tolerate such disrespect. You will show my stepdaughter into the drawing room, or she will leave this house."

Wilson offered a half-hearted bow and withdrew.

Raised voices rang through the hall.

Lydia swept into the room, wearing a jaunty pillbox hat and fashionable green pelisse. "This is utterly ridiculous. Hartford Hall is still my home. I'm allowed to have a private conversation with my sister without being threatened with eviction."

An argument erupted.

While everyone looked on, Melissa and Lydia hissed and quarrelled like back alley cats.

Melissa stamped her foot, her cheeks red with rage. "Whatever you have to say to Naomi, you can say in front of me."

"Very well." Lydia tugged a letter from her reticule and waved it at Melissa as if it were a lethal weapon. "I have the clerk's testimony. Mr Piggot states you paid him to write a new will and tricked the witnesses into signing the document."

"That's preposterous!" Jeremiah gripped the arms of

the chair with bony fingers and hauled himself up. "As God is my witness, I mean to throw you all out."

Aramis kicked Jeremiah's legs from underneath him and pushed him back into the seat. "If you move, you're a dead man. One way or another, we will get to the bottom of this mess."

He was tired of the endless questions and the constant search for the truth. He wanted to be alone with his wife. Somewhere safe. Somewhere quiet.

Naomi stepped into the fray, addressing Lydia. "Why didn't you tell me you planned to question the clerk? Why did you not include me in your plans to seek justice?"

Amid Melissa's spiteful remarks, Lydia said, "I cannot talk to you here. Step into the hall, and I shall explain everything."

"You can begin by explaining why you persuaded Mr Ingram to attack me. I've spent months fearing he might find me when it was all a ruse to force me to leave my home."

Lydia paled. "There's more to it than that."

"You see." Melissa pointed at Lydia's pallid cheeks and gave a smug grin. "Did I not say your sister was to blame?"

"Be quiet," Lydia cried before gripping Naomi's arm. "We'll continue this conversation outside."

They were almost at the door when Aramis intervened. He'd not let Naomi out of his sight. Not while the vultures were circling. He trusted her to defend herself against these deceivers, but every disastrous event in his life had caught him unawares.

"If you must speak privately, allow me to keep watch

from the door." He held Naomi's gaze. He was not the possessive type, but when a cynical man found love, he gripped it with both hands.

A smile touched her lips. Had he known tragedy was about to strike, that his heart was about to be torn in two, he would have hauled his wife into his arms and refused to let go.

Naomi stepped into the hall and gestured to the doorway. "Wait here. This will be over soon, and we'll spend a lifetime making every night memorable."

Who knew the words would come to haunt him in the passing hours?

Who knew the lord would forsake him again?

They stood ten feet away, though Lydia spoke to Naomi in a hushed voice. She gestured to the study behind them and called to the person hiding there, the name Edwin as clear as day.

A tall, broad man appeared wearing a greatcoat and no hat.

Edwin Budworth was not a man of many faces.

He had one face—a face that haunted Aramis' dreams. A face that should be buried deep in the dirt. Because the man standing next to Naomi was none other than Jacob Adams.

Chapter Eighteen

Naomi had seen Edwin Budworth a handful of times at the theatre. He ignored the actors, storming past them as if they were bland paintings on the wall. She often heard his raised voice booming along the corridor. He was glum and not at all attentive. It's what made his romantic relationship with Lydia so confounding.

Despite being brothers, George and Edwin were nothing alike. Edwin was strong, with a muscular physique. He had a full head of brown hair with only a trace of grey. His eyes reminded her of pebbles on an icy beach—cold and unmovable. Unlike Aramis, there was something quite ordinary about him. He was so ordinary it was difficult to believe he was capable of murder.

But when their eyes met, he studied her like a wolf sizing its prey. His pupils dilated. This man was hungry for blood.

While her blood froze in her veins, Lydia looked on as if he were the Messiah sent to rid the world of pestilence and famine.

Aramis stood in the doorway, blind fury marring his features. "Touch my wife, and I'll kill you with my bare hands."

Lydia scoffed at his sudden outburst, her own temper flaring. "You're not at Fortune's Den now, Mr Chance. You'll speak to my husband with a little more respect."

Husband!

Lydia had married Edwin Budworth? How? When?

Was that the reason for her secrecy?

Did she know he'd murdered his own brother? That said, it was all supposition at this point. What if they had made a dreadful mistake?

"You're not legally married to him," Aramis said, the strange statement proving the pressure of solving the case had affected his rationale.

Lydia was quick to prove Aramis wrong. "We were married in Highgate two days ago and have a certificate stating the banns were read. Despite what people say about the Reverend Smollett, I assure you, the marriage is legally binding."

Aramis took a hesitant step forward. "Not when your husband is a bigamist. There's no need to prove Melissa forged the will. She was never legally married to your father. The previous will stands."

Hearing the commotion, Melissa pushed past Aramis and stormed into the spacious hall. She took one look at Edwin Budworth and came to a crashing halt. "What the … How did …" The life drained from her face. Her eyes bulged in their sockets. "They t-told me you were dead."

Edwin's chuckle sounded sinister. "They made a

mistake. The devil sought to spare me. I'm sure he'll explain why when you're dining in hell."

"Thank heavens." Melissa smiled, doing her best to look pleased, not utterly terrified. "Why didn't you find me sooner?"

"You know why."

"Come here, Naomi." Aramis beckoned her forward, his tone firm though his hand trembled.

She was about to join her husband and ease his fears, but Edwin draped his heavy arm around her shoulder. "She's going nowhere. My wife needs a companion for our little trip abroad. We're to make for the coast tonight."

"You'll be dead before you reach the gatehouse."

Edwin raised the hand he'd kept hidden behind the folds of his greatcoat. "She'll come with me or die here." He pressed the cold muzzle of a pistol to her temple and clicked the hammer.

"Aramis." A whimper escaped her. It was clear this man was not Edwin Budworth. Based on the information gleaned so far, he had to be Jacob Adams.

Lydia looked just as confused and afraid. "Lower the pistol. My sister is no threat. She's on our side and is helping to regain our inheritance. It's Melissa and my uncle you need to hold at gunpoint." She turned to Aramis. "We've come to take them to the local magistrate."

Naomi stared at her sister in disbelief. "Poor darling," she began, giving Lydia a dose of her own medicine. "Who would have thought you could be so naive? He's using you for the inheritance. The question remains: how will he dispose of so many witnesses?"

"You weren't supposed to be here," the fiend cried.

"We would have killed them and buried their bodies, convinced the magistrate they'd fled to the Continent to escape the noose."

"Killed them?" Lydia looked horrified. "Why on earth would we do that? We have the means to prove they're liars. We'll claim the inheritance and live here in peace as we planned."

"We're leaving once we've tied up the loose ends. We'll return once all legal matters are in place. That was always the plan."

Melissa staggered back. She grabbed Aramis' sleeve to steady her balance but he tugged his arm away. "You can't take us all captive."

Aaron Chance entered the hall, his lethal stare fixed on Mr Adams.

Mr Adams turned to Lydia. "Be a good girl and do as you're told. We must even the odds, or we won't leave here alive. We need to take your sister as collateral."

Lydia's inner turmoil was evident in her furrowed brow. She'd been tricked by a man who had used her to settle a score. Heaven knows how he'd convinced George Budworth to pretend they were brothers. What it had to do with Mr Holland was a mystery. Though she felt sure the answers to both questions would be answered soon.

Assuming she survived the next hour.

She could tell from Aramis' focused gaze that he was calculating how he might disarm the villain. Aaron whispered something to him, and they both nodded.

But Lydia reached into her reticule, drew a pocket pistol and aimed at Melissa. "It's loaded. Please don't make me fire a shot. I've been practising for this moment, fearing you would do anything to prevent the truth coming to light."

"Come here, Melissa," Mr Adams barked.

One wrong move and shots would be fired. Melissa deserved to take a lead ball to the chest. Aramis did not. She'd not allow Jacob Adams to hurt him for a second time.

"Do as he says, Melissa." Naomi met Aramis' gaze. Guilt burned her throat. She shouldn't have dragged him into this godforsaken mess. "I shall go with them." She prayed this wasn't the last time she would look upon his handsome face or feel the tenderness in his touch. "I love you. But you must let us leave here before someone is hurt."

"Take me," he said, the bitter twist of his mouth showing how he loathed negotiating with a man he despised.

"No, Aramis." She blinked to stem her tears. "It's better this way. You know why." Mr Adams had every reason to dispose of him quickly. She had to leave now if there was any hope of them both surviving. "You must let me go."

The tension in his posture mirrored the conflict within. Common sense prevailed. "This isn't how it ends for us. Don't be afraid. You know I never break a vow."

Aaron placed his hand on his brother's shoulder. His dangerous, panther-like eyes remained fixed on Jacob Adams. "Leave now before I do something I'll regret."

In a sudden move that made her gasp, Mr Adams grabbed her around the neck in a stranglehold. He kept the pistol pressed so hard to her temple it would leave a bruise.

"If you follow us, I'll shoot her." He backed away slowly, heading for the front door.

Lydia faced her and mouthed, "He's bluffing. Be brave. All will be well."

The fool. When would Lydia wake from her stupor?

"I'm not leaving Hartford Hall," Melissa protested, while Uncle Jeremiah remained silent and hid behind Aaron. "You'll have to kill me."

"Very well." Mr Adams didn't seem to care if Melissa lived or died. "Shoot her, Lydia. Take aim like I showed you. She killed your father and stole what's yours. She deserves to pay with her life."

Lydia's hand shook as she straightened her arm and pointed the pistol. She swallowed deeply, trying to muster the courage to end Melissa's life.

"Please don't," Naomi whispered. Despite her selfish actions, Lydia was still her sister. "Melissa will come with us." Three people had a better chance of disarming the devil. "She'll hang for fraud if she remains here."

"Shoot her." Mr Adams was growing impatient. One slip of his finger on the trigger and her life would be over.

Lydia's hand shook. "Edwin, you promised it wouldn't come to this. You said no one needed to get hurt."

"Do it now, Lydia, or I'll leave you here with them."

"No! Wait! I'll come." Melissa came to stand beside Lydia. "I shall take my chances. Please. Put the pistol away."

Satisfied, Jacob Adams firmed his grip on her throat and dragged her out through the front door. The pain of him crushing her windpipe was nothing compared to the distress she saw in Aramis' eyes.

One curse after another left her husband's lips. He pinched the bridge of his nose before calling, "I love you."

Aramis clutched his chest. It felt as if his heart was being stretched to impossible lengths. Pulled so tightly it would invariably snap. While he had Naomi in his sights, he could breathe through the pain. But then the coachman flicked the reins, and the crunching of carriage wheels on the gravel tore the devil's own roar from his throat.

"As God is my witness, I'll kill Adams if he harms one hair on her head." He clenched his jaw, his fists, every damn muscle. "This is my fault. I'm to blame. I should have dealt with him ten years ago instead of behaving like a coward."

Aaron stepped in front of him, blocking his view of the drive. "Removing yourself from a distressing situation is a sign of strength, not cowardice." He gripped Aramis' shoulders, his fingers digging into the tense muscles. "Pull yourself together. Naomi needs you thinking clearly, not wallowing in regret."

"I let that bastard take my wife." The pain was like a vice crushing his chest. "I let him leave while I watched like a prized clown."

"As did I. We couldn't risk him shooting her."

"You hate her."

"I don't hate her. I hate liars and deceivers. I hate people who use others for their own gain." He grabbed

Aramis' cheeks in a pincer-like grip and forced him to focus. "You can't blame me for not trusting her, but she loves you. She left with that bastard to save you taking a shot to the chest. For that, I mean to ensure she is in your arms before nightfall."

"How?" He tried to fight the hopelessness, the fear of loss.

"By using the talents we honed on the streets." Aaron slapped him hard on the cheek. It was the shock needed to bring him to his senses. "You must use love as a strength, not a weakness."

Aramis rubbed his jaw. "Says the man who avoids female company like the plague."

"This isn't about me. Adams needs money, and he wants retribution. He will kill Melissa and Naomi unless we find them. Now think. Where might he go?"

He considered the options. Adams mentioned the coast but would avoid the main thoroughfares. He knew they would catch him before he reached the first turnpike. He'd not manage three hostages and board a boat without drawing undue attention. He needed somewhere to hide. Somewhere to punish Melissa without fear of interruption.

"Croft Manor is empty and some distance from the road. Holland's house is but five miles from here." They had destroyed the letter left by Miss Cooper. Adams had no idea they'd visited the house.

"Good. He won't be expecting us."

"Holland?" Jeremiah Grant said. "Henry Holland?"

Aramis turned to see Jeremiah lingering in the doorway, as pale and useless as a ghost. "What of it?"

"Melissa was friends with the man for many years."

There was an edge of bitterness in his tone. "I suspect they were lovers at one time. She used to visit him at Croft Manor." Jeremiah sneered at that. "There was some sort of disagreement after she married my brother. She received a letter from Holland a year ago, saying he wished he'd never met her and was moving abroad."

Aramis wished he'd never met Melissa, too.

But then Naomi wouldn't have had cause to kidnap him at gunpoint, to turn his life upside down and heal his heart.

Keen to be on his way, he didn't have time to question Jeremiah. "If you want to keep your neck from the noose, I suggest you leave England. If I see you on these shores again, you'll pay dearly for hurting my wife."

They didn't linger but took to their heels and sprinted down the drive to where they had left the hired carriage parked on the roadside. They found the coachman snoozing atop the box, but he confirmed Adams' vehicle had turned right out of the gates.

"Drive like the devil's at your heels, and I'll triple your fee," Aramis barked. "Don't turn into the manor. We'll walk from the road."

He joined Aaron in the carriage, exhaling deeply when the vehicle lurched forward and picked up speed.

"If I lose her, I'll never recover." He stared at the passing fields, a cavernous hole filling his chest. "I'll become every man's worst nightmare. I'll take your title as the most terrifying brute in London."

"It's not a title I want or have ever coveted," Aaron said solemnly. "But after everything we've suffered, it's helped us become the men we are today."

He could not disagree. Wealth and power were everything to a man desperate to drag himself from the gutter. Naomi had helped him see they came at a price. A price Aaron was still paying for dearly.

Perhaps he could help Aaron by being honest.

Perhaps he might breach his brother's barricades.

"Do you remember the night Father dragged me out of bed and wanted to make a man of me?" He was to fight in the pit so his father could recoup his losses. A boy pitted against a man twice his size.

You don't need to win.

Last two rounds, take a few punches.

A darkness passed over Aaron's features. "Some memories I wish I could forget. I've spent my life praying I could go back to that night, so I might knock the pillock on his arse."

Tell Aaron how you feel.

It may rid you of these nightmares.

Naomi's sweet voice slipped into his mind.

He prayed he could freeze time and hear it over and over.

"I've spent my life wishing I'd been strong enough to let him take me, not you." Emotion choked his voice. He remembered Aaron hauling himself out of bed, clutching his aching ribs. He remembered lying awake for hours, waiting for him to return. "You'd taken such a beating I hardly recognised you when you came home."

Aaron hung his head.

He took a few calming breaths before meeting Aramis' gaze. "I'd have died before I'd let him hurt you. I don't regret what happened. I regret those closest to me suffered in the process."

Love and respect for his brother swelled in Aramis' chest. "There's only two years between us, but you've been my brother, father and my trusted friend."

Aaron's left eyebrow rose a fraction. "My actions prove how I feel about you. There's no need to spout flowery nonsense." For Aaron, sentiment was like an ice at Gunter's. He indulged on rare occasions, though a spoonful proved sickly.

He considered telling Aaron about his nightmares and how he hated watching him fight. But he had more pressing matters to contend with. "When we rescue Naomi, I want her to live with us at Fortune's Den."

She might want to live at Hartford Hall, but that would pose a problem for him. He had a business to run and couldn't abandon his responsibilities permanently.

Aaron sighed, but the mask he'd perfected fell into place, hiding any personal emotions. "You own a few properties in town. It's only right your wife has a place to call home. A place you can be alone together."

Though he knew Aaron was right, they had never lived apart.

Sadness filled the space between them.

He could see Aaron sitting alone at the dining table. Sigmund his only companion on long winter nights. "Perhaps you want rid of me so you can spy on Miss Scrumptious in peace," he said to lighten the mood. "Don't tell me you've not imagined bedding her."

"What I do in my spare time is my business." Aaron averted his gaze to glance absently at the passing wheat fields. "Some men are meant to be alone. Women always want to change things."

"Not all women." Naomi was different. She was honest and intelligent and didn't try to manipulate him. "You need someone who isn't afraid of you. Someone who understands we all carry traumas from our imperfect lives. You need—"

"Don't tell me what I need." He gave a nonchalant shrug. "So, I might think about bending a certain woman over my desk. I might fantasise about seeing something other than disdain in her eyes. The reality is I need to own things. It's obvious I could never own her."

Aaron never spoke about his personal feelings.

It was a move in the right direction.

If only he could make Aaron see the beauty of a meaningful relationship. Perhaps that's how he would repay him for his many sacrifices. Help him to find the mysterious force that binds two souls together.

But to love a woman, a man had to embrace change. He had to be prepared to adapt and evolve. Love made a man challenge his old patterns and beliefs. That's why he feared Aaron would always be alone. He feared Aaron would never know the life-altering love he had found with Naomi.

Chapter Nineteen

Croft Manor
Uxbridge

The outside shutters were closed. The drawing room door was locked. Naomi pressed her ear to the wooden panel and tried to determine the strange scraping noise echoing through the hall.

She glanced at Melissa and Lydia. They hadn't stopped bickering since Jacob Adams threatened to shoot anyone who disobeyed his orders. "Please be quiet. Can you stop arguing for just a moment?" She was certain Mr Adams was hauling the console table in front of the door, an extra measure to prevent them escaping.

"Be quiet? The devil is going to kill me." Melissa paced back and forth, frantically wringing her hands. "He's going to kill us all. Why else would he bring us here? Where are the servants? Surely he's not killed them, too."

"Edwin is not a murderer," Lydia protested most vehemently. "He's been helping me to prove you're a deceitful witch."

Melissa threw her hands in the air. "Have you heard yourself? You sound like a raving lune. His name isn't Edwin. It's Jacob Adams, and he's been lying to you for months."

Lydia refused to listen and repeated the story they'd heard minutes ago. "My modiste introduced us during one of my trips to London. I met his brother. It was Edwin who persuaded George to hire me. It was Edwin who gave me the money to secure the apartment. He owns the Belldrake theatre. You have him confused with someone else. That, or you're inventing stories to shift the blame."

Naomi should add naivety to the list of Lydia's failings. Jacob Adams had been plotting his revenge. He had used her to punish Melissa and hoped to gain a small fortune in the process.

"Did your husband suggest you bribe Mr Ingram to attack me?" Naomi had been equally gullible in this game of subterfuge. She didn't want to think what Lydia had promised Mr Ingram in return. Aramis was right. Lydia could not be trusted.

"Mr Ingram had no intention of hurting you. It was all a ruse. I don't know why you're making such a fuss."

Such a fuss?

A man had stolen into her room at night. He'd pinned her arms to the mattress and pressed his body on top of hers. He'd ignored her pleas and dismissed her tears. It was the most terrifying moment of her life. That was until she'd been torn away from Aramis, fearing she might never see him again.

"I had to find a way to make you leave Hartford Hall," Lydia said, full of excuses. "How else were we to gain our rightful inheritance?"

"The inheritance Jacob means to steal from under your nose." Melissa moved to the window and peered through the tiny gap in the shutters. "People will probably die because of your stupidity."

"People have died," Naomi corrected. She was tired of Melissa's hypocrisy. "They're dead because you tried to kill Jacob Adams. Let's not forget you smothered my father with a pillow"—it was an educated guess—"forged the will and stole the inheritance. It's too late to play the victim."

Melissa did not deny the claims. "None of that matters now. If we want to live, we must work together."

"Edwin is not going to kill us," Lydia countered.

Melissa grumbled under her breath. "I cannot speak to an imbecile. And I thought Naomi was the simple one. There's more to her character than meets the eye. Aramis Chance is no fool."

The last comment roused Naomi's ire, a burning need to defend the man she loved. "After what you did to him, you don't deserve to utter his name. You used him in the most despicable fashion. Have you seen the scar on his arm? Do you know how he's suffered?"

When she left him at Hartford Hall, he looked defeated. But he was practical and logical and would comb the ends of the earth to find her. She just prayed he wasn't too late.

The turning of the key in the lock stole their attention. The drawing room door swung open, and Jacob Adams strode into the room. He waved his pistol at them, forcing them to shuffle back against the wall.

"Please, Edwin. Tell me what you plan to do." Lydia stepped forward, but he didn't threaten her or shoo her away.

"You know the plan. We're securing your inheritance and ridding ourselves of those who mean to hurt us. You swore to obey your husband. Now, be quiet and let me deal with this matter."

Lydia gave a relieved sigh. "Can we not call the magistrate and have him take Melissa into custody? I'm not sure why you need to keep us all locked in this filthy room. I swear I saw a mouse. And the chaise is damp and smells of brandy."

Mr Adams' stern expression softened. "You're in here for your own safety. We've spent months plotting revenge. Don't forsake me now. We need to tie up the loose ends and be on the ship tomorrow as planned. Our solicitor will take care of the rest."

So, they *were* leaving England?

She supposed it was the only way they'd escape the noose.

"Months? You've spent at least a year planning this," Naomi countered. More if one considered how long he'd been manipulating George Budworth.

Lydia shot her an irate look. "Be quiet, Naomi. Stop twisting the facts. I met Edwin eight months ago. We wrote to each other secretly until he convinced me it was better to leave Hartford Hall."

"You cannot escape your fate. They will convict you of murder in your absence." She hoped to make Lydia see that Mr Adams was orchestrating events to suit his own purpose. "A fugitive cannot inherit." She wasn't sure where the law stood on such matters. All she cared about was rousing doubt in her sister's mind.

But Lydia clenched her teeth and hissed, "When this is over, I've a good mind to lock you away in an asylum. It's not normal for a lady to be so obsessed with murder."

Despite Mr Adams' warning glare, Naomi pressed her case. "Then answer me one question, Lydia. Whose house is this?"

Lydia raised her gaze heavenward. "Obviously it's Edwin's house. He's had a terrible time keeping servants. That's why it's in such a state of disrepair. He means to sell it and move into Hartford Hall."

Good Lord! Their father must be turning in his grave.

Naomi locked eyes with Mr Adams. The man was a picture of smugness. No wonder he got on so well with Lydia.

Melissa spoke up, keen to correct the misconception. "This house belongs to Henry Holland. He's been in India these past twelve months. It's obvious why he left." She screwed up her nose as she scanned the filthy room. "He'll die of apoplexy when he learns his beloved home is in such a dreadful state. Doubtless you scared away his servants."

Mr Adams grinned. "This is my house, Melissa. Mr Holland left it to me in his will. It was the least he could do. I almost drowned because of him."

Melissa's eyes widened in horror. She started shaking, first her hands, then her whole body. "Henry is dead? You killed him?"

"You persuaded him to club me over the head and push me into the Thames. I'd have died had George Budworth not been enjoying a dalliance with a dockside wench."

"Thank heavens for your brother," Lydia said.

Naomi wondered if the stressful events had affected Lydia's brain. She appeared a little deranged. "Mr Holland is in the crypt along with the housekeeper."

A sob caught in Melissa's throat. "So he is dead. I thought it strange he only mentioned his trip to India once he'd left."

While Melissa dashed tears from her eyes, Mr Adams marched into the hall. She heard the loud scraping sound before he appeared, lugging the crude coffin into the drawing room.

"Holland liked playing with fire." He beckoned his coachman into the room, an evil-looking fellow with bulging eyes, and instructed him to pour the contents of his hip flask over the casket. "What say we honour him with a funeral pyre?"

The gravity of the situation was not lost on Naomi.

It did not take a genius to determine what Mr Adams planned to do. He'd proven he enjoyed using fire as a method of torture.

Naomi glanced around the room. The chaise did indeed smell like someone had emptied a bottle of brandy over the red damask. The outside shutters were closed, blocking the light and the most obvious means of escape. No one could identify the dead from a pile of charred bones. The only thing to do now was find a way to flee before Mr Adams torched the casket.

"Wait outside in the carriage, Lydia." Mr Adams didn't

give her time to obey his command but asked his coachman to escort her out. "We'll be leaving shortly."

It would seem Mr Adams still needed Lydia.

"What about Naomi?" Lydia tried to wrestle her arm from the rogue's grasp. "She's coming with us. We agreed to rescue her from Mr Chance's evil clutches."

Mother have mercy! How blind could one be?

"Wake up, Lydia. He's going to raze the house to the ground and get rid of the evidence." She hoped to shatter her sister's illusions. "It's too late to save us. You made a pact with the devil. You made the mistake of shutting me out."

A pained cry burst from Lydia's throat. She glared at Mr Adams. "No! That's not what we agreed. You said we would all live together at Hartford Hall once we'd got rid of Mr Chance."

Mr Adams scoffed. "I'm not sharing the inheritance with anyone. Now leave before I change my mind and force you to light the match."

Perhaps he couldn't get rid of Lydia until the Prerogative Court ruled in their favour. Perhaps he meant to pass himself off as Edwin Budworth and needed her continued support.

Lydia mumbled to herself, her eyes growing wide in disbelief. She'd been acting oddly since leaving Hartford Hall. Perhaps in her own way, Lydia did care. The evidence was there in her harrowing sobs.

Mr Adams motioned to the door. "Get her out of here."

The coachman grabbed Lydia and hauled her over his shoulder. Though she kicked her legs and thumped his back, he left the room, the thud of his booted footsteps echoing along with Lydia's cries.

Naomi turned to Melissa and lowered her voice. "He can only shoot one of us. I say we charge at him and hope for the best."

Melissa scowled like she'd scuffed her new slippers. "He'll shoot me first or pistol-whip the pair of us. I'll take my chances. We won't get far if we're lying unconscious amid the flames."

Mr Adams put paid to any plans of escape when he struck the first match. He aimed his pistol at their heads while tossing the lighted spill on the coffin. While Melissa tried to reason with him, he threw another lit match on the chaise.

"My husband will hunt you down unless you release us." Naomi jumped back as the furniture ignited with a sudden *whoosh* and a burst of amber flames.

"He hadn't the courage to challenge me ten years ago. I left him howling in pain, nursing his arm and cursing me to the devil."

A spiral of black smoke filled the air, making her cough. "He's ten times the man you'll ever be. When he finds you, I pray he makes you suffer in the most despicable way."

Mr Adams laughed and made to leave, but a shot outside wiped the sick grin off his face. He darted from the room, stopping to lock the door.

Melissa raced to the door, rattled the handle and thumped the wood with her fist. She called for help, pleading for someone to release them.

"There's no one here. The window is our best means of

escape." Naomi ignored the mounting heat as the fire spread. The smoke scratched her throat and clogged her airways. She tried to raise the sash but it wouldn't budge. Grabbing the silver candlestick from the mantel, she raced to the window and smashed the glass panes.

"I can prise the door open." Melissa had snatched a poker and was jabbing it between the frame and the jamb.

"Cover your nose and mouth and come here." Mr Adams had latched the shutters, but she pressed her face to the smashed pane and inhaled the fresh air breezing through the gaps.

Naomi turned to Melissa, but the woman was on her knees, coughing to rid her lungs of smoke and surrounded by a wall of flames.

They had a minute before the room became an inferno.

A minute before the fumes overwhelmed them.

No! This wasn't how her life was supposed to end.

Tears streamed down her face as she remembered her wedding day and the blossoming bud of hope she felt when Aramis kissed her. Every day since had been magical. Dreams did come true. Life was beautiful. And if by some miracle she survived, she'd not waste a second.

Hearing a commotion outside, she called to Aramis. It was foolish to waste her energy when she should be trying to force open the shutters.

But Aramis had promised to protect her.

To love and cherish her always.

And he never broke a vow.

By the time Aramis reached the drive leading to Croft Manor, his lungs burned. His chest heaved as he fought to catch his breath. Aaron sprinted beside him, determined to find Jacob Adams and make the devil pay.

Having left the coachman on the roadside, repairing the broken carriage wheel, they'd covered the last mile on foot. Not wanting to hinder their progress, neither spoke as they raced towards the manor. But the acrid smell of smoke reached Aramis' nostrils, and visions of his old nightmares returned.

"Adams is here. Is it my imagination, or has he lit a fire?" His heartbeat pounded in his throat as he considered all the ways the bastard might hurt Naomi. "What if he means to burn the house to the ground and destroy any evidence?"

Aaron cursed. "Be on your guard. If he means to escape the noose, he cannot afford to let us live."

But Adams wasn't hiding behind the poplar trees lining the drive. He didn't appear from the shadows, wielding two loaded pistols. A mere hundred yards ahead, he was shoving Lydia into his carriage while she protested. Then he slammed the door shut.

Was Naomi inside the vehicle, too?

"Adams!" Aramis locked eyes with the brute.

The fiend looked surprised to see them, though he didn't fire a warning shot or pull a blade from his boot.

While Aramis hurried to close the distance between them, Jacob Adams climbed atop the box. He gathered the reins and whipped the horses into action.

"You've lost more than the hairs on your forearm this time, lad," Adams cried as the vehicle charged towards them, gaining momentum. "Your wife is coming with me. Let's see who's the cuckold now."

They were forced to dive out of the way or risk being trampled to death on the driveway.

"If we run, we might catch him at the gatehouse." Aaron dusted himself off and tugged Aramis' sleeve, encouraging him to follow. "If not, we'll cross the field and cut him off on the road. I vowed you'd have Naomi in your arms by nightfall, and I mean to keep my damn word."

"Aramis! Help!"

He was about to take to his heels when he heard Naomi's desperate plea and the sound of shattering glass. He would know her voice amongst a thousand others.

"Aaron, wait!" Hearing loud bangs and thuds, he stared at the manor's facade. "Cursed saints! He's locked Naomi inside the house and lit a blasted fire."

Panic stole his breath.

"Help! Aramis!"

"Naomi!" He darted towards the house, treading on Lydia's pillbox hat and crushing it into the gravel.

Jacob Adams' coachman was rolling on the floor, groaning in agony and clutching the bleeding wound on his thigh. "She shot me."

He didn't have time to deal with the blackguard. "Tie

your neckcloth tightly around your upper thigh, and you'll live."

"Aramis! Quickly!"

He tugged off his signet ring, turned to Aaron and thrust it into his brother's palm. "If I don't make it out alive, give this to your first-born son. Tell him his heartless uncle chose love over vengeance." He didn't care what happened to Jacob Adams. He didn't care about anything but rescuing his wife.

Aramis was at the front door when Aaron grabbed him. "There's no need to enter the house. I'm certain she's in a room downstairs. Hurry. If she's smashed the windowpane, the rush of oxygen will act as an accelerant."

They raced to examine all the outside windows on the lower floor. The shutters were all closed and barred.

"Naomi!"

One shutter rattled. "Aramis. Hurry. It's too hot in here." Her voice was weak now, and she coughed after every word.

He was there in a heartbeat, unhooking the latch with shaky hands and yanking open the wooden screens.

The room was ablaze. Smoke poured out through the holes in the smashed panes. He tried to raise the sash, but the wood had swelled.

She thrust her arm through the window, desperate to touch him one last time. Blood dripped from minor cuts to her hand. Tears streaked down her dirty face. "I—I love you."

He met her terrified gaze. "Step aside. We need to kick the bars through. Move!" He'd not meant to shout, but time was of the essence.

Aaron stood beside him. They gripped each other's arms for balance and kicked the thin wooden bars. They snapped in seconds, fragments of wood and glass tumbling into the room.

Aramis reached for her, grabbing her arm and dragging her carefully through the gap. He fell backwards onto the ground, taking Naomi with him.

She didn't move. She didn't speak.

He lay still, too afraid to say her name in case the word was met with deathly silence. He held her tightly, tears filling his eyes. He'd not cried since the night Aaron almost bled to death on Mrs Maloney's floor.

Don't leave me.

Please don't leave me.

"I love you," he whispered against her brow. "I'll destroy that stupid list of demands. I'll do anything you ask of me, but please don't die. I need you. I've never needed anything so badly in my whole damn life."

Aaron crouched beside him. He brushed the tangle of hair from Naomi's face, then checked her pulse. His relieved sigh brought a glimmer of hope. "She's breathing but needs to see a physician. You must move away from the house before the fire takes hold."

Aaron gathered Naomi in his arms and carried her to a rusty bench at the bottom of the garden. He waited for Aramis to sit before placing Naomi on his lap.

"Wait here. I'll be back soon." Aaron shrugged out of his coat and draped it around Naomi's shoulders. He reached into his waistcoat pocket and returned Aramis' signet ring. "There's more chance of Delphine's parents descending in a shower of gold than of me having a son."

"Life may surprise you and catch you unawares." It might appear in the form of a woman whose heart was big enough for two.

"I lack the time and dedication needed to raise a family."

Naomi coughed, a hacking sound that had him patting his wife's back and saying a silent prayer to the Lord.

"I disagree," she said, catching her breath. "You're the best brother anyone could wish for." She sagged against Aramis' chest, so weak it proved worrying. "You'll be an excellent husband and father when you find the right woman."

Aaron shifted uncomfortably. "I might tell you to mind your own business, but in this instance, I'm forced to accept your compliment."

Naomi's light chuckle became another cough.

"She needs a tincture." Aramis' pulse drummed in his ears. He'd always been a man of action. He was unused to feeling so damned helpless. "She needs something to soothe the irritation in her chest."

"Wait here. I'll be back as soon as I can."

Aaron was about to leave but the crunching of gravel on the drive signalled the arrival of a carriage.

He gritted his teeth as he held Naomi. "If the devil has returned, I'll wring his damn neck."

But it wasn't Jacob Adams sitting atop the box. It was Gibbs. The vehicle came to a crashing halt. The door swung open. Daventry vaulted to the ground, instructing Gibbs to check the injured coachman.

Daventry came charging over. He looked at the flames

engulfing the house and made the obvious assumption. "Is she breathing?"

Aramis nodded. "But she's inhaled the fumes. She had the foresight to smash the window and inhale fresh air. I suspect that's what saved her." Though if he'd been a minute longer, she would have perished in the flames.

"I would send for a doctor," Daventry said, "but we can be in London in a little over an hour. We'll visit my personal physician. He's on hand day and night."

"This wouldn't have happened if you'd not left them here alone," Aaron said bitterly. "It's fortunate I don't give a damn about rules."

Daventry was one of the few men Aaron could not intimidate. "I couldn't take the chance of her being arrested for murder. I came as soon as I could. The innkeeper directed us here."

"There's no point arguing now." Aramis gathered Naomi in his arms and stood. "We need to leave for London. We can discuss the particulars on the way."

Daventry agreed. "I'll inform the innkeeper of the fire here. I'll visit Hartford Hall tomorrow with the local magistrate. We've enough evidence to arrest Melissa Grant for fraud."

Naomi pointed at the house. "She perished in the flames."

Aramis gave a quick account of what happened. "Edwin Budworth doesn't exist. He's a figment of Jacob Adams' imagination. Adams used the alias to lure Lydia from Hartford Hall while plotting revenge. They'll head for the Continent while Adams concocts another scheme to get his hands on Lydia's money."

Daventry sighed. "Chivers was right. He suspected Lydia was planning to leave England. He followed her to the shipping office, but she managed to elude him."

"We can discuss the details en route," Aramis said, his tone firm. "We're leaving." He studied the gentle rise and fall of Naomi's chest. He could think no further than her next breath.

Naomi's eyes flickered open. "Aramis."

"Yes, my love."

"Take me home."

"To Hartford Hall or Fortune's Den?"

She cupped his cheek and smiled sweetly. "Anywhere is home when I'm with you."

Chapter Twenty

Naomi stirred from her slumber, the deathly silence forcing her to open her eyes and examine her surroundings. Fortune's Den was never this quiet at night.

Though she was alone in bed, the potent smell of her husband's cologne drew her up on her elbows, for he was undoubtedly close by. She gazed about the candlelit room and noticed him sitting in the chair. A lock of dark hair hung over his brow as he stared at the floor, absorbed in deep thoughts.

Desire unfurled in her belly as she watched him.

Days had passed since they'd made love.

The memory of their last passionate encounter only intensified her craving. She'd survived her ordeal, but their troubles were not over. The need to know him intimately again before he left for the docks had heat pooling in her loins.

"It's so quiet," she said softly so as not to alarm him.

He inhaled sharply, his eyes finding hers in the dim

light. "Aaron closed the club tonight. He wants us to tackle this matter as a family."

The matter he spoke of was the possible capture of Jacob Adams.

Three days had passed since the fire at Croft Manor. Mr Daventry had returned to examine the ruins with officers from Bow Street. At Hartford Hall, Uncle Jeremiah still pleaded innocence when the magistrate carted him to gaol. Amongst Melissa's private effects, Mr Daventry's agents found personal letters from Mr Holland. Two things had prevented Melissa from marrying him. His lack of funds and the fear he'd one day hang for Jacob Adams' murder.

"What do *you* want, Aramis?" She would prefer to know he had his brothers' support when tackling the fiend. A terrible feeling in her gut left her fearing the outcome. Jacob Adams was unstable, unpredictable.

His gaze caressed her bare shoulder. "What do I want to happen at the docks? Or what do I want to happen when I return home?"

The huskiness of his voice sent a delightful shiver down her spine. "Let's tackle your imminent departure first. Might you change your mind and allow me to come with you?" Was it not better for Lydia to see a familiar face when she was arrested?

"I almost lost you once. I'll not risk losing you again." He brushed his hands down his muscular thighs and stood. Dressed all in black, his powerful aura made her sex pulse. "I will ensure Lydia is treated well, but you need to rest."

"I'm perfectly fine. The stress of the last few weeks has left me a little tired, that's all." She sat up, the sheets slipping off her naked body. "Which brings me to what you plan to do when you return home."

His tongue skimmed his lips as he stared at her breasts. "How is a man supposed to leave to catch a felon when his wife offers him every incentive to stay?"

"Perhaps your wife wishes to give you a parting gift." She touched herself, her fingers gliding over her breast and tracing her collarbone. "Perhaps she wants to ensure you return home safely, ready to enjoy what other delights she has to offer."

She climbed out of bed and padded towards him.

His mouth fell open. "Daventry will be here soon."

"Lock the door, Aramis." She splayed her hand over his chest, trailed her fingers down past the waistband of his trousers to cup his growing erection. "I'm sure you can indulge your wife for a few minutes. There's no need to undress. I shall save that pleasure for later."

A growl rumbled in his throat. He closed his eyes, his head falling back as she smoothed her hand over his solid shaft.

"I need you inside me before you go."

He looked at her, the heat in his eyes scorching hot. "Do you have any idea how badly I want you?" He cradled her throat and traced her lips with his thumb. "This will be a quick tupping, love."

"I don't care how quick it is. I need you. Hurry."

His guttural groan signalled his submission. He fiddled with his trouser buttons, releasing the placket, his impressive manhood springing free.

Before she could catch her breath, he'd lifted her off the floor and pushed her up against the wall. "Wrap your legs around me. Tell me you want me desperately because I'm entering you now."

He pushed inside her, so deep they both inhaled sharply.

"Aramis."

"You're so tight and wet." He gripped her buttocks, squeezing hard. "Nothing has ever felt so good. I'm at your mercy, love."

His eyes remained locked with hers as he filled her. The moist sound of their lovemaking heightened her arousal. Erotic words fell from his lips as he drove hard and fast.

"I mean to suck that little pearl tonight. You're not to touch yourself while I'm gone. I want you wet and aching. I want you dressed in that prim white nightgown, begging me to make you come."

His words alone had brought her to the brink. One strum of his masterful fingers and she would be lost to the pleasurable sensations.

But a sudden knock on the bedchamber door made him stop mid-stroke. "Yes?" His voice sounded strained, and he was trying not to pant.

"Daventry is here," Theodore called. "Are you ready?"

"Yes. I'll meet you downstairs."

Aramis uttered a curse as he withdrew. He didn't release her but captured her mouth, his tongue sweeping through her lips.

She threaded her hands in his hair, tugging hard, the intimacy deepening along with the kiss, desire flaring all over again.

He dragged his mouth away. "It's taking every ounce

of strength I have not to say to hell with Jacob Adams. Do you know how hard it is for me to leave you?"

She didn't want to think about the dangers he might face tonight. "Make sure you fasten your trousers before you do."

A wicked grin played at the corners of his mouth. "I love you. Keep the bed warm." He kissed her one last time before fixing his clothing.

"Don't take any unnecessary risks." Capturing Jacob Adams was vital to their future happiness—a ghost that needed exorcising. "I love you."

She loved him more with each passing day.

He pressed his forehead to hers. "I'll be back soon."

She watched him leave, the separation killing her. Now she knew how he felt that day at Hartford Hall when he had been powerless to act.

He would meet his nemesis again tonight.

All she could do was pray and leave everything to fate.

The Black Flagon was a sailors' den, a tavern crammed between warehouses on Brewhouse Lane near Dowgate, a small wharf on the north bank of the Thames. Daventry instructed Aramis to park his carriage on Upper Thames Street and ensure his coachman was ready to leave at short notice.

They all gathered in a dark alleyway near the tavern entrance. Amidst the drunken peals of laughter and bawdy song, one could hear the water lapping the dock and the creak of weathered timbers.

"Are you sure you can trust your informant?" Aramis had scanned the narrow street, wondering why Adams would rent a room above a ramshackle tavern eighty miles from Dover. "According to the shipping office, they were supposed to sail for Calais yesterday."

"My man followed Adams and Miss Fontaine here last night." As Lydia wasn't legally married, Daventry used her stage name. He glanced behind him, flicked a gold coin to the woman lingering in the shadows and demanded she move away. "They made the mistake of visiting Mrs Boyle, albeit once the shop was closed. I've had the emporium under surveillance for days."

There was no need to ask what they wanted from Mrs Boyle. Adams needed money for his extended trip abroad. "At least Chivers can reclaim his diamond cuff links."

"Adams threatened Mrs Boyle. She suspected the cuff links were stolen but had no choice but to pay."

"What's the plan?" Aaron kept his eyes trained on the men working on the wharf. "If Adams is inside, he won't get far. I suggest I enter the premises with Aramis and drag the scoundrel out."

Daventry thought for a moment. "We know Miss Fontaine is inside. My man said Adams left and is yet to return. Christian and Theo will stay with me. Enter the tavern and attempt to apprehend her. See if you can discover why they're here. I trust you have a weapon."

Aramis patted his coat pocket and nodded.

"I need nothing other than my fists," Aaron countered.

"Be careful," Daventry cautioned them both. "Adams may have friends inside. Call if you need help."

Keen to locate Adams and ensure his only destination was Newgate, Aramis was first to the tavern door.

Aaron joined him. "Daventry should attend the fights in our basement. Then he'd know why we find his last comment ludicrous."

If they were dealing with anyone other than Jacob Adams, Aramis might agree. "It's not Adams' strength we must be wary of; it's his ability to hurt those we love." He gripped Aaron's arm. "We won't kill him unless we have no option. We need the law on our side."

Aaron nodded. "I intend to be in the front row when he hangs."

The Black Flagon was like any other wharf-side tavern. The stubby candles on the worn wooden tables were barely spluttering. The place carried the pungent scent of the river and the stench of men used to hard work. Those huddled together in the gloom disliked anyone not deemed sea-faring folk.

All conversation died when Aramis strode to the bar. He met the gaze of the haggard man filling tankards from a wooden cask and gestured to his brother. "We'll have brandy. The best you have."

The fellow considered the quality of their clothes. "Happen you've taken a wrong turn, gov'nor. Those who drink here don't take kindly to strangers."

Aramis firmed his jaw. "Pour the drinks and there'll be no trouble. You don't want to spend tomorrow sourcing new premises." He slammed a sovereign on the counter.

"You clearly have no idea who we are. Help us achieve our goal, and we will leave you in peace."

The man looked at the coin. He pulled a dusty bottle of cognac from under the counter and poured two drinks. "That's all we have. Get to your business and be on your way."

Aaron grabbed the man's hand as he moved to take the sovereign. "We've come for the woman staying in the room upstairs. We can deal with the matter quickly, or we can start a brawl that will leave you with a bucketful of teeth in the morning."

"There ain't no one upstairs," he said, tugging his hand free.

A punter appeared at the bar, his weathered face at odds with his sprightly demeanour. He eyed Aramis as he spoke to the landlord, then returned to his seat once his tankard had been refilled.

Aaron drew a weighty coin pouch from his coat pocket and dumped it on the counter. "You're harbouring fugitives. The lady's husband is wanted in connection with four murders, kidnapping and fraud."

Aramis tossed back his drink, wincing at the bitter aftertaste. "We've men waiting outside. Decide which side of the law you're on."

The landlord took seconds to come to his senses. He leaned closer. "You'll find the woman tucked away in the corner. I'm to keep an eye on her until he returns. If you ask me, she's tuppence short of a shilling."

Aramis scanned the taproom, but couldn't see Lydia.

"She's sitting behind the pillar and hasn't moved a

muscle since he left. She keeps mumbling gibberish and weeping."

"Do you know where we can find her husband?" If Jacob Adams disappeared, Aramis would be forever looking over his shoulder.

Aaron pushed the pouch across the bar, tempting the landlord to examine the bounty. "He means to leave England. We need to know where and when he plans to make his escape."

The landlord took the bribe, unable to hide a satisfied grin as he weighed the pouch in his palm. "I can't be sure, but I heard he's paid for passage on Boyers' boat when he ships his dyed silk to Grimsby. They're leaving tomorrow at noon."

"Grimsby?"

The landlord shrugged. "That's all I know."

Aramis thanked the man and went in search of Lydia. He found her sitting at a small table in a hidden corner of the taproom. Her golden hair hung in a tangle of knots about her face. Her lips were sore and cracked where she'd nibbled them until they'd bled. When she met his gaze, her blue eyes looked vacant.

Aaron approached. He watched Lydia rock back and forth in the seat, frowning at her incoherent mumbles. "What the devil's wrong with her? Is she drunk?"

Perhaps Adams had fed her laudanum to keep her subdued.

"Lydia?" Aramis pulled out a stool and sat down. Thank heavens Naomi hadn't seen her in this state. He reached for her hand, and she didn't pull away. She was dirty and cold. "Miss Fontaine?"

She blinked rapidly as if familiar with the moniker. "She's such a silly girl, sir. Do this. Do that. Do the other. Watch me weave my web. No one even knows his name." Three times, she blew at the unlit candlewick. "You can't start a fire without a flame."

They watched her, trying to decipher her ramblings.

"She's not in her right mind," Aaron whispered.

After the traumatic event at Croft Manor, it was hardly surprising. What had triggered this lapse in her sanity? Jacob Adams' lies? Her unwittingly betraying Naomi? Shooting the coachman?

"He stole the gown, sir, and laid it out nice and pretty. Pretended they were a harlot's pink ribbons."

Aramis glanced at Aaron. "She's referring to the scene at the Belldrake. Adams framed Naomi for murder. It makes sense now. With Naomi out of the way, Lydia would have inherited the entire estate."

The landlord appeared, the rims of empty tankards pinched between his fingers. He bent his head and kept his voice low. "The gent you're looking for is talking to Murphy outside. It won't be long until he gets the measure of the situation. Best hurry if you want to catch him."

Aramis was on his feet before he could draw his next breath. He faced Aaron. "Stay with Lydia. I promised Naomi her sister would be treated fairly. I'll not have anything happen to her tonight."

Though clearly frustrated he'd been asked to stay behind, Aaron nodded. "Daventry better keep you in his sights, or there'll be hell to pay."

Aramis flew through the tavern, bursting onto Brewhouse Lane and scanning the dim street. Two men stood near a small warehouse ten yards away. Money exchanged hands as they planned and plotted.

It was Adams.

He had nowhere to run.

Nowhere to hide.

Aramis narrowed his gaze and scoured the shadows near the alley, his silent gesture alerting Daventry of his intention to attack. With measured steps, he prowled towards the brute who had left Naomi to die in the blaze.

Adams' companion glanced up, his mouth dropping open. Perhaps he saw the devil's own darkness in Aramis' eyes. Perhaps he sensed the thrum of danger in the air because he stepped back and raised his hands in mock surrender.

That's when Jacob Adams swung around.

His arrogant mask slipped.

Panic marred his plain features.

"It's the day of reckoning." Aramis clicked his neck and cracked his knuckles. "One of us will die. I'm damned sure it won't be me."

He charged at the rogue, landing the first punch squarely on Adams' jaw. It shocked the fiend and left him staggering back, trying to keep his balance.

"You won't win a fistfight with me," Aramis taunted. "I'm not the same man you tortured. I was forged in the fire of your vengeance. You'll perish beneath the power of mine."

A fight ensued.

Jacob Adams had plagued his nightmares for years.

He stood for everything Aramis had despised about himself.

Naivety. Weakness. Inadequacy.

Things were different now.

The crook was craven. He used the element of surprise to frighten his foes. He manipulated women. He killed defenceless men. In a face-to-face brawl with an opponent his size, Adams was decidedly weak.

It came as no shock when he pulled a knife from his boot and swiped the air as if warding off a wildcat. "Hit me again, and I'll slice you like a fish."

Aramis opened his arms wide. "Take your best shot."

The half-wit lunged—his first mistake. One well-timed kick sent the weapon flying into the Thames. With nothing to lose, he charged at Aramis, arms flailing—his second mistake.

Aramis landed punch after punch. He broke Adams' nose, split his lip and blackened his eyes. People gathered around to watch the spectacle. He didn't know if they were sailors, merchants or his beloved brothers. Nothing mattered but bringing Jacob Adams to his knees.

As with all reversals of fate, Adams proved he was a coward. Clutching his ribs, he darted along the wharf, knowing his only chance of cheating death lay in the cold, murky waters of the Thames.

He was about to jump when Aramis grabbed him by the scruff of his coat and hauled him back from the water's edge. "After what you've put me through, I deserve to watch you hang from the scaffold."

Daventry arrived with Gibbs in tow. "We'll take matters from here."

Adams wiped blood-stained spittle from his lips. He stared through eyes as purple as plums. "All's fair in love and war, lad. It won't be the last you'll see of me. I might visit you in your dreams."

Aramis resisted the urge to punch him again. "Once the hangman pulls the lever, I'll not give you a second thought."

Chapter Twenty One

Office of the Order
Hart Street, Covent Garden

"What's so important you would call us here at such short notice?" Naomi scanned the plush drawing room Mr Daventry used to greet clients, trying to stem her nerves. She tugged off her gloves and perched on the edge of the damask sofa. "The tone of your note suggests there's a problem."

Aramis sat beside her, his thigh touching hers, oblivious to the thrum of tension in the air. He looked relaxed, not agitated, and was in no hurry to press Mr Daventry for information.

Mr Daventry raised a calming hand and smiled. "I wanted to update you on our progress. Though I'm keen to know how Miss Grant is faring."

Naomi put her hand to her heart, wishing she had good news to report. "We went to visit her yesterday at Merryville." It was an odd name for an asylum, though the private facility afforded every comfort. There was a moment when she thought Lydia had recognised her. A brief flicker of affection in her sad eyes. "I'm afraid there's no real change. Her physician said complex matters of the mind can take years to unravel."

In one respect, it was a blessing in disguise.

Mr Daventry had spoken to the Home Secretary and explained how Jacob Adams had manipulated Lydia with a complex web of lies. It's the only reason she wasn't tried for aiding a criminal.

"Let's pray she makes a full recovery." Mr Daventry sat in the chair by the hearth. He took his leather portfolio from the low table and opened it at a particular page. "I'm told the Prerogative Court ruled in your favour and your father's original will stands."

Not exactly. A woman in an asylum was not considered fit to inherit. "We cannot make any long-term decisions at present, and so have decided to lease Hartford Hall." The money would pay for Lydia's care.

"On the subject of wills, I heard this morning that Mr Holland's sister is the heir to Croft Manor, though she'll be left with little option but to sell the land."

That harrowing day at the manor would live with Naomi forever. She still shivered whenever she smelled smoke. "After what happened to her brother, I suspect she will want a fresh start."

A brief silence ensued.

The housekeeper, Mrs Gunning, arrived with the tray. While the friendly woman poured tea, Naomi studied Mr Daventry. He had not called them to the office to discuss Lydia or the will. Why did he not get to the point?

Typically, he chose the moment Naomi was sipping her beverage to inform her Mr Ingram had been questioned for fraud.

She almost choked.

Aramis sat forward. "Where is he? I have a private matter to discuss with him. He needs to know his act of violence against my wife won't be tolerated."

Naomi touched his thigh. "We discussed this. We're not dwelling on the past." Mr Ingram would not bother them. Nor would Mrs Wendon now she had been threatened with gaol for giving false evidence. Still, the look in Aramis' eyes said Mr Ingram might wake one night to find a threatening shadow looming over his bed.

"The clerk stated Ingram was tricked into signing the will. He was released with a warning to be less trusting in future."

Aramis scoffed. "If there's evidence proving Ingram was duped, explain why Jeremiah Grant was sentenced to transportation, not the noose."

Mr Daventry gave an apologetic shrug. "Based on Lydia's mental state, the Lord Chief Baron believed there was an argument to suggest Jeremiah acted in the best interests of the estate."

Though Naomi despised her uncle, she did not want him to hang. "I think we all know greed was the motive." And Melissa was a master manipulator.

They drank their tea, and the discussion turned to the night she had taken command of Aramis' vehicle.

Mr Daventry chuckled. "I would have paid a king's ransom to see his face when you drew the pistol. Who knew Aramis Chance could be bested by a woman half his size?"

Naomi glanced at her husband, love filling her heart. "Make no mistake, sir, he is as dangerous as they say." But she had the privilege of knowing the caring man, the love-able rogue, the passionate lover. "But I believe we were destined to be together."

"Then you don't regret marrying him?" Mr Daventry looked at Aramis before his wary gaze fell on her. "What would you do if you suddenly discovered the Reverend Smollett had been arrested and your marriage was declared void?"

Her pulse skittered. She repeated the question silently, trying to convince herself she had misheard. But Mr Daventry was nothing if not precise.

"Forgive me. Are you saying we're not legally married?" More than a little panicked, she clutched her abdomen. She turned to Aramis, wondering why he hadn't grabbed Mr Daventry by his pristine cravat and demanded answers.

"There's no reason to believe your marriage isn't legally binding, though the matter is still being decided. I shall let you know the outcome in due course."

In due course? Naomi stared at Mr Daventry, tears welling.

Why was he so blasé?

Where did that leave them now?

While her head was a whirlwind of confusion, Aramis asked basic questions about the special licence. But where were the threats? Why was he not tackling the problem in his usual forthright manner?

"Aramis? For goodness' sake, say something!"

He placed his hand on her lower back. "We'll discuss the matter in the privacy of our carriage." He stood, helping her to her feet before addressing Mr Daventry. "We expect to be informed as soon as a decision is made."

Her mind was still a blur when Aramis assisted her into the carriage. She sat dumbstruck. Though the vehicle lurched forward, her heart was lodged in her throat. "After all we've been through, how is it possible?" she managed to say. "We need to visit Mr Sloane. He procured the licence. Surely he will know what to do."

He relaxed back in the opposite seat. "I'm certain Daventry procured the licence. There's no point worrying about it now."

"No point worrying? Do you recall what happened last night?" They had lost themselves in each other's bodies. Aramis had neglected to withdraw and had collapsed on top of her, exhausted.

A sinful grin touched his lips. "How could I forget what happened last night? You were incredible."

She narrowed her gaze, eyeing him suspiciously. "Is this some sort of prank? If it is, it's not at all amusing."

He held his hands up. "Daventry came to the club last night and told me about Smollett's arrest. He didn't express a need for concern. I was going to tell you when I came upstairs, but you were waiting in the bathtub, and I left all good intentions at the door."

The vision of them sweat-soaked and panting flashed into her mind. The power of his erotic kisses had left her mindless, too. "You could have mentioned it this morning."

He shrugged. "And spoil the surprise?"

"Trust me. I would have rather been prepared." She glanced out the window and noticed they'd missed the turning for Aldgate. "Are we not going home?"

"That's an interesting question." He reached into the leather satchel beside him, the one she had not thought to question until now. "I shall offer a detailed explanation once we're on the road."

"We are on the road."

"The road to Scotland." He pulled the iron handcuffs from his bag and dangled them on one finger. "I've taken command of you and your vehicle. Do you think I would sit idly and wait for Daventry to confirm you're not my wife?"

Relief replaced the blind panic.

"Scotland?" He meant to marry her over the anvil? "What about your responsibilities at Fortune's Den? I have no clothes but the ones I'm wearing."

"You don't need clothes. Delphine packed you a valise though I dread to think what's inside. Aaron gave me a three-week leave of absence. We can marry in Gretna Green, take a short tour along the Solway Firth, perhaps visit Dumfries."

That's why Delphine hadn't stopped grinning for most of the morning, and why Aaron had been a little subdued. "Delphine's insistence she needed three weeks to plan our belated wedding breakfast makes sense now."

"I told her I was taking you hostage. That I'd not release you until we'd exchanged vows." He tugged the fastenings and released both blinds, plunging them into semi-darkness. "If we're to marry, I have a comprehensive list of demands."

A coil of heat swirled in her belly. "If I'm to do your bidding, are you not supposed to offer me an incentive?"

His tongue traced the seam of his lips. "I assure you, you'll be thoroughly rewarded. Now, show me your stockings."

Feeling a flutter of excitement, she slid her skirts slowly up past her calves. "It's an awfully long way to Scotland. How will you entertain me during the arduous journey?"

The wicked glint in his eyes said he had a plan. "I thought we might begin with our favourite pastime. Who can last longest in the game of restraint?"

She laughed. "You lost to an amateur on the drive to Uxbridge."

"Yes, but I was unprepared."

"I've had quite a bit of practice since the last time we played." She raised her skirts a little higher and braced one foot on the opposite seat. "Now I know what arouses you, I have a clear advantage."

His breathing quickened as his gaze slid slowly up her thigh. "Is that you moving your pawn into position?"

She smiled. "You should topple your king now, my love. We both know I'll win before we reach the Great North Road."

Fortune's Den
Aldgate Street, London
Three weeks later

"What the devil are they talking about?" Aaron gestured to Naomi and Miss Lovelace sitting on the sofa in the drawing room, engaged in an amusing conversation. "Twice, they've looked in my direction."

Aramis grinned. "As I cannot read lips or minds, I have no idea. Perhaps Naomi is explaining how you helped to save her life."

"I mean to murder Delphine. I checked the guest list personally. It's enough that I have to tolerate Daventry and his men. There was no mention of suffering our competitor's company."

Aaron used his sullen mood as a crutch and had clearly forgotten he'd confessed to desiring the woman.

"Miss Lovelace is hardly our competitor. She owns a club for ladies, enjoys recitals and flower arranging. Nonetheless, I'm told she has a card room and the stakes often run high."

"She should be at The Burnished Jade balancing the books." Aaron observed Miss Lovelace's fashionable blue ensemble and grumbled again. "She pleads poverty, yet she's wearing another new dress."

A man rarely noticed what his nemesis wore.

Aramis might question why his brother cared.

"Naomi said Miss Lovelace is a skilled seamstress—a woman of hidden talents who makes all her own clothes. It's how she earned a living when her father's home was repossessed. It's how she saved the money to decorate The Burnished Jade."

Aaron snorted—the sound carrying a hint of pride. He glanced around the room, undoubtedly seeking a distraction. "Have you seen Delphine?"

"Not since we retired to the drawing room." He didn't mention Delphine's desire to find her parents. Did she have Spanish or Italian blood? Was her story one of neglect, or had she been torn from the arms of a loving mother? It mattered not. Finding them would be an impossible feat.

"She's been acting strangely since visiting her modiste yesterday. I had Theo accompany her, but he had nothing untoward to report."

"It must be hard living with uncertainties."

In sheltering Delphine from the outside world, Aramis feared they'd failed to prepare her for the truth. How would she fare if left to her own devices? What path would she choose when free of familial obligation?

"We raised her," Aaron replied defensively. "She's our sister and I dare anyone to say otherwise. What else does she need to know? We both know the truth is best left buried."

The truth was never buried.

It lay festering, waiting for an inopportune moment to surface.

"Perhaps I should visit Bedlam and question the crone." Delphine had accompanied him and Naomi when they moved Lydia to a private asylum. A haggard woman with straggly white hair had peered through the bars, taken one look at the exotic beauty and called her Sofia. They were a fool's ramblings, though the encounter had unsettled Delphine.

"You'll get no sense from anyone there," Aaron countered.

An uneasy feeling forced him to say, "Daventry means to resurrect the family ghosts. We've dealt with Lawton and Adams. Trouble is brewing. I feel it in my bones. I would rather help Delphine than watch her suffer." Daventry knew a man who found missing people. Despite being a peer's illegitimate son, Mr Flynn had once worked as a Bow Street Runner.

Aaron gave a resigned sigh. "Sometimes it's better to live with a dream than a harsh reality. But let me think on the matter." He glanced at Daventry's wife, who was with child again, and changed the subject. "Why would any man want to be a father? Since Daventry began interfering in our affairs, I've had the misfortune of inheriting two sisters. It's a drain on my time and patience."

Aramis patted his brother affectionately on the back. "It's about to get a damn sight worse. It won't be long before you're an uncle."

Aaron's curse would make Lucifer gasp. "Tell me you're joking. I need brandy. I need to fight in the ring. I don't need children crying in the club."

"How else will your legacy live on?"

"I won't give a damn. I'll be dead."

Whenever he had Miss Lovelace in his sights, Aaron's temper flared. Despite feigning indifference, he looked at her with shocking frequency.

"I shall leave you to mingle," Aramis teased, knowing

Aaron would escape to his office and lock the world out. "I need to gather a few things from upstairs before I leave."

He was moving to Salisbury Square with Naomi, to an elegant townhouse close enough to the club. He had hired Maddock to keep the debt-ridden drunkards from his door.

"What's the rush? You'll be working tomorrow night."

"Perhaps I'd like a quiet moment to reflect."

Aaron tutted. "Now I know why I never entertain women. Love has made you weak. Next, you'll be offering me spiritual guidance and burning those strange smells from the Orient."

They laughed together.

There was little point trying to explain the complex nature of love. If Daventry was the matchmaker everyone claimed, Aaron would discover the truth soon enough.

Aramis spent ten minutes sitting in a chair in his bedchamber, trying to picture his life before the night he met Naomi.

Join me for supper at the Belldrake tonight.
I shall make it worth your while.

He'd gone there blindly, not knowing his destiny awaited him. He never answered a woman's call, never accepted an invitation. Had he not been so damned angry, he would not have left Fortune's Den. Had he arrived half an hour later, he might have missed her, never knowing what he'd lost.

A light knock on the door drew him from his reverie.

"Aramis?" her sweet voice called to him like a siren's song. With some hesitation, she opened the door and peered inside. "There you are. Would you like company, or would you prefer to be alone?"

"There's a space on my lap if you'd care to join me."

She chuckled as she slipped into the room and closed the door. "I saw you escape. I know it will be hard leaving tomorrow." She sat on his lap and wrapped her arms around his neck. "We don't have to move to Salisbury Square. We can live here with your family."

"You're my family." He tucked a lock of hair behind her ear and laughed. "Aaron cannot abide children. After our accident, you might be with child. It would be my brother's worst nightmare. An innocent soul he would feel obliged to protect."

Her eyes brightened. "Might we have another accident tonight?"

"We can have one now if you lock the door."

She kissed him deeply, her essence chasing away any sadness he felt for leaving. "I've been thinking. I'm not sure your moniker suits you anymore. There's nothing black about your heart, Aramis. Perhaps you should trade titles with Theodore. You certainly excel at lovemaking."

"I excel at most things when I'm with you." He slid his hand under her skirts to stroke her soft thigh. They kissed until they were breathless. "Theo's moniker wouldn't suit me either. The King of Hearts loves many women. Until I draw my last breath, I shall love only one."

I hope you enjoyed reading *Temptress in Disguise.*

Why is Delphine being so secretive after her visit to the modiste? Who is the mysterious Mr Flynn and can he find her parents? Should she risk hurting those she loves in a quest for answers?

Find out in …

Lady Gambit
Rogues of Fortune's Den - Book 3

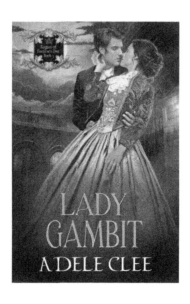

More titles by Adele Clee

Gentlemen of the Order

Dauntless

Raven

Valiant

Dark Angel

Ladies of the Order

The Devereaux Affair

More than a Masquerade

Mine at Midnight

Your Scarred Heart

No Life for a Lady

Scandal Sheet Survivors

More than Tempted

Not so Wicked

Never a Duchess

No One's Bride

Rogues of Fortune's Den

A Little Bit Dangerous

Temptress in Disguise

Lady Gambit

Printed in Great Britain
by Amazon

37468175R00182